RELIC

RELIC

A Folly Beach Mystery

BILL NOEL

ISBN: 978-1-937979-83-6

Enigma House Press
Goshen, Kentucky
www.enigmahousepress.com

Also by Bill Noel

Folly Beach Mysteries

Folly

The Pier

Washout

The Edge

The Marsh

Ghosts

Missing

Final Cut

First Light

Boneyard Beach

Silent Night

Dead Center

Discord

The Folly Beach Mystery Collection

Dark Horse

Joy

The Folly Beach Mystery Collection II

No Joke

Chapter One

A disestablished Coast Guard station, now known as Lighthouse Inlet Heritage Preserve, anchors the east end of Folly Beach, a tiny, barrier island located fewer than a dozen miles from downtown Charleston, South Carolina. This morning, I knew it as the place where Charles Fowler and I planned to shoot sunrise photos of the iconic Morris Island Lighthouse, precariously perched on the deteriorating Morris Island, visible from the Preserve. Tumultuous, early-July thunderstorms had rolled through overnight, jarring me awake three times, the final time a little after 5:00 a.m. I hoped that Charles would have seen the wisdom of postponing our photo shoot for another day.

Wisdom and Charles seldom appear in the same breath, so I wasn't surprised when his fist pounded on my door, with his annoyed voice saying, "Chris, we're late."

I shook my head, opened the door, and stood face-to-face with my best friend. Charles was a year younger than I. Although, this morning, my body felt like it was a decade older than my sixty-eight years. True, I've never been a decade older, so am guessing what it would feel like. Regardless, I wasn't ready to slosh through soaked sand and prickly sandspurs to listen to Charles pontificate on things in which I had no interest. After spending hundreds of hours with him since I'd moved to Folly, I knew it'd be a waste of words to point out the obvious reasons to not venture out.

Twenty minutes later, I finished dressing, grabbed my camera, and mumbled words that meant stupid, moronic idea, all while listening to Charles share how excited he was to be going on another photo adventure. We drove three miles to the end of East Ashley Avenue, the entrance to the Preserve.

Most days, street parking was at a premium since this was the entry to one of the most popular spots on the island. Today, there was one other vehicle parked on the sandy berm along the dead-end road, no surprise since it was still fifteen minutes until sunrise. To get to the best view of the lighthouse, we'd have to walk a quarter of a mile, much of it on what was once the road through the Coast Guard property, then the rest of the way over deep sand descending to the inlet.

I parked about a hundred feet from the stanchion, blocking all but emergency vehicles from entering the property, and was grabbing my camera from the back seat when Charles pointed to the other vehicle parked off the road between us and the stanchion. "Fitzsimmons."

"Strange name for a car," I said, to irritate the man who dragged me out of the house before sunrise.

"No, dummy. It's Anthony and Laurie Fitzsimmons' car."

"How do you know?"

"You know other Volcanic Orange MINI Cooper convertibles?"

I didn't even know that one. One of Charles's goals was to get to know every human on Folly, probably each human in South Carolina, plus their pets.

"Who're the Fitzsimmons?"

He pointed his hand-carved wooden cane at the MINI. "Met them in town last week. I was walking down Center Street, minding my own business, when they stopped me, asked if I went to Jacksonville University."

He almost lost me on *minding his own business*, an activity I'd never witnessed. Instead, I recovered. "Why'd they ask that?"

"Suppose because I was wearing a Jacksonville University T-shirt with Nellie on it."

"Who, or what, is Nellie?"

He sighed, unbelieving that someone wouldn't know Nellie. "The mascot, a dolphin."

In addition to Charles carrying a cane for no apparent reason, his torso was usually covered by a college, or university, T-shirt in summer, sweatshirt in winter, always long-sleeved. I don't ask why. It would be another waste of words.

"Again, why'd they ask about Jacksonville University?"

"They're from there, the city, not the university. Anthony was a high school math teacher; Laurie taught drama."

"Vacationers?"

"Retired last month to move here."

Lightning lit the sky off to the east; thunder rumbled in the distance. The weatherman said that the rain was out of the area, but I began to wonder. It didn't stop Charles from tapping his cane on the pavement while heading to the entrance.

I followed. "They buy a house?"

"Chris, give me a break. I didn't have time to get their life history, bank statements, Social Security numbers, blood types." He shrugged. "Anthony said they were late for something. They had to go."

Which meant my uber-nosy friend may not have their

blood types, yet it wouldn't have stopped him from interrogating them at a level that would make the CIA drool.

"Wonder why their car's here?" Charles said, more to himself than to me.

"Maybe that's their house." I pointed to a cottage near the car. There were five houses within a stone's throw from where we were standing. No lights were on in any of them, so they were either vacant vacation rentals, or the residents were still asleep, making them wiser than the two of us.

"Could be," Charles said with little conviction. He veered off the path to the Preserve to approach the MINI. He leaned close to the driver's side window then jumped back like he'd seen a ghost. He stumbled then regained his balance.

"What is it?"

He put his finger to his lips and whispered, "Laurie's in there."

"Asleep?"

"Hope so."

The MINI's door swung open, startling both of us.

Charles said, "Not asleep now."

"Crap! You scared me to death," said the car's occupant. She stepped out of the vehicle, twisted her shoulders around, like she was loosening a strained muscle. She stared at us, before saying, "Who the hell are you?"

"Laurie, it's me, Charles. We met in town the other day. Didn't mean to scare you."

Laurie stood five-foot-three, petite, with short, dark hair, and a bewildered look on her face. "We met in town?"

That was a blow to Charles's *everyone knows me* ego. He reminded her where they'd met.

Her look softened. "Oh, I remember. You're the guy with the long-sleeved Jacksonville University shirt standing in the blazing sun."

The sky began to lighten. Laurie's hair was matted; her tan slacks wet from the knees down. I stepped closer and told her I was Chris Landrum, Charles's friend, that we were on our way to the end of the island to photograph the lighthouse. I added that we were sorry to startle her.

Today's temperature was to reach the mid-80s, although the gusty breeze off the ocean, and the lack of sunshine, had the temperature currently hovering in the low 70s. Laurie wrapped her arms around her chest. She was shivering.

"Are you okay?" I asked.

"Umm, yes."

Charles stepped closer to her. "Where's Anthony?" He looked around, like he expected to see Laurie's husband pop up from behind the car.

Laurie looked down at the sandy berm, glanced back at her car, then turned to Charles. "He's... well, supposed to be with me. Umm, he's."

I waited for her to continue. She looked at Charles, at me, back at the ground, then said nothing.

"Laurie, you're shivering," I said. "Why don't we get in your car, where we can turn on the heat?"

"Good idea," Charles said before Laurie could respond. He was already on the way to the passenger side of the vehicle.

"Okay," Laurie said, barely above a whisper.

I held the door open while she climbed in and turned on the ignition. Charles opened the passenger door, moved a flashlight off the seat, pushed the front passenger seat up, and squeezed his five-foot eight, one hundred fifty-pound frame in the back seat. I walked around to the front passenger's seat. In the glow of the interior light, I saw gray roots from Laurie's brown hair. Even with her hair in disarray and wrinkled clothing she was attractive. She stared out the windshield and continued her silence. I was determined to wait for her to tell us what was going on.

Charles, a stranger to patience, leaned forward while pushing aside a four-foot long metal detector behind him on the seat. "Where's Anthony?" He said it like he hadn't already asked.

Laurie rested her arms on the steering wheel and leaned against her forearm. "He's … I don't know where he is."

"Help us understand," I said as calmly as possible.

She turned to Charles then back to me. "We were in whatever that's called out there." She pointed to the Preserve.

Charles, a stickler for details, said, "Lighthouse Inlet Heritage Preserve."

Laurie said, "Whatever."

I agreed with her. "Go on."

"We got here around seven… umm, last night now. We got caught up in, umm, our activities, didn't notice how dark it was getting."

"Activities?" Charles interrupted.

Laurie jerked her head toward Charles then glanced at the metal detector beside him. "Are you cops?"

It was a strange question. Before I answered, Charles said, "I'm a private detective, my friend here and I help the police occasionally."

Charles, who hasn't had a steady job since moving to Folly some thirty-two years ago, popped out of bed one morning, deciding that he wanted to be a private detective. He'd never studied the profession, nor apprenticed under a licensed private investigator, a requirement in South Carolina. He hadn't let those troublesome barriers stand in the way of self-proclaiming what he was, if only in his mind. When pressed, he'd said he read enough novels about private investigators to be "more than qualified," whatever that meant.

"Laurie," I said, "we're not police. Why?"

Charles said. "Humph."

She started to say something, hesitated, before continuing, "We were looking for Civil War relics in the woods when it started pouring. It was the first time that we'd, umm, explored that area. We got turned around."

The question about us being the police was beginning to make sense. It was illegal to use metal detectors, or to remove artifacts from the Preserve, owned by Charleston County.

Charles said, "What happened?"

"Before we knew it, we couldn't see five feet in front of us. The rain got harder. Lightning everywhere, thunder deafening. We were lost. Thank God we had flashlights." She took a deep breath. "We knew there was a trail somewhere. Umm, yes, we were on a sandy trail, maybe off it a little." She closed her eyes, her head vibrated like a tuning fork.

Charles said, "Then what?"

Laurie opened her eyes and blinked a couple of times. "Where was I?"

"On a trail," I said.

"We were? Oh, I guess so. Did I say we were lost?"

I nodded.

"It was really, really dark. Anthony told me to stay where I was. He'd find the way to the car." She hesitated, her hands trembled. "I told him we should stick together. He said no, for me to wait. I kept waiting for him to come back. I was huddled down under the densest tree cover I could find, anywhere to stay dry. It didn't work. God, the rain kept getting harder, thunder boomed, lightning turned the sky to daylight. I was so scared."

"What time was that?" Charles pushed, "What happened next?"

"Time, I don't know. Like I said, it was after dark. Maybe

ten, or eleven. I waited and waited. It seemed like hours. The rain eased, so I couldn't just sit there. I started walking in the direction of the ocean. At least, I thought that was the direction I was going. It was cloudy, but I could see a glimmer of moonlight when I broke through the woods. I saw the ocean, saw the beach. I figured that, if I turned right and started walking, I'd get to the houses near where we parked. Those over there."

She pointed to the structures adjacent the Preserve. "I saw the houses, so I had an idea where I was. Guys, I was so happy. Anthony would be in the car, waiting until the rain died down, to come get me. I knew he would." She turned, looked out the side window, then whispered, "He wasn't here. Why did I let him go? Why?"

Charles and I remained silent.

Laurie smacked her hand on the steering wheel. "If we'd gone together, I'd know where he was." She leaned forward. "Now I don't."

Then, she fainted.

Chapter Two

Other than Laurie being wet, exhausted, confused, and passed out, I had no idea what else might be wrong. I called 9-1-1 and told the dispatcher that help was needed at the east end of Ashley.

You'd have thought there was a three-alarm fire at the Preserve. In addition to the longest street on the island, next to Runway 15/33 at the Charleston International airport, Ashley Avenue is one of the straightest paved areas nearby. If it weren't for traffic, a twenty-five mile-per-hour speed limit, and regular police patrols, it'd be a perfect dragstrip. I saw strobing emergency lights, heard sirens from two patrol cars and two fire trucks long before they arrived.

The first responders earned their reputation. They were hitting their brakes five minutes after I called. Officer Trula Bishop was the first to arrive. Charles moved to the front seat of the MINI while I met Bishop behind the orange car.

"Mr. Chris, was that you who called?"

I nodded then gave her an abbreviated version of what'd happened. She told me not to run off then moved to the passenger side of the MINI to motion for Charles to get out so she could check on the distressed driver. Most Folly Beach Public Service Officers were cross-trained as EMTs and fire-fighters. This allows the small force to respond to not only police situations, but also to fight fires and stabilize those in medical distress until an ambulance arrives from Charleston.

The first fire engine squealed to a halt. Two firefighter/paramedics were next to the MINI. Officer Bishop let them do their thing and returned to me. Charles was close behind her as she suggested we might be more comfortable in her vehicle. I'd known Bishop since she joined the force three years ago. She was an outstanding officer, also one of the few females on the force. I also knew her suggestion to join her in her car was closer akin to a command. I got to the patrol car first and climbed in the back seat.

"Okay, Mr. Chris, what have you and your buddy got yourself into now?"

Charles answered before I could. "We were going for an early-morning saunter to take pictures of the lighthouse."

Bishop put her hand up, palm facing my friend's face. "Charles, is Chris a ventriloquist, or are you answering for him?"

I told you that she was outstanding. I smiled then took over for Charles giving her the unabridged version of what'd happened.

"She was asleep in her car with wet clothes," Bishop said, like she was trying to wrap her head around what we'd found. "How long was she asleep? When did she get back to the car? How could she fall asleep with her husband missing?"

I shook my head. "Don't know. She fainted before we learned more than what I told you."

"Were there other vehicles here when you found her?"

"Only her volcanic orange MINI Cooper," Charles said, providing Bishop more than she needed to know about the car.

Bishop pointed to the nearby houses. "Any lights?"

"No," I said. "No sign of life."

One of the EMTs tapped on the driver's side window. Bishop lowered the window, and the medic whispered something. She responded with, "Okay, keep me posted."

The EMT returned to the MINI when Charles said, "What?"

"Two things," Bishop said. "The ambulance is five minutes out."

"And?" Charles interrupted.

Officer Bishop glared at Charles then turned to me. "His patient is mumbling something about her husband should have come relic hunting with her tonight instead of…"

"Instead of what?" Charles asked.

"She didn't say. Her eyes rolled up in her head, and she was out again."

Charles twisted in the seat to look at the MINI. "Does that mean Anthony wasn't with her? That doesn't make sense."

"All I know, Charles, is what my guy said. You talked to her. Did she say anything that would make you think she was alone?"

"No, the opposite," Charles said.

A Charleston County EMS ambulance pulled up behind the MINI, followed by a silver Ford F-150 pickup truck occupied by Cindy LaMond, the island's director of public safety, aka police chief. Two EMTs from the ambulance rushed to the MINI, while Chief LaMond walked to where we were seated. She was in her early fifties, five-foot-three, well built with curly dark hair. She was also a close friend whom I'd known since she moved to Folly nine years ago.

Cindy glanced at the MINI then bent down and looked in the window of Bishop's patrol car.

"Crocodile crap," Cindy said, unchieflike. "When was the last time I rolled up on a crime scene without having to look at the two of you with your scraggly, wrinkled, Cheshire-cat-grinning faces, ready to ruin my day?"

"Good morning, Chief LaMond," I said. "Nice to see you this morning."

Cindy rubbed her lower back. "Get out of the car. My aching back doesn't take kindly to being bent like this."

The three of us exited and stood beside Cindy facing the MINI. "Okay, let's hear it?"

Bishop gave a police-speak version of what she knew. The chief turned to me to ask if that summed it up.

I said that it did as I watched the EMTs load Laurie Fitzsimmons in the ambulance.

Cindy walked over and looked in the MINI.

The rest of us followed.

"Okay," she said, "here's my question. How could whatever her name is, and her husband, get that lost back there?" She nodded toward the entry to the old Coast Guard property. "Hell, it's not that big."

"Eighty acres," added my trivia-collecting friend Charles.

Cindy glared at him then continued, "As I was saying, if you walk one direction, you hit the marsh, another, and you're staring at the lighthouse, head another way, and you're tippy-toeing in the Atlantic Ocean. Go the fourth direction and, *voila*, you're here at that god-awful orange car."

Charles pointed his cane at the MINI. "Volcanic orange."

Cindy lowered her head. "Charles, sayeth I in all sincerity, who gives a crap about the color's name? Can anyone answer my geography question?"

I glanced at Charles, waiting for him to give a more

detailed answer than anyone would have wanted. He didn't say anything, nor did Officer Bishop. I offered, "It's unlikely any of us would get lost, but she told us they were new here, it was storming, dark, plus it was their first visit out there. It's possible."

"So, was Mr. umm," Cindy looked at Bishop.

Bishop said, "Anthony Fitzsimmons."

Cindy nodded. "Was he with her, or not?"

"She told us he was," I replied.

Bishop added, "And told the EMT he wasn't."

It was nearly 8:00, the lingering clouds from last night's storm were offshore. Bishop said, since it was lighter, she'd walk around the MINI to see if she could find evidence that anyone else had been there.

Cindy called dispatch, requesting that more members of the Folly Beach Department of Public Safety join her at the end of the island. She leaned against Bishop's patrol car and rubbed the bridge of her nose.

I said, "Cindy, you okay?"

"Sure, umm… no. Chris, I'm three officers short. I have no business being out here fighting mosquitos, listening to you two blabbering, when I have a pile of paperwork taller than Mt. Rainier in the office." She pointed at the stanchion leading to the Preserve. "Now, we have Mr. Fitzsimmons missing, or not, depending on which mood his wife is in."

A City of Folly Beach SUV parked behind the second fire truck. Three men and one woman exited then gathered around their boss. She told them to grab the guys who were already here, spread out, and start a grid search for the missing spouse.

"Do we have a description?" said one of the officers I hadn't seen before.

Cindy closed her eyes then slammed her hand on the hood

of Bishop's car. "Tell you what, officer. Round up every man you find out there, bring him in, and we'll figure out if he's Mr. Fitzsimmons." Under her breath, she uttered, "Idiot."

No, she was not okay.

The search party spread out and started their slow canvass of the eighty-acre Preserve. Cindy said that, if she didn't get back up to full staffing soon, she'd reduce the force by one more with her resignation. Charles said he and I were going to continue toward the lighthouse to do what we came to do, although we were too late to capture images of the sunrise casting its glow on the lighthouse.

Cindy said, "If you think I'm dumb enough to believe that crock, then I don't need to be chief of anything."

She knew Charles well. The last thing on his and, to be honest, my mind was to take photos. I had no idea what happened overnight. Laurie's confusion about Anthony being with her, or not, muddied the story even more. What was clear was there was a chance that Anthony was somewhere on the property, so Charles and I wanted to be nearby when he was found. Charles's nosy gene had invaded my system.

The distance from where we found Laurie to the beach overlooking the Morris Island Lighthouse was paved, all but the last hundred yards. The road, built to serve the Coast Guard, bisects the wooded area between the ocean to our right, and the marsh to the left.

"More than fifty kinds of birds have been seen back here," Charles said as we walked along the road.

"You tell me that each time we're here."

In addition to collecting long-sleeve T-shirts, Charles collected books; enough to stock his apartment with nearly as many books as are housed in the Folly Beach Branch of the Charleston County Library. He also collected trivia and quotes from United States presidents, and was generous with spewing trivia and quotes at anyone who'll listen. In my case, I had given up listening five years ago. It hadn't stopped him from sharing.

"I know. I also know your memory ain't what it was when you were a young whippersnapper. I've got to keep telling you."

"If you say so."

I normally didn't mind his banter. Walking along this path reminded me of my first time here some ten years ago, when I had looked forward to a peaceful morning photographing the lighthouse. Instead, I happened upon a murder. That fateful discovery catapulted me into a nightmare that nearly got me killed, not quite a chamber of commerce preferred introduction to Folly Beach. That walk also allowed me to meet Charles, plus a handful of Folly folks who've become my friends.

We reached the spot where the paved road ended. Then, a sandy path led the way to the beach. I was startled from reliving the past when one of the police officers to my right yelled, "Over here!"

Charles stopped, pointed his cane the direction of the sound. "He's calling us."

He wasn't directing his comment at us, yet it didn't stop Charles from nudging me in the direction of the voice. The wind-swept trees and shrubs along the right side of the path made it impossible to see who'd called, plus there wasn't a path in that direction. Two officers emerged from the less-densely foliaged area on the other side of the path, shoved their way between the prickly shrubs, then maneuvered toward the sound of the officer who'd repeated his call. A City of Folly Beach ATV parked beside us. Its driver joined the two officers into the shrub-filled space.

Charles and I followed. Between the mushy sand, standing

water from the overnight storm, and prickly underbrush, it was slow going. The officers in front of us had created a semblance of a path for us to reach the spot where the police were gathered. It didn't take a devotee of TV crime shows, or a coroner, to determine three things: The person they were staring at was male. The man splayed out in the sand had taken his last breath. And, if I could find anyone dumb enough to bet with, I'd wager my life savings on the unfortunate soul being Anthony, the late husband of Laurie Fitzsimmons.

Chief LaMond was next to arrive. She waved her officers away from the body, took in the surroundings, told two of her guys to tape off the scene, then glared at Charles and me.

She shook her head, pointed her finger at the two of us before pointing the direction of the road.

"Get the hell out of my crime scene!"

Told you she wasn't okay.

Chapter Three

C harles was surprisingly quiet on the drive to town after we'd been evicted from the crime scene. His only comment was that he was scheduled to make a delivery for our friend, Dude Sloan, owner of the surf shop. Charles picked up a few dollars making on-island deliveries for Dude, helping restaurants clean after busy weekends and, until recently, when he'd started complaining about debilitating arthritis in his hands, provided help for contractors who needed extra hands on projects. None of these *jobs* had burdened Charles with reported income, withholding taxes, or those burdensome IRS regulations. His expenses were minimal, so little more than petty cash was needed to meet his standard of living. I dropped him in front of the surf shop then continued to the Lost Dog Cafe for an early lunch.

The Dog, located a half-block off Center Street, Folly's center of commerce, was my favorite breakfast, and lunch spot. The kitchen in my cottage is used about as often as a Wiccan priest attends services at the Baptist church, so I was in the restaurant more often than many of its servers. As usual, the popular restaurant was packed, the closest parking spot two blocks away. The hostess told me that there would be a fifteen-minute wait. I was on my way outside to wait for a table when I heard a familiar voice call my name. I turned to find Theodore Stoll, pointing to an empty chair beside his brother, Salvadore. I must've been distracted by the morning's discovery to miss seeing them when I came in. Theo had on an orange T-shirt; Sal wore a red, orange, and florescent green striped shirt that looked like it belonged in a 1960s lounge singer's closet.

I joined the men, and Theo said, "What's this I hear about you finding a body at the old Coast Guard station?"

Sal didn't give me a chance to answer. He removed his black, wide-rimmed glasses that looked like he'd had them since the 1950s and said, "Is it a full, or a part-time job, you have bebopping around Folly finding bodies?"

Theo followed with, "Who was it? Who killed him?"

I held up my hand. "Whoa. Good morning, guys."

Theo pointed his fork at me. "Okay, let's try again. Good morning, Chris."

"Better."

I'd met Theo a couple years ago when Charles and I joined a senior walking group at the behest of Larry LaMond, a friend of mine who's Chief LaMond's husband, to find anything we could about another member of the group who'd been suspected of trying to blackmail Larry. It hadn't entered my mind that a benign senior walking group could nearly cost the lives of so many people. Anyway, that's a story for another time.

Theo was the butt of jokes by others in the group, who'd nicknamed him ET for Energizer Turtle, rather than for the lovable alien from the movie *ET*. For the group to call Theo slow was hypocritical since the average walking speed of the others in the group was the speed of an earthworm. Sal, at age seventy-nine, was nine years younger than his brother. He'd moved in with Theo earlier this year. He was a stand-up comedian who'd spent many years on the road before giving up the nomadic life to live comfortably in Theo's McMansion.

Sal said, "With the polite stuff finished, answer Theo's question."

I wanted to ask which of Theo's three questions he wanted me to answer. Instead, I told him that, yes, I was at the Preserve when a body was found. I asked how he'd heard about it.

"Amber," he said, like it was all I needed to know.

It was. I'd known Amber Lewis since I moved to Folly. She was the longest-tenured server at the Dog, was also the go-to person if you're in need of a friendly, warm, smiling face, or the latest gossip.

As if on cue, she arrived at the table, patted me on the shoulder, and said, "Good morning, trouble magnet. Did finding another body stir up your appetite?"

"How'd you hear about it?" I thought it was a legitimate question since the lifeless Anthony Fitzsimmons was discovered less than two hours ago.

Amber nodded toward the counter, where three diners were in deep conversation. One wore a police uniform, so I knew the answer before Amber said anything.

"Officer Timmons told me. He said the guy had been shot. He didn't know who did it. Sad, so sad. I told Theo, since you're friends."

"Enough gibberish," interrupted Sal. "I need more tea."

Amber frowned at him. "You'll get more as soon as I get done talking to Chris and seeing if he wants anything to eat." She turned back to me. "Are you okay?"

Amber and I had dated my first couple of years on Folly.

We had remained friends since then. I could count on her being concerned.

"I suppose so. Did you know Anthony and Laurie Fitzsimmons?"

"A smidgen. They'd been in a couple of times. They're retired teachers, bought an old house, are fixing it up." She chuckled. "Laurie was fascinated by the dog photos on the walls. She kept asking if all of them had been here. I told her that a few had. Although, since there are a couple of hundred photos, many were given to us by people long after they left. Some had never set a paw on our dog-friendly patios."

Sal waved his hand in Amber's face. "You think talking about these damn dogs is more important than my tea?"

Amber gave him her best faux smile. "Of course not, Theo's rude brother. I'll stop being nice to customers and scamper over there to get you your tea because you are certainly the most important person in the building."

Sal smiled. "Miss Amber, I spent a half century around comedians. You're going to have to do better than that to insult me."

She rubbed her hand in his long, gray hair. "I love a challenge." She headed behind the counter to get Sal's tea.

I said to Theo, "Did you know Anthony and Laurie?"

"Nope."

"Me, either," said Sal. "What's a dog kennel?"

I started to ask why he wanted to know.

He held up his hand. "A barking lot."

I grinned.

Theo said, "I'm trying to housebreak my brother's habit of telling jokes.

"You're failing," I said.

Theo sighed as he shook his head.

Sal said, "You two old farts have no sense of humor.

Enough about the dead guy I didn't know. Theo, tell Chris about the call."

Theo twisted his napkin as he looked at his half-eaten chicken salad croissant. "He doesn't care about——"

"Doesn't care about what?" Amber interrupted then set a fresh glass of tea in front of Sal.

"Nothing," Theo said. "Chris, were you going to order?"

Amber turned my way until I ordered a Mahi salad."

She put her hand over her heart. "Lordy, Lordy, Chris ordering something healthy. Not sure my heart can take it."

Theo leaned closer to Sal and whispered, "Amber's been trying to get Chris to eat healthier since forever."

Amber was good at many things, succeeding with that task wasn't one of them. She was right, although knowing and doing were two different things. I was a few pounds over-weight, which I rationalized as a byproduct of aging. Rational-izing was one of my strengths.

"I owe it all to you, Amber."

She winked. "Yeah, right," then headed over to the kitchen.

I turned to Theo. "What call?"

Another of my strengths was listening. I never thought it was a strength until I observed many others who only want to hear what they have to say and appear oblivious to the thoughts, feelings, and words of those around them. Besides, Charles's nosiness was rubbing off on me.

"Okay. You know my son died a year or so ago. He——"

My turn to interrupt. "Son? Theo, I didn't know you had children."

"Oh. I thought I must've told you."

I shook my head.

Theo turned to Sal. "Why'd you have to bring it up?"

Sal held his hands out to his side in a *who me* motion.

"Yes, Chris," Theo said, "Theodore Jr, he went by Teddy. Probably my biggest failure. It's hard to talk about. We were never close. I spent all my time working. Eunice had to raise him nearly by herself. Teddy went out west to college, where he stayed. The only time we saw him was when he came home for the holidays." He shook his head. "He didn't do that often. Eunice and I tried to stay in touch, but he wouldn't return our calls. He was a chef, worked all the time. He said that he couldn't come to see us and discouraged us from visiting. He opened his own restaurant. Poor Eunice and I never saw it." He sighed. "I was a terrible dad."

"Not so great a brother, either," Sal added.

I supposed that was a joke. If it was, Sal was joking with the wrong audience.

I said, "Go on, Theo."

He stared at his plate, like he was studying his chicken salad. I didn't think he was going to respond, until he said, "He got married. Know how I found out? Got an invitation in the mail, an invitation postmarked a week after the wedding."

"I'm sorry, Theo."

He looked down at his plate, sipped his water, closed his eyes. Sal, for once, didn't crack a joke. I waited for Theo to continue.

He didn't get a chance. Charles stormed in the door, looked around, and made a beeline for our table.

"Guess who I just talked to. Guess what he said."

Sal looked at my out-of-breath friend, and said, "Big Bird. He squawked that you're a lunatic."

Charles opened his mouth, stared at Sal, then shut his mouth.

"It was a joke, Charles," I said. "Theo was saying something important. Can it wait?"

"Oh, sorry."

I asked Charles to have a seat. He judiciously did and remained quiet, a near miracle.

I turned to Theo. "You were saying?"

"Not now, Chris. I can't." He stood as he waved to Amber for their check. He leaned close to me. "Later." He dropped money on the table then told Sal that they were leaving. It was as quick as I'd ever seen Theo move. His green jogging shorts swished as he headed to the exit. Sal followed two-steps behind him.

Charles watched them go. "What'd I interrupt?"

"Nothing," I said, not wanting to get in an extended conversation about Theo's son and whatever he wanted to tell me, reluctantly tell me. "Who'd you run into?"

"You know old man Gant?"

"Abraham Gant?"

"That's the one."

I didn't know much about him, other than he'd lived on Folly most of his life and retired from the South Carolina Highway Patrol.

"What about him?"

"I was peddling back to town from, delivering a wet suit for Dude. Took it to a chubby guy living out near the end of East Huron. Don't know how he's going to wiggle into the suit. He said—"

"Charles, Abraham Gant?"

"No wonder you never know what's going on. Anyway, I parked my bike beside the Crab Shack, was headed in to enjoy a brew. Gant was standing on the corner by the bicycle rack. Did you know he preferred to be called Captain Gant?"

"No. How do you know?"

"Suppose because the first time I met him he said call me Captain Gant." Charles smiled. "Thought it sounded silly. First thing I thought of was Captain America, Captain Hook,

Captain D's, Captain Midnight, Captain Crunch, Captain—"

"Your point, Charles?"

"Okay, okay. Captain was his last rank when he was a cop. Anyway, I said, "Howdy.' That's all it took."

"For what?"

"For him to start ranting about relic hunters, scavengers. Now, here's the important part, Anthony Fitzsimmons."

"Explain?"

"Captain stuck his shriveled-up forefinger in my chest, said something like, 'Did you hear that old, blankety-blank scoundrel was killed?' He didn't say blankety-blank."

"Was he talking about Anthony?"

"Duh, of course. That's my point. How did Captain know about the murder? We'd just stumbled on it."

"What else did he say?"

"I'd heard he was eccentric, but didn't know about what. Now, I do. The old boy gets all riled up on the topic of the past, about what kinds of things happened then."

"Like what?"

"Ghosts, things, people from the past. Says what happened back there needed to stay back there. What's buried should stay buried. He spouted off something about the past is the past because it's not now. He said people who go digging up bones, or old stuff, are the scourge of the earth."

I was certain that what Charles said didn't make sense. "So?"

"Hang on, I'm getting to the good part. Captain Gant said those people who dig up the past should, now get this, be shot. Yep, that's what he said. S.H.O.T."

Chapter Four

I left the Dog after agreeing that Gant's comment warranted a call to Chief LaMond. I didn't believe his mini-rant amounted to a confession yet, unless I agreed to tell Cindy, I'd never hear the last of it. Of course, Charles could've called her. He said that she'd believe me before taking his word. History told me he was right.

A stop at the post office rewarded me with a brochure offering a "deal of a lifetime" on a "miracle" hearing aid that was about the size of a gnat but would allow me to hear the tiniest sounds, or not miss important words spoken by family and friends. I didn't know about hearing the tiniest sounds, something that seemed to be a distraction rather than an improvement, but knew my friends made sure they never let any of their "important words" get past me. I dropped the deal of a lifetime in the trash before calling Chief LaMond.

She answered with, "What took you so long to pester me about this morning?"

"Good afternoon, Cindy."

"Tell me one good thing about it. Come on, tell me one."

Cindy's moods occasionally ranged from mad at the world to life's grand. I was a good enough friend, so she didn't hesitate sharing both ends of the spectrum. Her frustrations with her no-win job occasionally seeped into her relationship with those who knew her deeper than by title. There weren't many of us in that category, so I gave her benefit of the doubt, if she appeared to be taking her frustrations out on me.

"It's a beautiful July afternoon."

"Oh, wait, let me get out of this rickety chair, stand on my tippy-toes so I can look over this damned pile of folders chock full of crap I need to review and, oh yeah, hang on while I throw the office phone in the trash so I don't have to see the red light blinking, the screen showing I have twenty-seven voicemail messages." She groaned. "Hell, yes, it does look like a beautiful day out there. Hope you're enjoying the heck out of it. Back to my question, what took you so long to pester me about this morning?"

I moved the phone away from my face, so she wouldn't hear my chuckle.

"Sorry to bother you. I was talking to Charles, who shared a conversation he had with Abraham Gant."

Cindy interrupted, "That's Captain Gant to you."

"Yes, Captain Gant told Charles something about the past needing to stay in the past, that people who dig it up should be shot."

Cindy sighed. "Let me guess. Your *faux* detective friend used his *faux* detective skills to figure that Captain Gant killed Anthony Fitzsimmons."

"That was his thought."

"Chris, do you know how many people Captain Gant has shared his warped views with about relic hunters, grave robbers, heck, anyone who happens to stump their toe on a Civil War frying pan uncovered by a storm?"

"No."

"Me, either. It's a bunch. I've heard it from several of our fine citizens. He's freely shared those views for years with anyone who'd listen. Tell Charles to go back to doing what he does best. That would be nothing, in case you're not sure."

"I'll do that, Cindy. Have you learned anything new about the murder?"

"I'm disappointed it took you this long to butt in. If it would be any of your business, which it is not, the answer is, "No.'"

"Have you heard how Laurie Fitzsimmons is doing?"

"That I can answer. The hospital kept her a couple of hours. She was Ubered home after being told to drink plenty of liquids, get plenty of rest. One of the Sheriff's Office detectives is going to talk to her this evening."

The Folly Beach Department of Public Safety was responsible for law enforcement, fire protection, even animal control on the island but, because of the size of the department, major crimes were investigated by the Charleston County Sheriff's Office.

"Which detective?" I asked, realizing how sad it was that this retired insurance company bureaucrat would even ask. Since moving to Folly, I'd, unfortunately, encountered several detectives and on a more positive note, had dated one.

"Callahan."

I'd met Michael Callahan a few years ago, when he was lead detective in the murder investigation of a stockbroker. A friend of mine was the prime suspect before Charles and I stumbled on information that helped prove our friend innocent.

"Good. So no suspects?"

Before hanging up she said, "One, Abraham Gant."

———

I took part of the doctor's advice to Laurie and took a nap before I was to meet Barbara Deanelli for supper at Rita's. Barb owned Barb's Books, a used bookstore which occupied the space that formerly housed Landrum Gallery, a photo gallery owned by, and creatively named for, yours truly. Owning a gallery featuring my photos had been a lifelong dream. Once it became reality, it turned to a nightmare, where costs exceeded income by amounts approaching the national debt. I shuttered the door two years ago. The space morphed into Barb's Books.

Barbara moved to Folly from Pennsylvania after her attorney husband, now ex-husband, was arrested for bribing state officials. Barb, also an attorney, had no knowledge of her hubby's nefarious activities, yet was judged *guilty by wedding ring*. She moved to Folly to restart her life, and be near her half-brother, Dude Sloan. Dude and Barb were as alike as Viagra was to Venus, yet, over the last year, he had managed to find common ground to inch closer.

To secure a table on the patio, I was at the restaurant a half hour before I was to meet Barb. Rita's was on the corner of Center Street and East Arctic Avenue, a prime location on the island. It's across the street from the Folly Beach Fishing Pier, cattycorner from the Tides Hotel, and across Center Street from the iconic Sand Dollar Social Club.

I was sipping on the house Pinot Grigio when Barb appeared in the doorway. She was my height at five-foot-nine, at sixty-five, three years younger than I, way thinner, with short black hair. She was wearing one of her trademark red blouses. Tonight, she had on tan shorts. Her perfectly coordinated, and probably expensive, attire contrasted with my faded blue polo shirt and wrinkled gray shorts. She didn't seem to mind my scruffy clothes, as she kissed my forehead, pointed at my wineglass, and said, "Where's mine?"

Kim, the server, was quick to the table and said she would get Barb's drink, "before you could say please." It arrived before Barb could tell me how busy the bookstore had been this afternoon. I would have been hard-pressed to tell anyone that the gallery had been that busy, ever.

Barb and I had been, as some of my friends called it, an item for a year or so. She had been slow to acclimate to the unhurried pace, and bohemian attitude, of many of the island's residents. She wouldn't admit it, yet I could see the mellowing in her hard-driving tendencies, and skepticism about the motives of others. Folly was becoming a part of her attitudes, and her behavior. It was a delight to see.

"Got a rumor to bounce off you," she said before looking around for Kim. "First, I have to get something to fill this empty stomach." She waved to Kim. "Blue crab and artichoke dip, please. I'm starved."

Kim nodded and headed to the kitchen. Barb could out eat a sumo wrestler, yet she was model-thin. I fluctuated between envying, and hating, her metabolism.

Barb told me about a customer who'd vacationed on Folly for the last nineteen years, staying at a different house, or condo, each year. I didn't see what was so unusual, but Barb couldn't imagine someone moving around that much. I wondered what that story had to do with the rumor she'd mentioned before she ordered the crab and artichoke dip.

"Did she tell you the rumor you mentioned?"

"No, I got off track. Now, for the rumor. This afternoon, one of my regulars told me a tale about a body the police found this morning at the old Coast Guard property. The customer didn't know who he was, or the circumstances about his demise."

Kim set the appetizer in front of Barb.

The story took a back seat to Barb's need to fill her stomach. Two bites later, she continued. "The customer didn't know anything about the body. Know what she did know?"

I was afraid that I did. "What?"

"An old geezer named Chris Landrum was the guy who called the police. Seems he was there with another geezer, Charles Fowler, plus a lady the customer didn't know." Barb pointed a fried tortilla chip at me. "It's funny that I'd hear something like that from a stranger rather than from the person sitting across from me."

Her hazel eyes showed a glimmer of what I hoped was humor.

"I didn't want to interrupt your day at the store. I figured I'd tell you tonight." I stuffed a chip in my mouth.

"So you thought a pleasant supper would be the perfect time to talk about a dead body and being out with another woman?"

"Well, umm, I—"

Barb laughed. "Kidding." Her smile faded. "Are you okay?"

I said that I was and proceeded to tell her about my fateful morning. Barb was a good listener, rare among my friends. She used her law school training, plus years of listening to clients, to grasp everything I said.

She chewed another chip, wiped her mouth with her napkin, before saying, "I've only been out there once. It didn't seem that large an area. Is it possible to be lost as long as Ms. Fitzsimmons said they were?"

"It's hard to understand, although she was a stranger to the area. That, combined with it being dark and stormy, could make it possible."

"You said they're in their late fifties."

I nodded.

"Did she seem in good health?"

"What do you mean?"

"Did she appear healthy? Any noticeable handicaps?"

"As far as I could tell she was okay. Why?"

"It's strange that a person in good health who, after being separated from her husband in a strange place, not knowing what was going on, would, after finding her way back to the car, fall asleep. I'd be worried sick, wouldn't be able to sleep."

"Putting it that way, yes, it's strange. What're you saying?"

Kim returned to ask if we were ready to order. Barb quickly said that she was and ordered the flounder. I was a sucker for Rita's hamburgers, so I ordered one.

"What am I saying?" Barb said as Kim moved toward the kitchen. "Suppose I'm a bookstore owner playing lawyer. Usually, when things don't make sense, there's more to it than meets the eye. If I was a defense attorney representing someone who'd been accused of murdering Mr. Fitzsimmons, someone other than his wife, that is, I'd be looking for suspects to throw at the jury. Ms. Fitzsimmons would be number one. She may be as innocent as a newborn, yet her unlikely story would go a long way toward creating reasonable doubt for my client."

I told her that the police would see the same things.

Barb said that she hoped so.

"Speaking of suspects," I said. "Do you know Abraham Gant?"

She nodded. "Cranky guy, insists on being called Captain?"

"So you know him?"

"Little, other than he stops in the store about once a week. Cranky, feisty fellow. Why?"

I told her about Gant's encounter with Charles.

"He's a history buff, spends most of his time browsing the history, or biography, sections. He bought a few books about the Civil War, one on slavery. He may not want anyone to literally dig up things from the past, yet he reads a lot about the past. That seems to be a form of dredging up history."

I seldom read anything other than the newspaper, and that's not often, so I didn't know how many books Barb had on the Civil War. She gave one of her endearing laughs when I asked.

"I've gotten several in, sold them as quickly to your friend William Hansel. He, like Gant, is a history buff."

"The Civil War?"

"He stops every Friday on his way home from the College of Charleston. He said he's a professor of Hospitality and Tourism, is deeply involved with Preserve the Past, the group with the goal of raising money to preserve the Morris Island Lighthouse. He always asks if I have anything new on the Civil War. William is one of my favorite customers. Others could learn a thing or two from him about politeness."

Our entrees arrived and the conversation, once again, took a back seat to eating. The sun was lowering itself behind the second story of St. James Gate up the street. While it was still in the upper eighties, we were in the shade, and comfortable. Neither Barb, nor I, returned to the topic of murder. We spent the next hour watching the steady stream of people walking along the nearby sidewalk, enjoying each other's company.

After leaving Rita's, we walked four blocks up Center Street, listened to the live music coming from Snapper Jack's upstairs outside bar, and the Crab Shack, before heading back down the street to her oceanfront condo. The day ended much more pleasantly than it had begun.

Chapter Five

Barb's questions about Laurie's actions stayed with me well into the next day. True, it was unusual that Laurie would find her way back to the car only to fall asleep while her husband's whereabouts was in question or if he was with her at all, yet did it rise to the level of making her a murder suspect? It wasn't my problem to solve, that was tasked to the capable hands of Detective Callahan from the Sheriff's Office and Chief LaMond of the Folly Beach Department of Public Safety.

Barb mentioning William Hansel reminded me that it had been several weeks since I'd talked to my friend. He was probably home from work so why not take the short, four-block walk to his house. I needed to lose a few pounds so, despite my aversion to exercise, the walk would do me good. Remember, I said to myself, it was simply me wanting to talk to an old friend, burning calories in the process, not anything to do with Anthony Fitzsimmons' death. Honest.

William's wife had died seventeen years ago, so he lived alone in a quaint, pre-Hurricane Hugo cottage on West

Cooper Avenue, two blocks from Center Street. He greeted me at the door, like there was nothing unusual about me dropping by unexpectedly.

"Ah, my friend," he said in his deep bass voice as he waved me in. He was thin, roughly my height, and four years younger than I. "To what do I owe the pleasure of your company?"

"Did I catch you at a bad time?"

"On the contrary. I just arrived home and changed from professorial attire to my gardening wardrobe."

If you took my friend sentence-challenged Dude's average words spoken, add it to William's, then divide the sum by two, you would come close to a normal sentence. William was a wonderful person with the best intentions but, occasionally, it was hard to stay awake once he started talking.

His gardening *wardrobe* consisted of jeans with a hole in the left knee, a long-sleeved denim shirt, and tennis shoes.

"Don't let me keep you from whatever you were going to do."

"Nonsense. The precocious, invasive weeds in my garden will wait until later for me to eradicate them. Is it possible that you have an agenda for today's visit?"

See my point?

"No. It's been a while since we've talked, so I thought I'd stop by."

"I'm pleased that you did. Could I interest you in iced tea?"

"If it's no trouble."

William headed to the kitchen, and I sat on the flower-patterned, wingback sofa facing a similarly-patterned wing-back chair. I gazed around the room to, once again, be struck by the feminine touches. Cream-colored doilies topped each table with glass angel figurines strategically placed on the coffee table. I had never asked, nor had William offered, but I suspected the house looked exactly as it had before his wife's death.

William returned to hand me tea in a vintage, cut crystal drinking glass. He offered sugar from a white sugar bowl. I declined, and William took a seat in the wingback chair.

He took a sip then said, "Chris, I value our friendship immensely, and I thoroughly enjoy our conversations. I also feel I'm well enough acquainted with you to share what my intuition tells me."

"That would be?"

"You did not appear at my door simply to *shoot the bull*, as my students would say. If I am mistaken, I apologize. If not, perhaps you would like to share your reason."

"Did you hear about the body found at the Lighthouse Inlet Heritage Preserve?"

"I was paying for gas this morning at Circle K, where I heard the person in front of me say something to the clerk about a deceased gentleman. I, of course, am not prone to infuse myself in conversations, unless invited, so I didn't learn anything further. Perhaps that is the body to which you refer."

I gave him a brief rundown about the body, and the circumstances under which it was found.

"Oh, my heavens, that's tragic. I am not familiar with them. Do they live on our island?"

I told him what little I knew.

"What were they doing in the Preserve overnight? My understanding is that it closes at sunset, albeit it's a rule diffi-cult to enforce since there are no barriers around the property."

"Hunting Civil War relics. They got caught in the rain, then darkness set in. There was a metal detector in the car."

William frowned. "Collecting artifacts from the Civil War,

or any other previous visitors or inhabitants of Folly, is strictly prohibited in the Preserve."

"That might be the reason they were there late in the day. There would've been few, if any, others nearby."

William looked in his tea glass, at one of the glass angel figurines on the table, then back at me. "It would appear someone else was there, unless Mrs. Fitzsimmons killed her spouse. Are you taking it upon yourself to investigate who might have terminated the gentleman's life?"

"Nothing like that. I found it interesting that she told me they were looking for relics. I'd heard you were a Civil War buff. I knew you had a strong interest in saving the lighthouse, but I wasn't aware of your interest in the Civil War."

"Quite frankly, I had little interest in the infamous conflict, until I learned about the gravesite of the nineteen soldiers from the 55th Massachusetts Volunteer Regiment found on the western end of Folly. The regiment was composed of free-born African Americans trained near Boston before heading south to fight the Confederacy.

"I perhaps had learned some about this during my secondary schooling, although if I had, it was long forgotten. I share a common race with those brave soldiers, so I took an interest in their plight before expanding that interest to the entire milieu and personality of those who fought in that war that divided our country."

"Barb told me you were a regular, always in search of books on the Civil War."

"That, and to gaze at the lovely bookstore proprietress." He winked at me and chuckled.

"That I can identify with."

"Are there specific questions that I might answer about the horrific time in our country's history?"

"Any ideas what the Fitzsimmons may've been looking for?"

"The gravesite I referred to is on the opposite end of the island from the Preserve although, from what I read, the eastern portion of Folly Island was important to the Federal army as a strategic base for the battle to take Fort Sumter. They constructed roads, primitive forts, living quarters, even an artillery battery out there." He shook his head. "I can't imagine how miserable it must have been surviving in the jungle-like foliage, the extreme summer heat, humidity, exposure to the ocean, lack of adequate shelter, and sanitation."

"What would've been left at those sites to pique the interest of the Fitzsimmons?"

"I would imagine little of monetary worth. Anything left would consist of trinkets of steel, or other metals, cookware, uniform buttons, tools. Remember a while back when Hurricane Matthew visited out humble island?"

I nodded.

"A man found a dozen or so rusted cannonballs on the beach near the Preserve. They were rendered harmless, yet would have been valuable to someone who collected, legally or illegally, ordnance from the Civil or other wars." William looked out the window, started to speak, then hesitated.

"What?"

"Chris, as I have shared with you on more than one occasion, I look askance at rumors and gossip. More than askance, I abhor them."

"But?"

"There've been rumors going around for decades that a British ship, or possibly more than one, sailed from Canada, carrying a cargo of guns and gold to the soldiers. One of those ships, the Constance Decimer, sank. It was later discovered near Charleston with no gold found. Old-timers swear that there were several other ships carrying gold.

"None of this has been proven, that's why I put it in the broad category of rumor. If the Fitzsimmons heard some of these stories, it's conceivable they thought the east end of the island could be the final resting place of the precious metal." William smiled. "Of course, there are an equal number of rumors that a hundred years before the Civil War, pirates sailed up and down the coast robbing merchant ships of gold, silver, other valuable commodities. Some of those pirate vessels were reputed to hide their bounty on the coastal islands, Folly included. Yet again, these are only rumors."

"I've heard stories about pirates."

"Does any of this help?"

"A little," I said. "One more question. Do you know Abraham Gant?"

"Captain Gant?"

"Yes."

"What about him?"

"Someone mentioned that he has strong opinions about relic hunters."

William smiled. "If by strong you mean that he thinks they all should be wiped off the face of the planet then, yes, he is opinionated. He'd attended a couple of Preserve the Past meetings. He seemed to be sitting on a cushion of nails, quick to comment on most anything. Once, when dear sweet Francene Gregory suggested that some excavating around the lighthouse might give the group a better idea of what it was like during the structure's earlier days, the Captain uttered something about sacrilege then stormed out of the room. He's not been back, nor has his presence been missed."

"Is that all you know about him?"

"Yes. It's more than I want to know."

We moved to a topic that was dearer to his heart, his garden, and ended on a lighter note. He told me not to be a stranger; I told him that he was welcome at my house.

I left the air-conditioned comfort and stepped into the heat that felt twenty degrees hotter than when I arrived. Add sweltering humidity, and I questioned the wisdom of walking instead of driving to William's. Instead of trekking all the way home, I stopped at the Surf Bar, located halfway between William's house and mine. An advantage of being retired was that most of the time I didn't have to be anywhere. I had a twinge of guilt about that freedom, as compared to most everyone else who had to work for a living. The twinge this time lasted until I grabbed a stool at the rustic bar and ordered a glass of wine. There were five other customers.

My appearance raised the average age of those present by roughly ten years. The popular bar catered to a younger crowd and, on most weekends, featured live music by groups I'd never heard of. From what I'd seen on how packed the bar was on weekend nights, I was in the minority when it came to knowing about the rock, funk, or whatever name captured today's popular music.

A couple of rock songs I did recognize filled the room, and the sound system was turned to a level more fitting to my elderly ears. That was fortunate since I heard my phone ring. Charles's name was on the screen.

He said, "Want to go with me tomorrow?"

"Hello, Charles."

I had been trying to get my friends to start conversations with radical words like, "hello," or even the shorter version, "hi." I'd been as successful as the pet collie I had as a child had been at climbing a telephone pole to catch a squirrel. Actually, the collie was more successful. It managed to leap three feet up the pole.

"Hi, Chris. So want to go?"

This wasn't the time to attempt a lesson in phone etiquette. "Where?"

"Gee, get with the program. To see Laurie."

"Silly me. Why didn't I know that?"

He ignored my comment. "Are you going, or not?"

"Charles, why are you, we, going to see Laurie?"

"To see if she's okay."

To paraphrase the Good Book, or possibly The Byrds, for everything there is a season. This is not the time, the season, to try to find out Charles's motivations. 'Tis the time to say, "Sure. What time?"

We agreed on a time, and I ordered a second glass of wine. I had a hunch that I'd need it.

Chapter Six

C harles told me that he'd used his "well-honed investigative skills" to learn that the Fitzsimmons's house was eight blocks off Center Street on East Erie Avenue. His well-honed investigation consisted of asking Officer Bishop where Laurie lived. With temperatures in the upper eighties, neither of us wanted to walk. He'd told me to pick him up at 10:00, so I was in his parking lot at 9:30 the next morning. On time, to him, meant thirty minutes before the rest of the world's interpretation.

He stepped out the door of his compact Sandbar Lane apartment, spotted my car, and looked at his wrist, where normal people wore a watch. Charles, never accused of being normal, didn't own a timepiece. He wore a long-sleeved, green and white, Bismarck State College T-shirt, tan shorts with a black ink stain on the pocket, and Adidas tennis shoes. His graying, ill-kept hair was sticking out the side of his canvas Tilley hat.

"Glad you made it on time," he said.

I smiled as he slid in the passenger seat and tossed his cane in the back seat. Two minutes later, we were driving east on Erie Avenue, while Charles looked for the address he'd been given. The houses on the left side of the road backed up to the marsh and the Folly River, giving them magnificent views of the sunset. The residences on the right didn't have nearly as good a view. Most were older with a sizable number built before Hurricane Hugo devastated the island in 1989.

Charles spotted the Fitzsimmons house a half block before East Erie made a sharp right turn to become Eighth Street East. The house was set back from the road on a lot surrounded by large live oaks, three palmetto trees, and straggly underbrush. My realtor friend, Bob Howard, would've described the house as "in need of some TLC." In non-realtor-speak, the word "dump" would have been appropriate. The one-story house had wood plank siding with several boards missing. The roof was covered with pine needles with mildew around the edges. Two sawhorses were near the front door with a four-by-eight-foot sheet of plywood spanning them. A red toolbox was shaded by the plywood, with an orange extension cord snaking from the side of the house to the sawhorses. A narrow gravel drive weaved around the trees. The MINI Cooper was in front of the house.

I was reluctant to go to the door, a reluctance not shared by my passenger. He grabbed his cane, bounded out of the car, then scampered to the door, as if he was late for a meeting with Laurie.

Well-worn front steps squeaked as we climbed them. The front door had been painted red, but had faded to pink; the brass-plated door knob had long lost its luster. Not seeing a doorbell, Charles knocked. There was no response, or sounds, coming from the house, so Charles glanced at me standing behind him, shrugged, and knocked again. Still nothing. He asked if we should leave when the door opened a couple of inches.

Laurie peeked out; her eyes darted from Charles to me. "Can I help you?"

"Hey, Laurie," Charles said like we were lifelong friends. "It's Charles and Chris. Remember, we were at your car the other morning?"

The door opened a couple more inches. The sunlight shone on her. Her eyes were bloodshot, her hair uncombed. Our visit was not a good idea.

"You were there when they took me to the hospital," she said, more of a question than statement.

"We were," Charles said. "Chris and I were nearby, and wanted to stop to see if you were okay, or needed anything. Have a few minutes?"

"Oh, umm, I guess." She slowly opened the door the rest of the way while motioning us in.

She wore a bulky, quilted robe, and was barefoot. She pointed to the living room to the right. "Have a seat while I throw something on." She headed toward the back of the house.

We sat on a burgundy-colored, leather sofa that appeared new. A black leather La-Z-Boy recliner was at a right angle to the sofa facing a large, flat-screen television. Nothing else was in the room. The new furnishings contrasted with the cheap wood-panel walls.

The double-hung window was missing all but the casing and jamb. Heavy, transparent plastic covered the entire window and was duct taped to the casing. An exposed electrical junction box was in the center of the ceiling which, at one time, must've held a ceiling fan, or a light. In front of the sofa, there was an eight-by-ten-foot dark green indoor/outdoor carpet that I suspected was hiding flaws in the floor.

Laurie returned. She had run a brush through her hair, put on a starched, white blouse, a black and white striped skirt, plus a forced smile.

I smiled, hoping it seemed sincerer than hers. "We didn't mean to intrude. I know this is a terrible time. We wanted to offer our deepest sympathy for your loss."

"Thank you," she whispered then turned to Charles. "I'm sorry, tell me your names again."

We reintroduced ourselves as she moved to the La-Z-Boy. Her petite frame was swallowed by the chair.

"I apologize for my memory," she said. "It's coming back now. You were at the car when I woke up. Charles, I also remember meeting you on the street when we asked if you were from Jacksonville."

Charles smiled. "That's right." He looked around the room. "You have a nice house. I'm so sorry you have to start your retirement on such a tragic note."

I wondered what house Charles was talking about. I kept my mouth shut.

"Thank you. Were you still there when they… when they found Anthony?"

Charles lowered his gaze to the floor. "Sadly, we were. We are so sorry."

Laurie stared at the spot on the floor where Charles had been looking. "I didn't know, umm, they didn't tell me about his passing until a detective came to the hospital. He waited for the doctor to release me." Tears filled her eyes. "Oh, God, if only I'd gone with him when he tried to find his way out of the woods. Why did I tell him to go ahead, that I'd be okay where I was? He might still be with us if I'd gone."

She was no longer confused about if he'd been with her that night like she'd told the EMTs.

Charles leaned forward. "You don't know that, Laurie. If you'd gone, maybe you'd have been… well, not with us now."

"I don't know."

Charles continued to lean toward Laurie. "Any idea who could've done it?"

I was beginning to get a hint of another reason Charles wanted to visit the grieving widow.

"No. We hardly know anyone here. We're retired teachers. Who'd want to kill us?"

"Did Anthony have enemies?" Charles continued.

"None."

Her tears had stopped flowing, and she seemed more comfortable talking.

I said, "You told us you all were in the old Coast Guard property searching for Civil War relics. Find any?"

She eyes opened wide. "I said that?"

I nodded and wondered if I should mention that she'd told the EMTs that Anthony wasn't there.

"No, nothing."

"Did anyone here know you'd be there?"

She shook her head. "The person who shot poor Anthony must be a nutjob, an escapee from a mental hospital who was there for… for, I don't know why. Poor Anthony was only trying to find his way to the car. Why did it happen?"

I said, "They'll catch whoever did it."

She slammed her fist on the armrest. "Will that bring my husband back?"

"No," Charles whispered.

Laurie shook her head. "I'm being a horrible hostess. Can I get you something to drink?"

Charles smiled. "Water would be nice. Could I help?"

Laurie declined his offer then went to the kitchen. Charles

leaned toward me. "It'll calm her. She needs someone to talk to."

She was quick to return with a plastic cup of water for each of us, even though I hadn't indicated that I wanted any. She went to the kitchen to get her cup then returned to the La-Z- Boy.

"How come you decided to retire to Folly?" Charles asked, as if the previous discussion of finding the body had never happened.

Laurie took a sip then stared in the cup. "My grandfather grew up here in the '30s. My parents and I used to come up from Florida each summer for a week or two. I remember Granddaddy spinning tall tales about various characters who lived here. He'd go on about how he thought the police were no better than the crooks yet, if anything bad ever happened to someone, all the people, good or bad, would band together to help whoever was having problems."

"The police aren't corrupt now," Charles interjected. "People still hang together if anything bad happens. You could say that's why we're here. What was your grandfather's name again?"

She hadn't said the first time.

"Harnell Levi." She smiled. "He was a character. Know what else Granddaddy talked about all the time?"

Of course, we didn't. I said, "What?"

"Buried relics. Civil War valuables. He said that he knew there was a lot of it. He just hadn't had time to look. I took it all with a grain of salt. Figured, if it was here, then someone would've found it by now. When I told Anthony about Granddaddy's stories, he took them to heart, started doing research." She stopped, took a sip of water, stared at the plastic covering the window. "If I hadn't told him those stories, he'd be with me today, tomorrow, and…"

"Again, Laurie, we're so sorry," I said. "We won't take more of your time. Is there someone we can call to be with you? Relatives?"

"Thank you, no. Anthony's only living relatives are distant cousins. They live in Miami. He never had contact with them. I doubt they'll come to his funeral. Mine are in Seattle. We're not close. Two friends are coming up from Jacksonville tomorrow. They're going to stay a few days to help with funeral arrangements."

"Good," Charles said. "Let me give you my number. Please call if there's anything you need or if Chris and I can help."

She took the number then walked us to the door. "Thanks again for stopping by. Sorry I wasn't good company."

The inside of the car felt like we were in an oven with the heat turned to 350 degrees. I switched the air conditioner to high and turned to Charles.

"What do you think?" I asked.

"What do I think about what? The poor lady lost her husband. Now, she's stranded on an island where she doesn't know anyone. She's a mess. That's what I think."

"I agree, although did you catch what she said about why they were separated the night Anthony was killed?"

"Sure. She said she told him to try to find his way back to the car, that she'd be okay where she was."

"Yes, that's what she said today. Remember what she told us when we found her at her car?"

Charles rubbed his three-day old whiskers. "Sure. Umm, maybe."

"She said Anthony told her to stay where she was. He'd find the trail to the car. She then told him they had to stick together."

"Now that you mention it, yeah. Two different stories?"

I nodded. "She could've been confused that night. The rain, being lost, sleeping in the car, being confronted by two men she didn't know."

"We need to tell Cindy?"

"I don't know."

"I do," Charles grabbed my phone off the console and handed it to me.

The chief's voicemail kicked in after five rings. Charles rolled his eyes, like Cindy had the nerve not to take such an important call. I left her a message to call when she had a chance.

Charles looked over at the house. "I'll grant you that Laurie could've been confused about her stories, or she's having trouble keeping her story straight. Remember, when she was talking to the EMTs she was confused about if Anthony was even there. Confusion would be simple, if it's all a lie."

Chapter Seven

I began the next day with a cinnamon Danish from my next-door neighbor, Bert's Market. My culinary skills exceeded a butterfly's ability to bake a cherry pie, but not by much. If it wasn't for Bert's, the island's only grocery, and the Lost Dog Cafe, I would've shriveled up and blown away. The humidity was low, the temperature cooler than it had been for a couple of weeks, so I took the Danish, a cup of complimentary coffee, then walked two blocks to the Folly Beach Fishing Pier.

After walking to the far end of the thousand-foot long structure, I stopped to observe five surfers sitting on their boards, waiting for a wave, and two men on paddleboards creating their own excitement by paddling through the calm surf. Chief LaMond hadn't returned my call, so I was tempted to call her until I realized that the inconsistencies in Laurie's stories were minor, easily explained. I didn't want to be an alarmist, or worse, a Charles. I also replayed the rest of the conversation with Laurie, but nothing else struck me as important.

Laurie saying that she and her family weren't close reminded me of what Theo had confided about his son. I also remembered Charles interrupting his story. Did Theo want to tell me more, or what was important about a phone call that Sal mentioned? One way to find out. I didn't know him as well as I knew William, so I wasn't comfortable showing up at his door unannounced.

Instead of calling Cindy, I punched Theo's number in the phone. I told him I felt bad that our conversation at the Dog had been interrupted and wondered if he wanted to share more. He said he would, then hesitated before saying it really wasn't anything to burden me with. That was all it took. I asked if he wanted to meet for lunch. He said he would but had promised to take Sal to the mall for shoes. I told him I was nearby and could come to his house. He hesitated before saying okay.

When Theo opened the door I had to bite my tongue not to laugh. He was wearing red, white, and blue striped jogging shorts, well, they'd be called jogging shorts on anyone other than Theo. On him, shuffling shorts came to mind. He also wore a tank-top T-shirt, or as trivia-collecting Charles had informed me was called an A-shirt, the *A* standing for athletic. It had a paint stain on the side. Rounding out his attire were his knee-length, black, support socks.

Theo waved me in, then ushered me to the great room where floor to ceiling windows provided a panoramic view of the marsh and the Folly River. I'd been in the room several times, was always impressed with the high-end, aka expensive, furnishings, with original oil paintings on three walls. Theo had founded a window-replacement company where he discovered a gas he sandwiched between two panes of glass, helping keep cold air in when it's hot outside, warm air in during the winter. He'd tried to explain the chemistry to me, although all I understood was that he'd sold the company for several million dollars.

"Where's Sal?" I asked after I took a seat on the oversized, latte-colored leather sofa.

Theo pointed toward the ceiling. "Still asleep. He seldom stirs before noon. After years performing late nights in comedy clubs, his circadian rhythm pattern is asunder. When we saw you at the Dog, I had to wake him up to go with me."

In non-technical talk, I supposed that meant that Sal slept late. "You were used to living alone. How are things working out with him?"

"It's been an adjustment. He stays out of my way, spends most of his time in his room. After sleeping in hotel rooms for decades, he says he's comfortable in the small space. That's fine with me. How about coffee?"

I said it sounded good then followed him to the kitchen that looked like it was taken from the pages of *Charleston Living Magazine.*

"At the Dog, you were talking about your son. Sal mentioned a call, but you didn't get to tell me about it."

I stopped hoping he'd pick up on the conversation. He handed me the drink, then we returned to the great room.

"I told you I wasn't a good dad. His mom was great, encouraged him in school. He had straight A's in high school. I wanted him to follow in my footsteps and go into engineering, maybe law school. In hindsight, it was a mistake. We had a major blowout over it. He rebelled, left home the week he finished high school. Chris, I shouldn't have pushed."

Theo looked at the floor and shook his head.

"What happened?"

"He moved to Southern California, taking a series of low-paying restaurant jobs. The only reason I know is because he kept in contact with his mother. Eunice told me that he worked his way up to be a cook at better restaurants. We didn't hear anything for five years, then we got a note saying he and another guy were opening a fish restaurant, said he was happier than he'd ever been." He shook his head like he was shaking out memories. "Did I tell you he got married?"

"You'd mentioned it before Charles interrupted."

"Sure you want to hear this?"

I said that I did.

"The next time I heard from him was when we got the wedding invitation, got it after the wedding. When Eunice died, I found the name of his restaurant in one of the letters he'd sent her. I called. It was strange talking to Teddy after all those years. You know what he told me?"

I shook my head.

"It was busy season. He couldn't get away to come to the funeral. He sent a big arrangement of flowers to the funeral home. Chris, I hate to admit it, but I wanted to hurl them in the trash." Theo twisted the corner of a throw pillow in his lap.

"Theo, you don't have to tell me unless you want to. You said he died a year or so ago. What happened?"

Theo stared out the window. A walking pier extended from the back of the house, across a narrow strip of marsh, to the edge of the river.

"I was out at the end of the pier, this time of day, in fact. The phone rang. A female voice with an accent, possibly Caribbean, asked if I was Theodore Stoll, father of Theodore Jr. I told her I was and asked who she was. Her name was Grace, said she was my son's wife. He was dead." He stared at the pillow in his hands. "I was stunned."

"What happened?"

"Grace, umm, Teddy's wife, said he was on his motorcycle on the way to work when a car swerved to avoid hitting a dog. It struck Teddy's front wheel. The motorcycle flipped, Teddy was thrown over the handlebars, his head hit the raised curb. He wasn't wearing a helmet. Killed instantly."

"I'm sorry."

He shook his head. "It took me a few minutes to grasp what she'd said. Finally, I asked about funeral arrangements while mentally trying to figure out how I could get there. I needn't have. The woman said he'd been cremated. She and Teddy's friends spread his ashes in the Pacific." Theo threw the pillow across the room. "My son didn't want me around when he was alive. Didn't want me there in death."

I repeated how sorry I was.

After a long pause, Theo said, "You asked about the call. Grace said she was on the way to Charleston. She wants to meet me. Chris, I don't know one iota about the woman." He held his arms out, palms up. "Why would she want to meet me? Why would I want to meet her?"

"Don't suppose you'll know until you meet her. When's she getting here?"

"Two days." He stared out the window before turning back to me. "Will you go with me?"

———

Chief LaMond returned my call that evening and apologized for taking so long, something about a two-day training session in Charleston for local police chiefs. I asked how the sessions were. She unceremoniously said that she had learned more painting her toenails while daydreaming about Brad Pitt. She added the meals were better than Larry could fix on his outdoor grill. That meant the meals were nothing to write a culinary magazine about since Larry was almost as good a "chef" as I was. I told her that I was sorry, she added a couple of her native East Tennessee profanities, then added that her officers benefitted by her being at the meetings instead of pestering them. She ran out of steam griping about the training session then finally asked why I'd called.

"Couple of reasons. I was curious if you've learned anything else about Anthony Fitzsimmons's death, or—"

"I knew it," she interrupted. "Larry owes me a steak dinner at Halls Chophouse. Halleluiah!"

Halls was one of the top restaurants in Charleston.

"Let me guess. He bet I wouldn't call to ask about the death?"

"Yep, the boy will never learn. That's after I told him you already left the message."

"Congratulations. So have you learned anything?"

"Hang on a second. Let me get the taste of that scrumptious filet mignon out of my mouth before I scream at you for sticking your cute little nose in police business, business that's none of your business."

"Cindy, I'm not butting in. Charles and I found Laurie. I was curious."

"Butting in, nosy, curious, inquisitive, all the same. You, and I suppose your sidekick, are for what, the seventieth time, playing detective, assuming the highly-trained police professionals couldn't find their noses during allergy season."

I choked back a chuckle. "So anything new?"

Cindy uttered a loud sigh, followed by, "Autopsy results indicate time of death was Sunday between midnight and 4:00 a.m. Cause of death didn't need an autopsy to determine. A bullet hole in the head ruled out prostate cancer. Even us dumb cops got that right." She hesitated and said, "This is the point where you're supposed to say, 'Now, chief, that's not true. I have faith that you and the other cops will figure it out. I will stay out of your way to let you do your job.'"

"Did you learn anything else?"

Another sigh. "Not really. The rain washed away any prints. The shot was from close range. A couple of the nearby houses were occupied, everyone claimed that they were asleep after midnight, didn't hear, or see, anything. None of them even said they saw the glow-in-the-dark, orange car parked near their house. A lot of lightning was nearby so, if anyone heard the gunshot, it could've been mistaken for thunder. That's about it. Don't worry. I'm sitting here at my expensive police-chief desk waiting for the damn killer to walk in to confess. To think, you don't believe us cops know what we're doing."

"Cindy, I know you know what—"

"Chris, no need to say it. I'm frustrated, letting off steam. We have nothing. It feels like crap. You called for two reasons."

I could almost hear her shout *butting in* before I told her the second reason. "Charles and I went to see Laurie Fitzsimmons yesterday. She said—"

"That's not butting in?" the chief shouted as I moved the phone away from my ear.

"Charles thought—"

"That's two damn words that should never be neighbors."

"We thought since Laurie told him that she and her husband were new to Folly that they might not know many people here. We wanted to see if she needed anything."

"Chris, that's about the biggest pile of moose manure I've heard this year and, believe me, I've heard piles of it."

It was my turn to sigh. "Chief, do you want to hear what we learned or want to continue your harangue?"

"What did you and your social worker friend learn when you went to help the damsel in distress?"

"When we found her that morning, she said Anthony told her to stay where she was. He'd find the trail to the car. She told him that they had to stick together."

"So?"

"When we met yesterday, she said that she told Anthony to try to find his way back to the car, that she'd be okay where she was. Don't you think those are significant differences?"

"Chris, they're different but, under the circumstances, doesn't it make sense that she could've been confused, especially when you first met her? Her husband was missing. She'd been asleep. It'd been storming. She was in a strange place. And, you and Charles appeared out of nowhere. If I ran into someone looking like Charles under those circumstances, he'd scare the, well, you know what, out of me."

"You're right, of course."

"But you don't believe it?"

"Cindy, my gut tells me it's more than confusion."

"Is your theory she killed him?"

"Okay, I'm butting in a little. If I was a detective, I wouldn't rule it out."

"You do realize you're not a detective."

"Of course not, chief."

"Right. What do you and your fake private eye friend think her motive was?"

"No idea."

"If she was asleep, had been out there all night, what did she do with the gun?"

"No idea."

"That helps. I don't know how I'd keep Folly safe without such incredible citizen support."

Cindy was good at passing out grief and sarcasm. She was

also an exceptional law enforcement official. From numerous discussions over the years, I knew that she'd taken me seriously. Even if she didn't acknowledge it, she'd follow up on whatever I shared. She was a good cop, an even better friend.

"Cindy, what's going to happen next?"

"No idea."

Chapter Eight

I ran into Dude Sloan the next morning in front of Planet Follywood. After a brief discussion, the only kind possible with Dude; I agreed to have lunch with him at Loggerhead's. We'd often talked but seldom broke bread together, so I was looking forward to the meal, sitting outside on a beautiful summer afternoon, while sharing partial sentences with the surf shop owner.

I was seated on the deck at a table near the railing overlooking the Oceanfront Villas, an expansive four-story, oceanfront, condo complex, when Dude appeared at the top of the steps. The aging surfer was five years younger than I, three inches shorter, a ton of pounds lighter. His face looked like a cross between Arlo Guthrie and Willie Nelson. He wore one of his many florescent tie-dyed T-shirts with a peace symbol dominating the front, along with one of his many confused looks on his face. He spotted me then weaved his way around several tables. The patio was nearly full, with two servers working at Mach speed to keep up.

Dude looked at me then at his watch. "Christer be early."

It was a malady I'd caught from Charles.

I pointed to a chair on the opposite side of the table. "I wanted to make sure we got a table."

Dude looked around at the crowded seating area. "It worked."

Tiffany, a server who'd waited on me several times, always with a friendly smile, and a kind comment, was quick to the table and asked Dude if he wanted something to drink.

He looked at the glass of white wine in front of me. He said, "Martini, *tres* green fruitees, stuck with wood." He grinned at Tiffany. "Please."

Tiffany looked at me, still with the smile on her face, and shrugged.

"Gin martini with three olives," I said.

Dudespeak often required a translator, and like gin martinis, was an acquired taste. Tiffany seemed satisfied as she headed to the outdoor bar.

"Be snugglin' with fractional sis?"

Since I'd started dating Barb, Dude's half-sister, a little over a year ago, he'd gone out of his way to have more contact with me. We talked a couple of times a week at the Dog, and he and Pluto, his Australian Terrier, had stopped by the house a few times. He and Barb had never been close; their professional lives had little in common until she moved to Folly. Their current common interest was they both owned retail stores, although the surf shop had been wildly successful for years while Barb's Books was new, struggling to gain a profitable customer base. They'd become closer a year ago when a tragic event touched each of them. They're now protective of each other.

"We had supper the other night."

"*Donde?*"

As If Dudespeak wasn't hard enough to understand, he's

been throwing in Spanish. I'd asked if he was learning Spanish. He'd responded with, "*Un poco*," which I'd remembered from high school Spanish as meaning "a little." I suspected that *donde* meant "where," so I told him Rita's.

Tiffany returned with Dude's martini. He took a sip, gave a thumb's up, and said, "Cool."

Brief, but English. We told Tiffany to give us a few minutes and we'd order. There were a couple of groups waiting for tables, several people seated appeared to be ready to leave, so I didn't feel rushed. We were in the shade of a large umbrella and I was in no hurry to leave the deck. I asked about business. He threw together a handful of words that meant business was good. He asked if I'd heard about the murder, if so, was I helping the police catch the killer. I told him yes and no. He didn't seem to believe me, so I changed the subject to the weather.

I hadn't paid attention, but the table beside us had opened. The hostess was seating three people, one being Laurie Fitzsimmons. She wore a mid-thigh length black skirt, and a dark gray blouse. She looked much better than when Charles and I visited her house. She sat on the opposite side of the man and woman, a couple about Laurie's age. The man was overweight, mostly bald, average height. His companion was slightly taller than the man, not heavy, not thin with no memorable features.

Laurie glanced at us and looked surprised. "Oh, hi, umm …"

"Chris," I said.

"Chris, of course." She smiled. "It's good to see you."

Her forced smile, added to the way she held her arms across her chest, didn't seem to share her words.

Dude, not to be left out, said, "I be Dude, bud of Christer. Who be you?"

This was Laurie's first exposure to Dude, so she probably wouldn't know how to respond. I stepped in, figuratively, and introduced Laurie to my surfer friend. Laurie told us her friends were Dean and Gail Clark.

I remembered that she'd said that a couple from Jacksonville was coming to be with her for a few days.

"Dean, Gail," I said, nodding their direction. "Nice to meet you. Are you from Jacksonville?"

Dean started to answer, when Gail interrupted, "Yes, we're here to help Laurie get through the next few days."

I said, "Sorry you're here under such terrible circumstances." Our tables were three feet apart. With the crowd noises, it was difficult hearing, plus I felt like I was intruding on their private time. "I'll let you get to your meal."

Laurie gave a sincerer smile. "Good seeing you again."

Dude, seeming oblivious to my desire to let them have their privacy, said, "Slip slide tables together. You be joining us."

Laurie looked at our table. "Thank you, Dude, but—"

Gail interrupted, "Great idea. It'd be nice for us to get to know Laurie's friends."

Friends wouldn't be how I'd describe our relationship since I'd only seen Laurie twice. She'd known Dude for as long as it takes to smack a mosquito that just bit my arm. Before I could say, "Thanks, but no thanks," Gail was *slip sliding* their table our way. Tiffany returned to our combined tables to see if Dude and I were ready to order, and if Laurie, Gail, and Dean wanted drinks. I said Dude and I would wait a little longer. Gail, without input from Laurie, or Dean, ordered a bottle of white wine.

Gail turned to me. "Laurie wanted to sit in her house and order pizza. I told her she needed to get out, get fresh air, get her mind off Anthony's death."

Laurie looked at the menu, ignoring what was being said.

Dude waved his hand toward Dean. "Be from gator state?"

Had he missed Gail's earlier answer to the same question?

"Jacksonville," Gail said, answering for Dean. "We've been friends with Laurie and Anthony for years. Neither of us have kids. We have lots in common. Played cards a couple of times a month. Dean and Anthony are, sorry, were history buffs. The second Laurie called to tell us what happened, I said we'd be up to stay through the funeral. I don't work so I had the time." She hesitated, nodded toward Dean. "My husband taught for five years with Laurie and Anthony, before taking over his dad's tire business."

I wondered if Dean was permitted to speak when he was at work. I'd wager it was rare at home.

Dude bobbed his head. "Cool."

Tiffany returned with the bottle of wine and set glasses in front of the newcomers. "Ready to order?"

Gail said not yet, again, without consulting her tablemates.

Dean took advantage of the break in discussion. He turned to me. "Have you known Anthony and Laurie since they moved here?"

"Not really," I said. "I met Laurie the day Anthony died."

"Oh," said Gail. "I thought you, oh well, never mind. Did she tell you Dean and I were supposed to be here that day? We were going relic hunting with them, but Dean had to go to a tire retailers' meeting in Tallahassee." She put her hand on Laurie's hand. "If we'd been here, Anthony may still be with us. Laurie, I'm so sorry."

Dude leaned toward Dean. "Me found injun head penny once. Be relic?"

Dean leaned closer to Dude. "Well, it could—"

"By the strict definition of relic, yes," Gail interrupted. "Our interest is more in line with artifacts from the Civil War. Anthony had been telling us about the history of Folly Beach during that war. Laurie's grandfather told her stories years ago. We were excited about joining our friends. Again Laurie, sorry we couldn't be here."

"You're not as sorry as I am," Laurie said. "Let's order. I'm certain Chris and Dude aren't interested."

Gail waved Tiffany to the table, and each of them ordered. I was pleased Gail didn't order for everyone. Tiffany looked at me, I nodded for Dude to say if he was ready. He and I ordered, while Laurie started talking to Gail and Dean about funeral arrangements. I heard Gail tell Laurie that Dean had to get back to the store in the morning, but she would be staying until after the funeral. Dean would return for the funeral then take Gail home the following day.

We ate mostly in silence. Our tables were touching, although our conversations, however brief, remained apart. Dude was determined to tell me about four vacationers from Maine who were in the surf shop where they got in an argument about who was the best surfer. It seems none of them had ever been on a surfboard. They were arguing based on how athletic they were on the golf course. Dude thought it was hilarious; I thought it was mildly amusing.

Dude and I finished before Laurie, Dean, and Gail, so we waved bye. I told them it was nice meeting them and again expressed condolences to Laurie.

On our way down the steps, Dude said, "Gail chick be big bundle of bull."

Not necessarily articulate, yet one-hundred percent accurate.

Chapter Nine

The next morning, low-hanging clouds and light rain blanketed the area, so I was surprised to hear a knock on the door a little after eight. I was even more surprised to see Charles standing on the screened-in front porch. He wore a purple, long-sleeve, T-shirt with Alcorn State University in gold, block letters on the front, a canvas Tilley hat with water dripping off the brim and carrying a bag from Bert's Market. His classic 1961 Schwinn bicycle leaned against the front of the house. I wondered why he'd peddled over rather than driving. I didn't ask.

He pushed his way past me on his way to the kitchen. "You're a wimp, so I figured you wouldn't come out to meet me for breakfast. You're a pitiful excuse for a cook, so I figured you wouldn't have anything here to eat. I picked up donuts next door, figured we could eat in your never-used kitchen."

What I figured was that it was too late to say, "Good morning, Charles. How are you today? What brings you out on such a lousy morning?"

I may be a pitiful excuse as a cook, if that good, but I was a wiz at fixing coffee in a Mr. Coffee machine. Charles found one of my three clean mugs, poured a cup, plopped down on a kitchen chair, and tore open the box of prepackaged donuts. He seldom appeared at my door without an agenda. If I asked what it was, he'd respond by saying something like, "Couldn't I want to see a friend?" I wasn't ready to play that game, so I sipped my drink waiting for the agenda to unfold. It didn't take long.

"I was thinking," he said then took a bite of donut.

"Would you like to share what?"

He pointed the mug at me. "Harnell Levi."

It took me a couple of seconds to remember who that was. "Laurie Fitzsimmons's grandfather."

Charles shrugged. "You know any other Harnell Levis?"

"I didn't know the one who was Laurie's grandfather. What about him?"

"The geezer died six or seven years ago. I knew him from when I did some cleaning at the Sandbar Restaurant."

The Sandbar Restaurant had been behind Charles's apartment building, and was one of Folly's most popular eating spots for ages but has been closed a few years. It'd overlooked the Folly River, and had a memorable view of sunset.

"Why didn't you tell Laurie you knew him?"

Charles started on his second donut, took a sip of his drink, then said, "Teddy Roosevelt said, 'If you could kick a person in the pants responsible for most of your trouble, you wouldn't sit for a month.' That was old man Levi. Figured if I couldn't say anything good about her gramps, I'd better keep my mouth shut."

"Tell me about him."

"The old coot was short, doubt more than five one, portly, if he could smile, I never saw it. The old man was plum cranky. He was also paranoid, always looking around like a

KGB agent was hiding around every corner. I never saw him when he wasn't mumbling something, or whispering."

"What about?"

"Best I could decipher, he'd found some Civil War artifacts. Told me once he'd been a prospector in the old west. It didn't make a lick of sense since the old west was long gone before he could've been there. Some of his mumble-talk was about relics and other stuff, said he knew where it was."

"Other stuff, like what?"

"He never said. Probably wasn't frankincense, or myrrh. I'd lean toward silver, or gold."

"You never heard him say silver or gold."

"Nope. He was one weird dude."

"Laurie seemed to have been close to him. If he talked to you about *relics and other stuff,* he probably shared more with his granddaughter. You think that's why they were hunting relics?"

"Yep."

"And he claimed to know where some were."

"Yep."

"It's possible that they either found something of value, or had a good idea where to look, then someone else found out about it. That could've been motive for killing Anthony."

"Yep."

I hoped that Charles would stop imitating Dude and add something more to the discussion. "If that's true, who would've known? Laurie and Anthony hadn't been here long. If they truly had an idea where to find buried relics, or treasure, why would they tell anyone?"

"Therein lies the mystery."

After three more donuts, two more cups of coffee, Charles noticed the rain had stopped. He decided that he needed to get to his apartment before the weather turned worse. On his way out, he said I should meet with Chief LaMond to tell her what he'd learned from Harnell Levi. I asked why he didn't want to meet with her. He said that she would believe me before believing him. I said I'd think about it.

The phone rang before I could give it more thought. Theo called to remind me that I'd agreed to go with him when he met with his daughter-in-law. I told him that I remembered.

"Good," he said. "She just called, said she's in Charleston, and asked if I could visit today. Are you available?"

Even if I didn't want to go, I didn't have enough time to think up a reason why I couldn't. Besides, I was curious about his daughter-in-law.

"Sure."

"Great. I'll pick you up at noon."

————

Theo wasn't as time obsessed as Charles, so it was five after twelve when his late-model, black Mercedes pulled in the drive. Knowing that Theo walked at turtle speed, I'd been watching, so I could meet him at the car before he got out. He thanked me for going three times before we'd made the short trip off island, twice more on the half-hour ride to the hotel.

Theo's daughter-in-law was staying at a Comfort Inn near downtown Charleston. Theo was to call her cell once he was at the hotel. He was slower than usual as we walked from the car to the lobby of the attractive, seven-story building. It took him a couple of minutes to catch his breath after he flopped down on a sofa in the lobby. He was breathing heavily as he stared at his phone.

"Are you okay?" I asked.

"Scared. Chris, I don't know if I can do this."

"It'll be fine. Besides, you're in better shape than she is. Imagine how she must feel meeting her late husband's father."

Theo smiled. "Good point." He tapped her number in his phone.

She was quick to answer. Theo said he was in the lobby but, before he could say anything else, she must've said she'd be down.

"She sounded excited," Theo said as he stood and walked to the large windows overlooking the parking lot. When the elevator door opened, Theo jerked around to look in its direction. Two men dressed in seersucker suits, and engrossed in a conversation, emerged. Theo sighed as he returned to the sofa.

The elevator door opened again, a dark-skinned woman stepped into the lobby. She was short, roughly five-foot-two, trim, in her early-fifties, with a short-cropped Afro haircut. She had on a black blouse, dark-gray Capri pants, and flip-flops. We stood and looked her way.

Theo whispered, "Think that's her?"

The woman saw us standing fifteen feet away, smiled, then headed over. Theo's question was answered.

She stopped in front of us, nodded, and said, "Gentlemen, would one of you happen to be Theo Stoll?"

Theo said that he was.

The woman's smile increased; she held out her arms and wrapped them around his waist. He got a startled look on his face, which, fortunately, the hugger couldn't see.

"Then, fine, sir, I am honored to say that I am Grace, your daughter-in-law."

Her Caribbean accent, combined with an endearing smile, made her both pleasant to look at and listen to. She unhooked her arms from Theo's waist and took a step back. Theo struggled with what to say, so I stepped forward, told her who I was, adding that I was Theo's friend. The center of the lobby wasn't the best place to continue our conversation, so I asked if she was thirsty.

"A drink would be pleasant," she said as she continued to smile. Her teeth were glowing white, and flawless.

Theo didn't respond.

I ushered them to the breakfast area then to a booth along the wall as far as possible from three guests huddled around a laptop. Large photos of scenic spots in downtown Charleston adorned the walls. I went to get drinks from a refrigerator in the corner of the room. Theo had found his voice by the time I returned.

"How was your trip?" he asked.

She smiled. "Long, exhausting. I'm pleased to finally have reached my destination after four days on the road. Thank you for meeting me. I know this must be awkward."

Theo smiled for the first time. "True for you as well."

Grace took a sip of orange juice. "Yes. I don't know how to say this other than to say, I'm so sorry for the death of your son."

Theo shook his head but didn't respond.

I said, "Grace, I'm sorry for your loss."

"Thank you. It was devastating."

Theo's head jerked up, he leaned closer to his daughter-in-law. "You must know I had little contact with him. I didn't know he was getting married until I got the wedding invitation. I only knew your name because it was on the invitation I received days after the event." He took a deep breath. "Grace, I don't want to sound insensitive." He took another breath. "Why did you come all the way across the country? What do you want?"

I was startled by Theo's stinging words to someone whom he'd just met moments earlier. Grace jerked back like Theo had slapped her.

The conversation went downhill from there.

"Mr. Stoll, I'm terribly troubled that I've offended you. I was aware of your lack of closeness with Teddy, but—"

"Lack of closeness," Theo shot back. "I hear nothing from him in years. He couldn't find time to attend his mother's funeral. Then, he gets married to someone I'd never heard of. Now, you appear out of nowhere, smiling like everything's hunky-dory." He sighed. "Like we're one big happy family."

Grace's shoulders appeared to fold inward; she sank down in her seat; a tear appeared in the corner of her eye. I was shocked. I'd never seen Theo this agitated. He glared at her while shaking his head.

"Grace," I said, "I hope you understand that hearing from you and now your arrival has thrown Theo's world upside down. Perhaps you would like to share with him, with us, what inspired you to come from L.A. Did you say you were on the road for four days? That had to be a grueling trip."

Theo continued to glare while remaining silent.

His daughter-in-law looked at him, then turned to me. "Yes, Mr. Landrum. Last night was the first night I stayed in a hotel since leaving California."

"Where'd you stay on the road?"

"I have a sleeping bag in the food truck. It wasn't horrible; rough on the back." She tried to smile. It fell short.

I wondered if that meant she didn't have any money. It was best not to ask. "Do you have family on the East Coast?"

"Just…" she nodded toward Theo.

Theo's glare softened, although not much. He tapped his finger on the table. "Where's your family?"

"I grew up in Topeka, Kansas. Mom was from there. Dad was from a tiny, tiny town you've never heard of near Kingston, Jamaica. My parents are no longer with us. It is my understanding that you are Teddy's only living family."

Theo shook his head. "Teddy has an uncle. My brother, Salvadore, lives with me."

"Oh, I am sorry. Teddy didn't mention him."

Theo tapped his fingers harder on the table. "Of course, he didn't. Probably didn't remember him. He would've had to stay in contact with his family to know about such things."

Grace lowered her head. She didn't need more grief from Theo, so I moved the conversation to more positive topics. "Charleston is a beautiful city. How long will you will be visiting?"

She looked at Theo. In a low, singsong voice said, "I'm moving here."

"For good," Theo said.

"Mr. Stoll, I couldn't stay in California. Our restaurant, the business that Teddy and I built from scratch, the business we had another partner in before he stole most of our profits before absconding, went under. Teddy died there. I have nothing but bad memories from California. I tried, but couldn't remain there. I know no one in Kansas who is still living. I never got to know any of Dad's relatives in Jamaica. Truth be told, I've never been to Jamaica." She hesitated then continued. "I thought I could know at least one person here and open my food truck. Perhaps it was a mistake to think that."

Theo waved his arm around the room. "Will you stay here?"

"I wish. This is a lovely place. The bed felt so good last evening. My resources are limited, so I will be staying in my truck until I've saved enough to find an apartment. Thank you for asking."

In the Pollyanna world in which Charles resides, the one I occasionally visit, this would be where Theo offers Grace a room at his house which is ten times larger than he needs.

Even though Sal is there, he has extra bedrooms collecting dust. I know him to be a kind, compassionate, trusting soul, regardless of today's behavior.

Theo nodded to Grace. "You've spent several nights in it, so I suppose it's comfortable. With your experience, you should be able to find business for your food truck."

She smiled, something I wouldn't have been able to muster under similar circumstances. "That's what I'm counting on. Do you know if they grant food trucks permission to set-up on the island where you live?"

There are a couple of food trucks that have seasonal locations on Folly, although I didn't know anything about the requirements for operating one. I also realized I had no idea what Grace sold out of her truck.

"Grace, there've been a couple. What type of food do you sell?"

"We, umm, I've tried several things. It's been hit or miss. Hamburgers didn't do as well as anticipated. Sub sandwiches fell flat. Our niche seems to be hot dogs. Not just run of the mill mustard, or ketchup on hot dogs. I sell fifteen combinations, ranging from the traditional Chicago-style dog, to one I call the 'everything but the kitchen sink dog.' "

She looked at her watch. "You must be terribly busy, so I don't want to keep you. Besides, the hotel privileged me with a late check-out time, so I need to start moving out. Mr. Stoll, umm, Mr. Landrum, it was a true honor to meet you. I'm sorry it had to be under such unpleasant circumstances."

She stood and reached to shake Theo's hand.

He offered it to her, although it was as enthusiastic as if he would reach to shake a polar bear's paw.

She gave it a brief shake then reached for my hand. I felt terrible for her, yet I didn't know what to do. We shook, then I gave her a quick hug, before she headed to the bank of elevators.

We were in the car ten minutes before Theo said anything other than agreeing with me about the heavy traffic. I wanted to ask why he was so cold, no, make that rude, yet I knew he'd talk when he was ready.

We were five miles from Folly when he said, "I was shocked she's black. I was stunned with the realization I not only had no idea who she was, I didn't have a clue who my son was, or who he'd become. She drove all the way across the country to... to what? What does she want from me? What on God's green earth should I have said to a total stranger?"

"Theo, you know as much about her as I do, so I don't have answers. There may be an ulterior motive for her being here. I get that. You were burned earlier this year when Sal brought three comedians with him who, for all practical purposes, moved into your house."

"Damned near got me killed."

"Yes, despite that, look how you and Sal have bonded after years of being strangers."

"So?"

"So, you don't know what Grace wants. She didn't ask for anything. It's possible she meant it when she said you were her only family left. She loved Teddy; she may hope to find some of him in you."

Theo didn't say anything as he stared at the road in front of us.

"Theo, do you have a problem with her being black?"

I knew Theo and William were friends from their time together in the walking group, I didn't remember him ever saying anything derogatory about anyone because of race.

"Chris, I'm eighty-seven years old. I grew up in a time when race relations weren't what they are now. I wouldn't say my parents were racist, wouldn't say I was yet, when I was young, black people had their place. It wasn't the same as ours. It was the way it was. Segregation, although I didn't know what the word meant, was the law of the land. I'm an old dog, but think I can learn a few new tricks."

"When I had my company, two of my top engineers were black, African American. They were great engineers, great people. That's a lot of words to say I probably have vestiges of racism in me. I think I've overcome most of it. Yes, I was shocked when I saw Grace. Was it because of her color? I honestly don't know." He smiled for the first time since being in the car. "Hell, Chris, I would have been just as shocked if she was six-foot-five, or if her hair was glow-in-the-dark purple."

"You're saying your reaction was because she was different than you'd expected?"

"I'd like to think so."

Theo returned to silence until I was letting him out at his house, when he said, "You know what that doesn't answer?"

"What?"

"Why she's here."

Chapter Ten

I didn't have time to think about Theo's antagonistic reaction to Grace. The phone rang as I walked in the house.

The conversation opened with Charles's machine-gunning me with, "What's she like? What did Theo say? Does she have a dog? When will I meet her?"

I gave him a brief rundown of our meeting. I made it through the first minute of the summary before Charles did what he does best, interrupt with more questions. I proceeded to tell him, in no particular order, what Grace looked like, what she had on, how Theo reacted to her, how long it had taken her to drive from California, and if she had a dog. I was unable to tell him what her food truck looked like since we hadn't seen it. Most importantly, I couldn't tell him why she was here.

After more elaboration than necessary, he asked, "What does she want?"

"I don't know."

"Why didn't you ask her?"

"Charles, it wasn't my place. She was here to see Theo."

"Seems to me that's a little strange. I think Theo has a legitimate point thinking she wants something. He's rich, has a big house, is old as dirt, and just as fast. Sure, Sal's Theo's blood relative, but after him who's in line to get Theo's wealth when he kicks the bucket?"

"Charles, when did you get so jaded? Theo's not going to let her pull anything over on him. He's bright, but considering the way he reacted, I'd be surprised if he'll reach out to her, much less rush to put her in his will."

"Have you already shed enough brain cells to forget how Theo was hours from being taken in two years ago by a con artist? Nearly gave him a million bucks."

"I haven't forgotten. You didn't see how Theo reacted to Grace. He was borderline nuclear. If she'd asked for money for a soft drink from the vending machine, I think he would've turned her down."

"Whatever," Charles said, then took a deep breath. "Now let me tell you why I really called. Laurie Fitzsimmons called."

"Oh."

"Yeah, oh. Know what she wanted?"

"You want me to guess?"

"No. She wants to have supper."

"Did she say why?"

"I suppose because she's hungry."

"You know what I mean."

"She didn't say. Remember Gail, Laurie's friend from Jacksonville?"

"Sure."

"She's still here, hubby headed home. Laurie and Gail are going to St. James Gate tomorrow night. She asked me to join them. Does that sound strange, or what?"

"What'd you say?"

"After I got over the shock, I said, 'Why not? Chris and I'd love to join you.'"

"Charles, did she invite me?"

"No. I did. Why?"

"Never mind. What'd she say?"

"She mumbled something, held her hand over the phone, then said something to I assume Gail. She returned with, this is a direct quote, 'Six-thirty, meet you there,' and hung up."

Hanging up was something I should've done as soon as Charles said, "I suppose because she was hungry." Theo asking me to go with him to meet his daughter-in-law, now Charles asking, correction, telling me I was having supper with Laurie, a person I'd met twice, and Gail, someone whom I'd met once. Do I look like a human psychiatric service animal?

———

In Charles's world, six-thirty meant six o'clock, so I was standing in front of St. James Gate when he walked up wearing a long-sleeved, gray T-shirt with what looked like an eagle over University of North Florida in blue on the front. Unlike his unlimited supply of T-shirts, he had on the same frayed, tan shorts that had been with him since we'd first met.

He pointed to the logo on his shirt. "Bet you think it's an eagle."

He would've been hurt if he knew I hadn't given it any thought. I shrugged.

"It's an osprey."

Instead of saying, *Who gives a flying flip?* I said, "Oh."

"Wore it in honor of Gail. It's in Jacksonville, you know." He peeked in the restaurant's open front window. "Speaking of Gail, are the ladies here?"

I reminded him that Laurie probably assumed that six-thirty meant six-thirty. He responded with an articulate, "Whatever."

Erik Swartz, a friend of mine, walked up behind Charles, said "Hi," then pointed at Charles's T-shirt. "Eagle?"

"Osprey," I said before Charles could go into an extended explanation of who knows what.

Erik said, "Oh."

My thought exactly.

Erik turned to me. "Glad I ran into you. Figured out who killed Anthony?"

"We're working on it," Charles said, before I could deny trying and telling Erik it was in good hands with the police. "Did you know him?"

Erik nodded toward the restaurant's door. "Not really. I met him in there once. I stopped by to talk to John, the owner, about a musician I was booking. I had to wait, so I grabbed a beer and started talking to Anthony, who was drinking a Guinness a couple of chairs over."

Erik was a talented musician who booked musical acts in a few local businesses.

Charles said, "What'd you talk about?"

"Nothing really. I asked how long he lived here. He said he retired from teaching a few weeks earlier. He and his wife bought a house."

"Anything else?" Charles the Nosy asked.

"Nothing important. I was trying to make conversation until John was free. I asked what he was planning to do now that he was retired."

Erik chuckled.

"Funny, now that I think about it, he said something about not doing much, except fixing up the house. He said it needed a lot of work. I said it sounded like a money pit; he smiled, said I hit the roofing nail on the head. He said for me not to worry. He laughed, said he'd dig up the money to pay for it."

I said, "Do you think he literally meant dig up the money?"

"Didn't at the time. After what happened, I'm not sure. I hear he was out at the old Coast Guard station with a metal detector. He must've been looking for something."

Erik laughed.

"He could've been looking for all that gold that rumors have been flying around about for decades."

Charles had been neglected long enough. "Think there's gold buried on Folly?"

"Talk's cheap. I've been around here going on a dozen years and have heard stories about buried treasure. If you ask me, which you did, I think I have as good a chance stumping my toe on a gold brick here on the sidewalk as Anthony would with a metal detector." He looked at his watch. "Gotta run, guys. Nice talking to you."

Charles watched Erik walk away then looked at his empty wrist. "Laurie and her friend are late."

Of course, they weren't. I started to tell him so, when I saw them crossing the street.

Laurie wore an oversized, black blouse over black slacks, and an oversized frown. She was still in mourning. Gail, a half-foot taller than Laurie, wasn't as grieved. She had on a celery-colored blouse with a tan skirt.

Gail smiled when she saw Charles, then pointed at the logo on his shirt. "Ozzie the Osprey."

Charles smiled, like he'd stumbled on a gold brick on the sidewalk.

Gail ignored her friend and shook Charles's hand. "Thank you for joining us."

"My pleasure," said Charles. "I hope you don't mind if I

brought Chris with me. If we play it right, we'll get him to pay."

Laurie said, "It's okay."

Not quite a resounding yes.

I told the ladies that it was nice to see them again then suggested we go in before the restaurant filled.

It was fortunate that we arrived when we had because it was nearly full. We were seated at a table in the front corner of the restaurant that had just been vacated.

A server finishing cleaning the table asked what we wanted to drink.

The ladies each ordered a Guinness, Charles stuck with a Bud Light. I ordered white wine.

Laurie seemed ill at ease, something her friend didn't share. Gail said, "Do you know why we chose here?"

I shook my head; Charles said, "Why?"

"This was Anthony and Laurie's favorite restaurant. They ate here two or three times a week. Isn't that right, Laurie?"

"Yes, we—"

Gail interrupted, "That's why I thought it'd be a good place tonight. Isn't that right, dear?"

Laurie nodded, probably because she knew she wouldn't be able to get a complete sentence out without Gail interrupting.

The server returned with our drinks, and Laurie was quick to take a sip. I didn't blame her. I told the server to give us a few minutes to decide on what to order.

Gail said, "Anthony's funeral will be Friday. I begged Laurie to take the body back to Jacksonville so their former teaching buddies could attend. But, no; she said, 'Don't be silly.' Folly was now home; Anthony would be buried near where she lives." She reached over and patted Laurie's leg. "I told her not to worry. Dean would come back, and I'd already be here for the service. Isn't that right, Laurie?"

Laurie took a larger gulp of beer, turned to Gail, and said, "I don't think our friends want to hear about a funeral. Let's talk about something more pleasant."

Gail said, "Oh. I was mentioning it because I'm sure they'll want to attend. Isn't that right, guys?"

"Tell us where and when, we'll be there," Charles said without glancing my way.

"See," said Gail. "There'll be a graveside service at two o'clock at the Holy Cross Cemetery, on, what's the name of the street, Laurie?"

Laurie looked at her drink and mumbled, "Ft. Johnson Road."

Charles said, "You can count on us."

"Now," Gail said, "that's out of the way. Charles, Laurie tells me that you're a private detective. That must be exciting, must be dangerous."

"I don't know about exciting. Dangerous, definitely. I, along with some of my friends, including Chris here, have helped the police a few times."

Gail turned to Laurie. "Why don't you ask Charles to help find the person who, murd… umm, took poor Anthony's life?"

This didn't appear to be the way to turn the conversation to more pleasant topics, so I said, "Gail, I know the detective from the sheriff's office assigned to the case. I also know the Folly Beach Police Chief. They're both good at their job. I have confidence they're doing what they can to solve it."

Laurie appeared to perk up. "That detective, think his name's Callahan, came to see me yesterday. He had me go over what happened again. There's no doubt he's thorough."

The server returned, we ordered, and the conversation drifted to lighter topics.

Gail asked how long Charles and I had been on Folly and what I had done before retiring. She talked about a factory where she'd worked before it moved its operation offshore. She shared way more information than we needed about how Dean had quit teaching, how he'd taken over his dad's tire store.

I started to tune out the conversation when Gail began telling us how the two couples had met, how neither had any children, how they shared a common interest in history and cooking, plus how they played bridge twice a month. Most I'd already heard.

Telephone calls were seldom pleasant interruptions, but I was pleased when my phone rang around the time Gail was telling us a "fascinating" story about the time she and Laurie had prepared the "most delicious" bison meal for their husbands.

Chief LaMond said, "What's that noise in the background? Am I interrupting something?"

I wanted to scream, *"Yes, thank you!"* Instead, I told her who I was with and that she wasn't interrupting.

"Interesting. Can you stop by the office in the morning? I've got a couple of things to share about the murder."

We agreed on a time. I returned the phone to my pocket while wondering why Cindy had said, "Interesting," then realized that the interruption hadn't slowed Gail from regaling Charles with more "fascinating" tales.

I had little interest in most of what she was saying, although it was nice that the topics veered away from Anthony's untimely demise. Laurie interjected how much better it was living on Folly, with its laid-back residents, and slower pace. Gail continued to finish most of Laurie's sentences. Laurie didn't seem to mind. I would've been tempted to smack her annoying friend.

The food arrived, and we ate in silence before Charles leaned toward Laurie. "That reminds me, I was wondering if there were other cars out there when you arrived with Anthony. When Chris and I got there, we only saw your MINI."

I wondered what Laurie, more accurately, Gail had said that reminded Charles of that. I didn't ask since I was interested in her answer.

Laurie blinked a couple of times. "It seems like there were three or four. There weren't as many when I got back to the car after stumbling around finding my way out. I think there were two. Why?"

She must've understood that one of the vehicles could've belonged to the killer, that is if she hadn't killed her husband. I asked, "Do you remember what they were?"

"Not really. I'm not good about cars. Most look alike."

"What color were they?" Charles asked.

"It was dark. I couldn't tell. They weren't white, or silver. They were dark. Could've been black, gray, blue. I don't know."

I said, "You never saw anyone after you entered the Preserve?"

"No," Laurie said. "Oh, I get it. One of cars could've belonged to the person who shot Anthony."

"Possible," I said. "Although they could've belonged to the people staying at the nearby houses."

"It doesn't matter. I couldn't identify any of them. Besides, Anthony is still dead." She lowered her head and put her hand over her face.

So much for a lighter topic.

Chapter Eleven

After Laurie and Gail headed to Laurie's house, I told Charles about the meeting with Cindy. As expected, he asked if he could join us. I told him that it was fine with me. If the chief didn't want him there, then she'd kick him out, preventing me from having to bear the grief of telling him, "No."

The Folly Beach Department of Public Safety was in the salmon-colored City Hall. The main entrance to the seat of local government was on Center Street, but the entry to the stairs to Cindy's office was around the corner on Cooper Avenue, directly across from the Surf Bar. The door was open, and Cindy was behind her oversized desk, staring at a foot-high pile of manila folders when I knocked on the doorframe. She looked up, glanced at her watch, and said, "Well, if it isn't Tweedledumb and Tweedledumber."

She wasn't smiling, so I took the higher road. "Morning, chief. Do you have time to meet with us?"

"Us, as in the person I asked to come by, plus his shadow?"

"Yes."

She pushed the pile of folders aside, waved for me to close the door, then motioned us to the chairs in front of her desk.

"This job's going to be the death of me," she said as she turned to the large window behind her. "You know how many loud-noise complaints this serve-and-protect office received last night?"

I said, "No."

Charles said, "Seventeen."

Cindy stared at him, like he was a tarantula crawling up her arm. "Nine. What in blue blazes am I supposed to do about it? Do I have my guys run all over town to see if their eardrums burst when they should be patrolling for bad guys? The death of me yet."

I said, "Sorry, Cindy," before Charles asked about each complaint.

"Never mind. That's not why I asked *Chris* to stop by." She paused, stared at Charles long enough for him to get the message, before turning to me. "I've known you long enough to know you're getting as nosy as your buddy sitting there."

"Inquisitive," Charles corrected.

Cindy rolled her eyes. "So, Chris, since you, and yes, you, too, Charles, awakened the sleeping Mrs. Fitzsimmons the morning we found her late husband, you'll have your antenna up, soaking in all the local gossip about what we've learned. Most of what you hear will be pure BS. I know that you'll keep whatever I tell you in confidence. You will, too, Charles. Right?"

Charles nodded. I couldn't see if he had his fingers crossed.

Cindy returned his nod. "Chris, I have a couple more questions about the morning you two found Mrs. Fitzsimmons. Something still doesn't feel right. I can't put my finger on it."

"Fire away."

Cindy tapped her desk. "Was she really asleep when you found her?"

"I have no way of knowing. She acted startled when she jumped out of the car. Her eyes were bloodshot, her hair a mess. I'd say yes."

Cindy smiled. "I know I'd be startled if someone looking like Charles stuck his face against my window. What do you think, Charles?"

"I agree with Chris."

I was pleased that he ignored the chief's insult. I said, "Why?"

The chief tilted her head. "If Larry and I were out there in a storm that was pitch black, and if we got separated and I found my way to the car, the last thing I'd do would be to fall asleep. I'd be worried, I'd call for help, I'd stare out the window. Fall asleep, never. Would you?"

That'd bothered me from the beginning. "I hope not."

Charles said, "I wouldn't have been able to sleep."

"Exactly," Cindy said. "Let me ask something else. Do you believe her story?"

Charles glanced at me before saying, "I don't know what Chris thinks. It makes sense to me, all except falling asleep."

I nodded. "We're all different. It seems strange, although I couldn't say how Laurie would react in the same situation. What do you and Detective Callahan think?"

"Callahan isn't sharing much. You know the sheriff's office and lowly city cops aren't always on the same page. Hell, most of the time, they don't put us in the same book. All to say, I don't know what he thinks."

"What about you?" I said.

Cindy said, "Tell me about your supper with Mrs. Fitzsimmons and her friend, umm, what's her name?"

"Gail," Charles said before I made the transition from

asking what Cindy thought about Laurie being asleep to our dinner. "We met Laurie and Gail at St. James Gate. Gail's from Jacksonville, has been friends with Laurie for years. They played bridge—"

Cindy put her hand in front of Charles's face. "Whoa. Hold the history lesson. All I want to know is why were you having supper with them?"

I thought, *Please don't say because they were hungry.*

"Laurie sort of bonded with us after we woke her up. She wanted to tell us about Anthony's funeral. Come to think of it, she didn't say why."

I said, "Cindy, why do you ask?"

"I'm trying to get a better picture of Laurie. Tell me about what you talked about." She pointed a finger at Charles. "Not what you had to eat, not who else you talked to, not all those itsy-bitsy facts you accumulate, you know, the ones having nothing to do with anything. Let me narrow it down more. Was anything said that could have anything to do with Anthony's death?"

That said volumes about what she thought about Laurie's story. "You think she's lying?"

Cindy sighed. "Did you miss my question about dinner?"

I said, "Laurie wanted to talk about their past, until Gail said she heard that Charles had helped the police catch bad guys. She asked him if he could find Anthony's killer."

Charles waved his hand in the air. "She asked both of us."

"Oh, great, just what we need. Where did she hear that?"

Charles said, "Laurie told her."

Cindy turned to me. "What did you tell her?"

"The police were good, that they'd figure it out, that there wasn't any need for us to be involved."

"Thanks, I suppose. Anything else?"

Charles said, "I asked her how many cars were nearby

when they got to the Preserve, then how many were there when she came back to the car."

Cindy rolled her eyes. "How does that say that you didn't need to get involved?" She exhaled. "Never mind. What was her answer?"

I shared what Laurie had said. After Cindy mumbled something about us being nosy, butting in police business, how she should be shot for talking to us about the case, she said Laurie's story about the other vehicles was consistent with what she'd told the police at the scene.

"Cindy," I said, "do you think she killed her husband?"

She shook her head. "Don't know. What I do know is her story's fishy, could be true yet, still fishy. She had opportunity. We haven't found the gun, so there's no way to know about means. And the big question, until late yesterday, was motive."

"It would have been easy for whoever killed him to fling the gun in the ocean," Charles said as he made a throwing motion. "Splash, it's gone."

"Never to be found," Cindy added.

I wasn't paying attention to their recreating flinging a gun. "Cindy, what do you mean about motive and late yesterday?"

"Before I tell you, let me ask, did Laurie say anything to indicate she and her hubby had problems with each other?"

"No," I said.

"Like problems enough to kill him over?" Charles said.

Cindy said, "That'd be the kind."

Charles shook his head. "Not that I heard."

"Chris, back to your question," Cindy said and pointed at me. "It's nice that one of you listens to what I'm saying. Len, one of my officers, was talking to his insurance agent yesterday about a life insurance policy. He got married a few months ago and, now, his wife's pregnant. We have a good policy through the office, but he wanted to add to it in case, well, in case something happens. Anyway, you know the agent, David Darnell."

I nodded.

"David asked Len if we'd caught the killer. Len said, "No," then David said the Fitzsimmons were his clients. Len, being a good cop, told me what David said, so I called the agent to ask about the Fitzsimmons' insurance. He started to give me the runaround about needing a warrant to get that information. I said I would and started to hang up. Good ole David stopped me, said since Anthony was no longer among the living he guessed it was okay to share that Anthony and Laurie had taken out a half-million-dollar life insurance policy on each other."

"Motive," I said.

Cindy shrugged. "Know when the policy was written?"

"When?" Charles blurted.

"Two months ago."

Chapter Twelve

I stopped at Bert's for bread after meeting with Chief LaMond. My last loaf had turned several shades of blue and green, attractive colors in a painting, not so much for lunch. Mary Ewing, one of the store's personable clerks greeted me at the door. A thin, attractive, twenty-something, she gave a high-wattage smile. "Hi, Mr. Landrum."

I'd met Mary a couple of years ago, when she and her two young daughters were homeless. With the assistance of surfer friends, they were squatting in vacant vacation rentals. True, the assistance came in the form of breaking into houses, although the intentions were admirable. Since then, a local minister helped her find legal living arrangements.

"Mary, I've told you, please call me Chris. How are the girls?"

Her smile increased. "Joanie turned four last week." She laughed. "Big sister, Jewel, threw her a party."

"Jewel's eight?"

"Going on twenty."

"I bet it was fun."

"Joanie said it was the best birthday she'd ever had. The two women we share the house with were there, one had her five-year old son, the other lady brought the three kids she babysits. It was a hoot."

"I can imagine."

Mary started to respond, looked over my shoulder, then waved. "Hi, Captain."

I turned to see Abraham Gant return Mary's wave. He was in his mid-eighties, probably had been six-foot tall during his heyday but was now around five-foot-nine.

"How's my favorite clerk?" Gant said as he hugged Mary.

Mary told him that she was fine.

"Who's your friend, Mary?"

"Captain, this is, Mr. Landrum, I mean Chris. We've known each other nearly as long as I've been here."

Gant gripped my hand and smiled. Calling his grip bone-crushing would've been an exaggeration, although not by much.

"Chris, I'm Captain Gant. If you're a friend of Mary, you're a friend of mine."

Mary patted me on the back. "Captain, you two have something in common."

He laughed. "Something other than being old farts and having you as a friend?"

I was glad that Mary considered me a friend, although I didn't see any humor in the octogenarian Captain thinking I was an old fart, or otherwise.

I turned to Mary. "What do we have in common?"

"Both were law enforcement. Chris, the Captain is retired from the South Carolina Highway Patrol. He was a captain so that's where his name came from."

Gant turned to me. "Were you a cop?"

"No, I—"

Mary interrupted. "Chris helps the police. If you can believe it, he's caught some killers. He's—"

My turn to interrupt. "Some friends and I've been fortunate a time or two when we learned things that the police weren't aware of. It helped them solve a couple of murders. Nothing like what you spent your career doing."

Gant's smile lessened. "Oh, you stuck your nose where it didn't belong?"

Time to change the subject. "We were fortunate to help the police. How long have you lived on Folly?"

I didn't think he was going to answer. Finally, he said, "My parents moved here in the late 1930s. Dad was in the Coast Guard. I wasn't much older than Joanie." He smiled at Mary.

I said, "I've been here ten years. I wish I'd been here longer. It's great hearing stories from the old-timers. Do you know Charles Fowler? He's a good friend who's lived here way more years than I have."

"The T-shirt guy, sure, although I don't know him well. We run into each other occasionally."

"Hate to interrupt, guys," Mary said. "Work calls."

I said it was nice talking to her then the Captain gave her a fatherly, grandfatherly hug.

"She's so sweet," Gant said as Mary moved behind the counter to check out a woman carrying a white poodle.

"Charles said you'd told him about Anthony Fitzsimmons' death."

"I told him about it, but should've known he already knew. Your friend has a reputation for knowing everything that goes on."

I remembered Charles's comment about being surprised that Gant knew about the death such a brief time after the body was found.

I smiled. "He does have a way of accumulating rumors,

sometimes the truth. How'd you hear about the body?"

Gant stared at me like I was a suspect in a crime. "Don't recall. Must've heard it from someone at breakfast. Why?"

"No reason."

"Did you know the SOB?"

"I never met Anthony. Charles talked to him and his wife once. I take it you didn't like him."

"He had me fooled. Met him in Planet Follywood, where he started up a conversation. He and the Mrs. bought a house here, retired schoolteachers, he said. After I told him I'd been here since the invention of fire, he asked me all sorts of questions about what island life was like way back when. I don't get to share my stories much anymore. Most of my cronies are gone; most of the youngsters don't care. He wondered if I knew his wife's grandfather, Harnell Levi. I told him, 'Yes,' although I didn't know him well." Gant grinned. "I didn't tell him Harnell was a serious nut case who was ignored by most folks."

"Nut case?"

"The old guy was always blabbing about treasure, pirates' gold, striking it rich. He reminded me of those old, scruffy prospectors in black and white movies who were always chewing tobacco, telling anyone who'd listen about gold in *them thar hills*."

"No one took Harnell seriously?"

Gant shook his head. "What would you think if you saw an old man walking down the beach carrying a rusty shovel while singing 'Some Enchanted Evening' at the top of his lungs?"

"Good point."

Gant's smile faded. "Anyway, Anthony and I were getting along pretty good, until he said his hobby was relic hunting. He went on and on about digging up the past."

"What happened?"

"I'll say it once, only once." Gant pointed to the concrete floor. "What's buried should stay buried. Period. Those who've come before us lived their lives the best they could. Some were good. Some were bad. All are gone. They need to stay gone. We have no right digging them up, no right digging up their things, their bones, their past. I'm not saying there're ghosts, not saying there ain't. There've been stories over the years of people on Folly seeing ghosts of soldiers, of nurses, of average folks. I haven't seen any, myself. I'll tell you what, I know of honest people who've seen them. Relic hunters, and people digging for buried treasure, are disturbing the souls of the wonderful people who've come before us. Bad things should happen to them. It's illegal to go digging up anything out where the SOB was murdered." He glared at me. "Got him killed."

"Have you heard rumors about who might've killed him?"

"Chris, I don't traffic in rumors."

"If he was killed because of what he was doing, I wonder who knew he'd be there."

Gant rubbed his hand through his short, gray hair and stared at me. "Twenty-five years ago, it would've been my job to figure that out. I'm glad it isn't. Know why?"

I shook my head.

"He deserved what he got."

Gant pivoted and walked away, nearly running over Stanley Kremitz as he stormed out the door. I couldn't help but wonder if Gant knew that Anthony Fitzsimmons was going to be at the Lighthouse Inlet Heritage Preserve that fateful evening.

Stanley was my height, thin, in his late sixties, although he looked older. He moved to my side then looked at the door. "What'd you do to put a bee in his bonnet?"

Stanley was a friend of Chester Carr, a man I'd met five

years ago. I'd become better acquainted with Chester two years ago when Charles and I joined a walking group he'd formed.

"We were talking about the man killed at the old Coast Guard property. Apparently, Gant didn't take too kindly to him."

"People in glass houses shouldn't throw stones."

If Stanley wasn't Chester's friend, I'd avoid him or, as he would say, "I'd avoid him like the plague." He was a nice man, friendly, but had never met a cliché he didn't like, or worse, repeat.

"What do you know about him?"

"You know I always look on the bright side. That's hard to do when it comes to Gant, who insists on being called Captain. He's got a quick temper. It doesn't take much to set him off."

"Think he'd get mad enough to shoot someone?"

"He was a state cop. He'd know how to pull the trigger. You can take that to the bank."

The store was getting crowded, and I ushered the retired pipefitter out of the aisle, and said, "Did you know Anthony and Laurie Fitzsimmons?"

"A little. Met them in here, right back there by the bin of fruits." He laughed. "Laurie was picking up an apple. I stepped up and said an apple a day keeps the doctor away. She must've thought I was weird. Stared at me like I was a three-headed hippo." He rolled his eyes. "Go figure."

I didn't see anything wrong with Laurie's reaction. "Was that it?"

"No. Anthony found humor in what I'd said. He told me who they were. I said it was nice meeting them. Laurie finally seemed to catch on that I was teasing. They're both retired teachers, live here full-time now."

"Did you know about them relic hunting?"

"Anthony had a pack of batteries in his hand, so I made a joke about using them to run the apple she had in her hand. You know, like the Apple i-stuff, the iPhone. They didn't laugh. Can you believe that?"

Absolutely, I thought. "Looking for relics?"

"Yeah," Stanley said. "Anthony finally said they needed batteries for flashlights. It was as bright as Charmin outside. I joked about them not needing flashlights. Anthony, or maybe it was Laurie, said they like to fish around in wooded areas. They sometimes need the extra light to see. That begged the question, fishing around for what, so I asked. Anthony glanced at his wife then said something about them having an interest in the Civil War. They've heard that old military stuff, buttons, other metal things can be found around here. I asked if they'd found anything."

"Had they?"

"Anthony looked around, like he was about to tell me where the fountain of youth was and didn't want anyone else to hear. Then, he looked at Laurie. I didn't see her reaction. Anthony sure did. He changed direction in mid-stream and said, 'Nope,' they hadn't found anything."

"Was that it?"

"I suppose."

He didn't sound convincing, so I said, "You sure?"

"Yeah. Terrible about what happened to him that morning. I hear Laurie was the only other person out there, and she didn't see what happened. Someone said she didn't know anything happened to Anthony until the morning. Chester tells me you're good friends with the chief of police. Is that how she tells it?"

I thought it was a strange question, one that I wasn't comfortable answering, well, answering truthfully. "Don't know. We haven't talked about it."

Chapter Thirteen

I met Charles the next morning for a late breakfast at the Dog. After sparring with Amber about my choice of French toast, over her ongoing crusade to get me to eat healthier, Charles asked for the latest on Anthony's death. I told him I didn't know anything new, then shared my conversations with Gant and Stanley Kremitz.

Charles rubbed his three-day-old beard. "Gant goes apoplectic when anyone mentions ghosts, or diggin' up bones. The old boy's got a bag of screws loose when it comes to the past. I still think it's possible he shot Anthony."

"He became agitated talking about Anthony and relic hunting. I asked if he'd known Laurie's grandfather. He said, "Yes' then shared that Harnell was considered a nut. I couldn't tell if that was Gant's opinion because Harnell was digging for buried treasure, of if others felt that way."

"Chris, it bothers me that Gant knew about Anthony's death so soon after the body was discovered. Plus, being a retired state police officer would've given him the skill to kill."

"I don't know how he heard about it, but you don't need to

be a retired cop to be able to shoot someone. Don't forget, people who weren't in law enforcement have shot at us."

Charles held out his arms, wiggled his left leg. "Shot at by amateurs. We're alive. Anthony ain't."

Amber returned with breakfast, and to add sanity to our conversation. She asked if we'd heard about the heavy rains that were supposed to hit this afternoon, or the sale at two T-shirt stores.

I answered, "Yes" to the rain. I didn't care about the sale.

Charles added that he would've been interested in the sale if they sold college T-shirts. They didn't, so he wasn't.

Amber left to wait on a family of five who'd taken a table in the center of the room, when Chief LaMond entered and headed our way.

She motioned for Charles to slide over, sat beside him, then said, "Have you heard?"

"Heard what?" I asked.

Cindy opened her mouth wide, raised her hand, and made a motion with her forefinger, like she was making a mark on a whiteboard. She said, "Is this a historic day, or what?"

I said, "What're you talking about?"

"I never thought I'd live to see the day when something bad happens on *my* island, when you didn't know about it before I did. Damned historic day."

Charles jerked his head toward Cindy, almost knocking over his bell jar of water with his hand. "What happened?"

"Be patient," she said. "I'm savoring the moment." She took a notebook out of her pocket. "At nine-hundred this morning, Mrs. Anthony Fitzsimmons called 9-1-1 to report that an unknown person attempted to make her the late Mrs. Fitzsimmons. She—"

"Whoa!" Charles interrupted. "Details?"

"Thought that'd get your attention. Laurie called to report

someone fired a shot through her window. We responded posthaste, for you amateurs, that's police talk for super swift. Our mayor looks askance at citizens being shot at. Go figure. Officer Bishop was first on scene. She reported that Laurie wasn't hit, whoever pulled the trigger was long gone. I was nearby, got there next."

Charles did what he does best. He interrupted, again. "Did she see who it was?"

"Shut up and listen. You'll find out," Cindy said, doing what she does best. "She didn't see anyone. That would've been too easy. She said she was in the bedroom when the first thing she knew was the window beside her shattered. She jumped back, tripped on the side of the bed. By the time she got to her window, the perp was gone, plus there was a bullet hole in the wall on the opposite side of the room."

"Where was Gail Clark?" I asked.

Cindy flipped a page in her notebook. "Gail Clark, oh, yeah, her Florida friend. Laurie sent Gail to Harris Teeter to get food for lunch." Cindy smiled. "She, Laurie, that is, said she needed alone time. Something about being tired of Gail finishing her sentences. Said she was finishing sentences that Laurie was only thinking about. Seems nerves are frayed between the friends."

"Any witnesses?" I asked.

"No. The bedroom faces a vacant lot with lots of trees, shrubbery, weeds as tall as me. Whoever was in there could've been doing a naked rain dance, and no one would've noticed."

I took a sip of coffee and said, "Don't suppose Laurie had any thoughts on who it was?"

Cindy shook her head. "She's pretty torn up. Hell, I would be, too, if someone took a shot at me when all I was doing was standing in my bedroom. Think of how much worse it is for her, considering it came a few days after her husband was murdered, came the day before his funeral."

Charles said, "Don't suppose the shooter left the gun and his driver's license?"

Cindy cocked her head. "Gee, Charles. We forgot to check. No wonder you think you're a detective."

I said, "What happens now?"

"Detective Callahan's been to the house. He's having crime techs search for anything that might've been left in the vacant lot. I doubt they'll have any luck." She pointed to Charles. "Unless he, or she, left a driver's license."

I looked around to see if anyone was near enough to hear, then asked, "Cindy, could she have faked it, took the shot herself?"

Charles stared at me. Cindy nodded. "That entered my mind. You think she did it to deflect suspicion that she killed her husband?"

I shrugged. "It still strikes me as strange that, after getting lost from her husband in the middle of the night, she'd find her way back to the car then fall asleep. Add to that, the half-million-dollar insurance policy would be a strong motive."

Cindy continued to nod. "It's an interesting coincidence that she sent her friend to the grocery before the incident."

Charles took a sip of his drink then said, "Did you search her house for a gun?"

"On what grounds? The woman calls us in hysterics to report being shot at. We show up and say 'That's terrible. While we're here, can we search your underwear drawer?'"

Charles said, "That mean, "No'?"

"Can't fool you, Charles."

"Trying to help."

"Thank you," Cindy said, slobbering sarcasm.

"While we're talking about possible suspects, I was talking to Abraham Gant yesterday. He—"

Cindy waved her hand in my face. "Captain Gant, to you."

"Captain Gant went on a rant about relic hunters, specifically about Anthony Fitzsimmons."

"That's nothing new. Rant and Gant not only rhyme, they're redundant."

"True, although I thought it was a bit strong when he said Fitzsimmons got what was coming to him."

"Let me see if I have this straight," Cindy said, "You think Laurie and the captain were standing outside Laurie's window this morning shooting up her bedroom?"

I sighed. "No, I'm saying each had a motive for killing Anthony."

Charles said, "Add Gail Clark to the list."

"Why?" Cindy asked.

"She leaves Laurie to go to the grocery, then someone shoots through the window."

I shook my head. "Motive?"

"Don't know." Charles motioned toward Cindy. "That's for you to figure out."

"Halleluiah," Cindy said. "*Faux* detective Charles finally leaving something for us civil servants to do." She looked at her watch. "I've had about all the fun I can have with you two. Got to get back to the office to pretend like I know what I'm doing." She stood and took a step toward the door, before turning back to us. "I can't believe I knew something before you did."

I asked Charles why he thought Gail was a suspect, other than being out of the house when the shot was fired. His phone rang before he answered. Up until a year ago, he didn't have a cell phone, or an answering machine. The reason he got the phone was because he and his then girlfriend, Heather

Lee, had moved to Nashville for her to pursue a music career. He wanted to be able to give me updates on their move. Her career never got off the ground, so they returned to Folly. Not long after, Heather left Charles. He kept the phone.

The phone conversation was brief. The half of it I heard consisted of, "Yes," and "Okay, we're on our way."

"Where?" I asked as he slipped the phone in his pocket.

"Laurie's."

Chapter Fourteen

The house looked as much a work in progress as it had during our first visit. The only difference being, instead of Laurie greeting us, Gail met us at the door. She motioned us in saying Laurie was in the kitchen.

Laurie wrapped her arms around Charles, like he was a long-lost relative. She had tears in her eyes as she loosened her grip and stepped back. She gave me a hug that lasted half as long as the one she'd given Charles.

"You won't believe what happened," she said in Charles's direction.

Charles didn't admit he knew. "What?"

Gail, from the doorway, said, "Laurie, perhaps your friends would like coffee."

"Oh, sure. Sorry for being rude. Coffee, brownies? The next-door neighbor brought over more than we could ever eat."

I said coffee, not because I wanted it, but hoping it'd calm Laurie if she was doing something. Charles glared at me, like I was keeping her from telling what'd happened. Charles and I took chairs at the kitchen table. Gail grabbed one of the two remaining chairs, like she expected to be waited on by the woman who'd been the alleged target of a bullet hours earlier.

Laurie delivered a plate of brownies then went for our drinks.

"Nice kitchen," Charles said as he looked around.

This time, he wasn't simply being kind. Much of the house needed work, but the kitchen was immaculate. New stainless-steel appliances fit the spaces between the granite countertops. White cabinets and a white subway-tile backsplash were the perfect contrast from the mint green walls.

Laurie rubbed her hand over the granite counters. "Thank you. Anthony thought I was spending too much. After seeing the finished kitchen, he said it was wonderful." She looked at the tile floor and whispered. "He'll never get to enjoy it."

Gail interrupted Laurie's melancholy moment. "Laurie, don't you need to tell your friends why you called?"

Laurie brought our coffee before taking the remaining seat. She glanced toward the bedroom. "Somebody tried to kill me." She looked in her cup as she slowly shook her head.

Gail reached to squeeze her friend's arm. "Now, dear, tell your friends everything."

Laurie twisted her arm out from under Gail's hold and turned to Charles. "We'd been trying to see what food we needed for the next few days. People brought plenty to eat, but we were out of the basics. I was feeling queasy, so Gail offered to go to Harris Teeter. She left. I want in the bedroom to tidy up. To be honest, I thought about lying back down. Instead, I came in here to get a glass of water when I heard it." Her gaze returned to the cup.

"Tell them," Gail said.

She was as impatient as Charles.

Laurie continued, "All I remember is shattering glass. My

first thought was, *That's just what I need, a rock breaking the window. Anthony's funeral tomorrow, now this.* I went in the bedroom ready to look out and scream at some kid when I realized there was a hole in the wall opposite the window, glass all over the floor." She glanced at me and turned to Charles. "Guys, if it'd been seconds earlier, I'd be dead."

Chief LaMond already answered the question, but I asked, anyway. "Laurie, did you see anyone?"

"I was scared, so confused. When I realized it was someone shooting, I ducked, afraid to look outside. By the time I got the nerve to peek, I didn't see much. There was someone walking out of the lot next door, or I thought there was. I was so scared."

She'd told Cindy she hadn't seen anyone.

"Can you describe the person?"

"Not really. I think it was a guy. He could've had on a ball cap, no, he did have one on."

"Height, age, weight, anything else about him?" I asked.

"No. By the time I saw him, he was past the tree line, so I didn't get a good look. Even if I got a clear view, it might not have been the person who shot at me. I was so shaken that it may've been a minute or two before I looked out the window. I don't know, honest."

"Did you tell the police what you saw?"

"I don't remember. I was shaking when they got here, my stomach was doing somersaults." She wiped a tear from her cheek then smiled for the first time. "I wasn't my best."

"Of course, you weren't, dear," Gail said as she returned her hand to Laurie's arm.

Charles looked toward the bedroom. "Laurie, do you feel like showing us where it happened?"

Gail responded for Laurie. "I don't think she—"

Laurie stood. "Yes."

We followed her to the bedroom. The room was painted a soothing green, a shade darker than the kitchen. A queen-size sleigh bed was against the far wall with its bedspread, covering the sheets, although not neatly. A large double-hung window was on the left side with a piece of cardboard covering the lower half. The wood paneling on the opposite wall had a two-inch diameter hole a couple of feet below the ceiling. It looked like it had been made by a woodpecker, although more likely the work of the crime techs digging out the bullet.

Laurie saw us looking at the window. "Chief LaMond's husband owns a hardware store. She called while she was here. He rushed over. He didn't have a piece of glass that fit, so he taped the cardboard up there until he could fix it. The black officer, Bishop, I believe, swept up the glass. Such nice people."

I told her that I'd known Cindy, her husband, and Officer Bishop for years and that they exemplified most of the people on Folly who would do anything to help their neighbors. I added, "Laurie, you said you were in here then went to the kitchen before the shot was fired?"

"Yes, went to get a drink."

Charles stood on his tiptoes to see out the top half of the window, and said all he could see from that angle was the top of the trees in the adjacent lot.

Laurie's hands began to shake, so I suggested that we return to the kitchen.

This time, Gail refilled our cups while Laurie put her elbows on the table, her head between her hands.

In a couple of minutes, her breathing returned to normal, and her hands stopped shaking.

Charles said, "Is there anything we can do?"

Instead of answering, she said, "I don't know what I'll do. I don't know how I'll live, how I'll afford it."

Gail returned to the table. "Now, dear, the insurance will keep you from having to worry."

"Insurance?" Charles said, never fearing to tread where no man should go.

Laurie moved her hands from her face, glared at Gail, and turned to Charles. "When we retired, Anthony insisted we take out a large insurance policy. I argued it was morbid, that we shouldn't do it. He said it was his way to show his love for me. He never wanted to leave me wanting." Tears rolled down her cheeks.

Once again, Gail put her hand on Laurie's arm. She shook it off and rushed to the bathroom.

Gail watched her go. "Anthony was a wise man. Laurie will need that money. All she has is her teachers' pension, and a house that needs more work than they expected. Dean and I tried to talk them out of buying this place." She glanced at the closed bathroom door. "I think she was sure they'd find a buried treasure, not have to worry about money."

"What made them so sure?" I asked.

"Her grandfather gave them——"

Laurie opened the bathroom door, Gail stopped mid-sentence.

"Chris, Charles," Laurie said, "I hate to run you off. I need to lie down."

We stood, and Laurie gave me a hug and thanked me for coming. She moved to Charles, squeezed him, whispered something, then escorted us to the door.

Charles didn't say anything until we were in the car with the air-conditioning blowing full blast. "Chris, how many times did Laurie say she'd been in her bedroom then went to the kitchen when she heard the window shatter?"

"Twice that I recall. No need to say it. Laurie told Cindy she was in the bedroom when the bullet hit."

"Good old Abe Lincoln said, 'Be sure to put your feet in the right place, then stand firm.' Seems that Laurie had to do some fancy footwork to be in two places at the same time."

"A red flag, yes. It's also possible she was traumatized, confused when she talked to Cindy."

"Do you believe that?"

"Don't know. Either way, we need to tell the chief. She can follow up."

Charles looked back at the house. "You bet we do. And how about the insurance policy that Laurie argued against buying? Sounds fishy."

"Maybe," I said.

"Without a psychic, it's going to be hard to ask Anthony." He adjusted the air flow. "Why did she latch on us?"

"Latched onto you. I was along because you invited me."

"Strange," Charles said. "I didn't think she was going to let go once she got her arms around me."

"What'd she whisper when we were leaving?"

"Don't be a stranger."

"Oh."

" 'Oh,' is right."

———

I deposited Charles at his apartment and went home to called Chief LaMond to tell her what we'd learned.

"Why were you and your nosy friend there?"

I told her I was there because my nosy friend invited me. He was there because Laurie called him.

"Why did she call Charles?"

I thought about how happy she'd been to see him. I'd wondered the same thing. Instead of going into the hugging and whispering, I said, "Don't know. He's one of the few people she knows here."

After a moment of silence, Cindy said, "With those non-answers out of the way, why are you calling?"

I shared the discrepancy between what Laurie had told the police about where she was when the shot was fired opposed to what she'd told us.

Cindy said that it was interesting, although, in the grand scheme of things, considering the amount of stress that Laurie had been under when she'd told her version to the police, it wasn't that unusual. She went on a mini tirade about how many of the witnesses she interviewed over the years told stories that proved to be nowhere near what happened. She pointed out that they weren't intentionally lying, their stories were "royally screwed up" by shock, selective memory, other "psychological gibberish" that the "ignorant police chief from the hills of Tennessee" wasn't bright enough to understand.

I wasn't going to argue, although she's one of the smartest people I know. She proved it when she ended by saying she'd talk to Laurie again.

In a rare concession, she thanked me for calling. Of course, she ended the call on a more familiar note. "Oh, yeah, if I find out you two are sticking your snotty noses where they don't belong, I'll throw both of you in jail, charge you with driving a police chief coocoo."

She hung up before I could say, "I love you, too."

The phone rang, so I thought she was going to give me another chance.

No such luck.

"Chris, this is Theo. Could I buy you a drink?"

I'd never heard those words from Theo. "Yes."

"Good, could you meet me at The Washout. It's a nice night, I'd like to walk. I'll leave now, be there in a half hour."

The Washout was a ten-minute walk from Theo's house, so thirty minutes sounded about right for the man who moves slower than the Lincoln Memorial.

I live three times as far from the restaurant, as does Theo, so I made the trek and was sitting at the outside bar fifteen minutes after hanging up. A conversation with the bartender about the hot weather, and the rash of vacationers on the island, and twenty minutes later, an out-of-breath Theo limped up to the bar.

He wiped sweat off his forehead, took the seat beside me, and said, "Whew. You would think all the walking I do would have me in better shape for these long excursions."

His white T-shirt was gray from sweat. I was afraid, instead of ordering him a drink, I'd have to order an ambulance. Theo took a gulp of water from the glass the observant bartender set in front of him, then said, "I hope I didn't take you away from anything important."

I didn't tell him that my other options had been to ponder a solution for world peace, wonder if climate change was real, or fixing a peanut butter sandwich for supper. I stuck with, "I wasn't busy."

"I suppose you're wondering why I asked you to meet me."

"It crossed my mind." I left out, *about fifty times.*

He took another gulp. "I would've invited you to the house, except Sal was there. Don't get me wrong, my brother's wonderful. It's great getting to know him, again, after all the years he was on the road. It's nice having family nearby. It's been lonely since I lost Eunice." He hesitated and looked at his glass. "Did you know that we'd been married fifty-two years?"

He'd told me several times. "That's a long time, Theo. You must miss her terribly."

"Yes," he whispered. "Anyway, it's good that Sal is living with me."

He sighed, as I waited for "but." I didn't have long to wait.

"But my brother is driving me crazy. Chris, not a day goes by, correct that, not an hour goes by without him telling a joke. The old boy's got a million of them. They must've been funny forty years ago, when he shared them with a room full of drunks at a smoky comedy club in Oshkosh, Wisconsin. Occasionally, one of them strikes my funny bone. By occasionally, I mean one in a hundred. The old boy's going to joke me to death."

"Have you said anything to him?"

"I've tried. He nods like he's listening."

"And?"

"He cracks a joke. Anyway, that's not your problem, not the reason I wanted us to share a drink."

The bartender returned to give us the chance to order drinks, something other than water. We each asked for a glass of white wine, the bartender said, "No problem," a phrase which, in my opinion, had no place in the vocabulary of any server or bartender. He left to get our drinks.

"Chris, was I too hard on Grace?"

I wasn't ready for the transition from Sal to Grace. When in doubt, I turn the question around, something that'll never work with Charles. "Do you think you were?"

Our drinks arrived, Theo took a sip before saying, "She took me by surprise. I didn't know what to think, what to expect. When she stepped off the elevator, I didn't know what to do." He shook his head. "I blew it."

"Theo, I can't imagine what must've been going through your mind. It'd been years since you had contact with your son. Then, you learned he was gone. Now there was a stranger saying that she's your daughter-in-law. I don't know how I would've reacted."

"Chris, it's not her fault Teddy is dead. Why did I take it out on her?"

"You were shocked. You didn't know her. You didn't know what to expect. You didn't know why she came across the country. All reasons to be skeptical."

"Not a reason to be rude. For heaven's sake, she's my daughter-in-law."

"You could've handled it better. That's easy to say now. If I were in your shoes, I'm not sure I would've done anything differently. What're you thinking?"

"She said she was going to live out of her food truck. That tells me she doesn't have much money. She asked about moving her truck to Folly. That means she wants to be here. She didn't ask for anything. Is it possible she's sincere about wanting to be near her father-in-law, to be near me?"

"It's possible." I repeated, "What're you thinking?"

He leaned over to pull up his black, knee-high support stockings. In such a faint voice, I nearly missed what he was saying. "Asking her if she wants to move in my house until she gets on her feet enough to get a place of her own."

"Oh."

"Think it's a good idea?"

I smiled at the thought of the incongruity of Theo's house inhabited by an over-the-hills comedian, a half-Jamaican widow, and a retired engineer. All I said was, "I don't know. You still aren't sure what, if anything, she wants."

Theo watched a mini-van turn on West Hudson Avenue from Center Street. He then turned back to me. "I think it's a good idea. I'll call her tonight."

"What does Sal think?"

"Don't know, haven't told him."

"That should be interesting."

"He'll probably have a joke about a Jamaican, a comedian, and a geezer walking into a bar."

"Theo, you're a tough audience."

He chuckled, the result I'd been hoping for. He turned serious. "Chris, I'm dominating the conversation. Have you heard anything else about the murder of the retired schoolteacher?"

"Not much. Laurie called Charles, so we went to see her today."

"I didn't know they were friends."

With everything going on with Theo, I didn't need to discuss the attempt on her life. "She'd met him once before we found her in her car the day of her husband's murder. Seems she's bonded with him."

"That's great. Charles is a good person to have on your side. When's the husband's funeral?"

"In the morning."

"Should I go?"

"Did you know them?"

"Never met. I thought going to the funeral would be the Folly thing to do."

"I'm sure the widow would appreciate it." I gave him the details. He said he'd better get home to call Grace.

"Are you going to talk to Sal before you call her?"

"No. If she says, "No," he didn't need to know I offered. If she says, 'Yes,' I can show him I may not know jokes, but I can spring a surprise."

Go, Theo, go!

Chapter Fifteen

nthony's graveside service was to be held eight miles from Folly in the Holy Cross Cemetery on Ft. Johnson Road. The temperature was in the mid-eighties, with humidity pushing the heat index to near triple digits. A low cloud cover kept direct sun off the mourners. I was pleased by the number who attended considering how few people the Fitzsimmonses knew on Folly. Two rows of white folding chairs were in front of the coffin with Laurie, Gail and Dean Clark occupying the front row.

Both ladies wore long, black dresses. Dean looked out of place in a navy, three-piece suit. Everyone else was casually dressed, including Charles in one of his few non-logoed, long-sleeved T-shirts. Good to his word, Theo was there and, as a concession to his age, was offered a seat in the second row. He was joined by William Hansel and three ladies I didn't recognize. Stanley Kremitz and a woman I assumed to be his wife were standing with a group of six others behind the row of chairs. Charles and I joined that group.

The service was brief, a good thing considering the stifling heat. The women beside Theo spent most of the service waving their faces with fans featuring an image of a church on them. The fans gave them away as regulars at Lowcountry outdoor funerals. I worried about Theo since he didn't have a fan, and his face turned redder as the service progressed. Dean sat ramrod straight, and Gail kept her arm around Laurie's shoulder while she had her head bowed the entire time.

As the service ended, I moved behind Theo to see if he was okay. He said he would be as soon as he was in his air-conditioned car. Charles went to offer condolences to Laurie, William joined Theo and me for the short walk to our vehicles. I wanted to make sure Theo made it safely to his car before speaking to the widow. By the time Theo was resting in air-conditioned comfort, Laurie was walking toward the three elderly ladies who'd been seated behind her. She had on black, high heel shoes and gingerly traversed the bed of pine needles near her car. The ladies took turns hugging the widow before they became engrossed in conversation.

Stanley led the woman he was with over to me. "Chris, allow me to introduce my better half, Veronica."

I said that it was nice to meet her and appreciated them attending.

"I didn't know the deceased," Veronica said as she squeezed Stanley's arm. "Stan had met them, so I thought it would be nice for the widow to see that her island neighbors were sympathetic to her loss."

Stanley nodded a couple of times. "Every cloud has a silver lining."

I was trying to come up with a cliché that meant, *How do I get away from Stanley* when Veronica said they were in a hurry to meet a friend in Charleston? I pretended I hated to see them go.

Charles moved beside me. I told him that I wanted to

speak to Laurie. He said that there was no need because we were meeting her, and the Clarks, for lunch at the Crab Shack.

We got in the car, and I said, "Charles, I don't want to infringe on Laurie's time of grief."

"It was her idea. She insisted that we join them."

"We?"

"Sure," Charles said while adjusting the air-conditioning vent. "She asked me to have lunch with them. I told her you were driving. She nodded meaning she wanted both of us."

Not my interpretation. Arguing with Charles would have been as fruitful as arguing with the live oaks standing sentry around the perimeter of the cemetery.

Charles wiped sweat from his neck as we pulled back on Ft. Johnson Road. He pointed his thumb toward the back window. "Ever been to Ft. Johnson? It's a mile behind us."

"No."

"It goes back a long way. Named after Sir Nathaniel Johnson back in seventeen-something. He was the Proprietary Governor of the Carolinas, whatever that is."

Charles was somewhat of a history buff. My interest in history ended when I was in the ninth grade and the teacher, Old-Bitty Jenkins, asked me what Abe Lincoln and Jefferson Davis had in common. I said they were both dead. She threw a piece of chalk at me. Apparently, I was right, but also wrong.

"Oh," I said, showing little interest.

He mumbled something about the fort's role during the American Revolution, then during the Civil War, and how most of the land now belonged to the South Carolina Wildlife, and Marine Resources Department. I zoned out until I heard him finish the lesson with something about the College of Charleston having its Grice Marine Laboratory on part of the land.

I knew Charles enough to know something was bothering him. He was using the history lesson to take his mind off whatever it was.

The roar of the air conditioner lessened the temperature in the car until it reached a comfortable level. "What's bothering you?"

He readjusted the air vent again. "I'm worried about Laurie. Gail's leaving tomorrow. She'll be alone. She knows a few people at the most. She said that she's still not over being shot at. What's going to happen to her?"

Was someone trying to kill her, or did she fire the gun to deflect suspicion that she killed her husband? I shared that question with Charles.

"Don't be ridiculous. Of course, she didn't fake it. Did you see how torn up she was back there?"

I didn't remind him that she'd taught drama.

"Charles, remember eight years ago when that guy who lived at the Edge shot himself in the arm with the crossbow?"

The Edge was a large seaside boardinghouse owned by a lady who rented rooms to those who couldn't afford the costlier condos along the beach. It was destroyed by a hurricane, a hurricane with the added assistance of a killer who came within moments of ending Charles's and my lives.

"Duh, nearly got us killed."

"Yes, he shot himself so the police would think he was a victim like the two people he'd killed."

"Did you miss the part about not forgetting what happened?"

Then why was he being so dense about what I was suggesting?

"Charles, don't you see how this could be the same thing?"

He shook his head. "This is different."

"How?"

He slammed his hand on the center console. "It just is." He then whispered, "Chris, it just is."

Not another word was spoken, until we found a parking spot across Center Street from the restaurant.

———

The Folly Beach Crab Shack was one of the island's longest-tenured restaurants. Laurie and the Clarks hadn't arrived, so we had the choice of a table on the covered patio or inside. I would've preferred the patio but, after standing in the heat at the funeral, and considering the clothing worn by our luncheon companions, we opted for inside.

A server appeared with water for each of us when the other three arrived and were escorted to the table. Laurie and Gail had replaced their high heels with flats. Dean had abandoned his tie, vest, and suit coat. He looked like he'd walked through a sprinkler. We stood as Laurie hugged each of us then took the chair beside Charles. The Clarks sat on the other side of the table.

"Thank you for choosing inside," Gail said. "The cool air feels good. We were afraid you'd be on the patio."

The newcomers were quick to say water when the server, who announced she was Selene and would be taking care of us, returned to ask what they wanted to drink. The color in their faces had turned from standing-in-a-sauna red to pale Caucasian.

Laurie glanced at me then turned to Charles. "Thank you for coming to the funeral. It was nice seeing so many people there who I don't know that well."

Gail added, "Laurie's worried about being here with so

few friends. Dean and I've encouraged her to move back home."

Laurie jerked her head toward Gail. "Gail, I appreciate your offer. I told you in the car that this is my home. I'm not going anywhere. Let's talk about something else. I'm certain these gentlemen aren't interested."

She didn't know Charles.

"Laurie," he said, "you're one of us now. Look how many people attended the funeral. They were there for you. We stick together. You don't have to worry about making friends."

Gail interrupted, "I'm just saying—"

Laurie interrupted Gail's interruption, "I'm saying the topic is closed. Let's order."

I motioned for Selene before the women exchanged blows. Charles put his arm around Laurie's shoulder, showing which side he was on. Dean asked Gail if she wanted to head home this afternoon instead of in the morning.

She looked at the menu then said, "No. I promised Laurie we'd stay to help straighten up the house."

"It's not that big a mess," Laurie said, subtly sharing her vote on the Clarks leaving early. "I can take care of it."

Dean had leaned back in the chair and watched the antagonistic ping-pong match between the women before saying, "Either way is fine with me."

Gail said, "What time is your meeting tomorrow?"

"After lunch," Dean said. "There'll be time if we leave in the morning."

"Then, it's final," Gail said, "We'll wait until tomorrow."

Laurie's glare looked more hostile than one of grief. Selene had stood at the table with pen in hand waiting for the debate to end before offering to take our order. We ordered, and the conversation took a more civil turn. Laurie talked about the restaurant's colorful walls and the murals. Gail talked about the considerable number of restaurants on Center Street, while Dean stuffed his mouth with peanuts he scooped from a barrel beside the patio door. We ate in silence for a few minutes after the food arrived.

The silence was broken when Laurie said, more to herself than to the rest of us, "All Anthony dreamed about was moving here, finding buried treasure. He said we wouldn't have to worry about money again."

Gail, in a gesture of peace, put her hand on Laurie's arm. "Yes, dear, I know. We'll miss him terribly."

I'd heard, over the years, that Civil War relics had been found on Folly Beach. Uniform buttons, belt buckles, knives, cooking utensils, and cannonballs were the items I'd heard most often mentioned. If that was what the Fitzsimmons were looking for, I couldn't see how they could benefit financially to where they wouldn't have to worry about money.

Charles must've had similar thoughts. "Laurie, what kind of buried treasure were you looking for?" His face broke into one of his loveable smiles that made it difficult to be mad at him regardless how personal the question. "Is there a pot of gold out there I don't know about?"

She dropped her fork on the plate. "No, of course not. It was… nothing. Gail, I think I need to get home. This has been a draining morning."

Gail looked at Laurie's plate. "You sure you don't want to finish eating?"

Dean said, "Gail, didn't you hear her. She's ready to go."

Charles said not to worry about the check, he'd get it. Laurie stood before Gail could give her more grief about finishing lunch, or moving back to Florida, or whatever else she wanted to gripe about. Charles was quick to his feet. He gave Laurie a hug before the trio made their way to the exit.

Charles watched them go. "Wow. If those are best friends, I'd hate to hear Laurie's enemies."

I agreed, yet didn't say anything. I was reeling from Charles's offer to pick up the check.

Chapter Sixteen

William Hansel and Theo entered the restaurant while we were eating. They didn't appear as bothered by the heat since they were on the patio. Charles and I finished. He paid, then suggested we visit William and Theo.

As we approached their table, William looked up from his fish sandwich and smiled. "I see where you gentlemen were engaged in social intercourse with the widow and her acquaintances from Florida."

Uninvited, Charles pulled up a chair. "If that means we were talking with them, yep."

The professor smiled, took a sip of iced tea, and Theo said, "William convinced me we were hungry after leaving the cemetery."

I didn't think it was necessary for him to explain why they were at a restaurant at lunch time.

I said, "William, I was pleased to see you at the funeral."

He nodded. "As you know, I wasn't familiar with the family, yet when Theo indicated an interest in attending I felt compelled to accompany him. I postulated that attendance would be minimal, so I didn't want Mrs. Fitzsimmons to feel that no one was saddened over her spouse's passing."

Theo nodded. "I'm glad he did. I didn't want to go by myself. As cruel it is to say, I didn't want to invite Sal. I was afraid he'd see those gathered as an audience and start cracking jokes."

Charles said, "Wise."

Selene brought fresh glasses of water to Charles and me then told us to wave if we needed anything.

William took another bite then said, "Chris, I've been thinking about what you said about buried treasure being on Folly. I did some research in the college library, found several references to buried artifacts in proximity to our location. In addition to the gold from the Civil War I told you about, I found information on historic occurrences a hundred years prior to the Civil War."

"Rumors about pirate ships you mentioned?"

"Precisely."

Charles leaned closer to William. "What'd you learn?"

William glanced at the ceiling, like he was recalling something from the far reaches of his memory. "According to two sources, pirates frequented the waters off Folly in addition to other barrier islands. They hid their vessels in and around the isolated islands and pounced upon unsuspecting supply ships sailing to coastal locations." He stopped and took another bite.

Charles, who doesn't take kindly to interruptions in something he wants to hear, said, "What happened?"

I said, "Charles, let the man eat."

William smiled. "Are you familiar with an English gentleman named Edward Teach?"

I shook my head.

Charles said, "Who's he?"

"Perhaps you are familiar with his more common moniker, Blackbeard."

Theo raised his hand. William pointed at him.

Theo said, "One of the most famous pirates to sail the ocean blue. He had a house on Folly."

"Correct."

Charles, who didn't want to be left out, added, "I knew that. A hurricane blew his house away."

You know my opinion of history, so I remained silent.

"Mr. Teach, Blackbeard, is the subject of numerous myths, rumors, perhaps an occasional fact. What does appear to be substantiated is that in his day he had one of the mightiest ships ever to sail. He used it to his full advantage. His ship carried more than forty cannons, making it more formidable than any other he encountered."

William paused and glanced around the patio before continuing. "Blackbeard was also three hundred years ahead of those who make a living in our media-saturated, image-obsessed world by aiding politicians or successful businesspersons with how they are perceived by the public. Before going in battle, the famous pirate would garb himself in black, affix pistols to his torso, then at that point don a large, black captain's hat."

"Scary," said Charles.

William looked at him with a gaze I suspected he used on students who had the audacity to interrupt the professor's lecture. "There's more, Charles."

Charles waved his palm in William's face as an apology.

"One reference book said he would put slow-burning fuses in his greasy black hair and beard then ignite them. The fuses sputtered giving off smoke, which gave Blackbeard the appearance of the devil rising from the depths of hell. When opposing ship captains saw the spectacle, gentlemen, they surrendered without firing a shot."

Charles switched from saying scary to uttering, "Cool."

William ignored him. "One of Mr. Teach's travelling companions for a time was Stede Bonnet, another famous pirate."

Charles said, "Hanged at the Battery in Charleston."

"How do you know that?" I asked.

Charles smiled. "Historic marker at the Battery. It says Stede, and twenty-nine of his crew, were hanged in seventeen something. Sorry, don't remember the year. Another pirate dude and nineteen members of his crew were also hanged there. Their bodies were thrown in the nearby marsh that was eventually filled in. That area now houses some of the mansions in the Battery."

"1718," William added, showing his penchant for accuracy.

Enough of the history lesson about what happened in Charleston. I wanted to get back to Folly and buried treasure. "William, did any of the references specifically say Blackbeard, or other pirates, buried their bounty on Folly?"

"Mind you, I didn't spend a great deal of time in the library. I found no documented references to pirates burying or hiding their ill-gained treasures on our island."

Charles said, "That doesn't mean they didn't."

"Of course not," William said. "I did find references to handed-down stories about buried treasures, but none of them mentioned Folly, or Coffin Island, as it was then called."

Charles rubbed his chin. "So Laurie and her late husband were on a quest with nothing to indicate it would pay off?"

"I can't speak to their intentions," William said. "There were no documented instances that I could find. I did discover one interesting tidbit, albeit not footnoted with credible citations. You see, I'm constantly reminding my students that if they are going to reference something in their papers, they must cite the source. That's so future——"

Charles interrupted, "The tidbit, William?"

"Yes, of course. There were stories that one large cache of gold and silver was buried along the North or South Carolina coast. The interesting part of the stories was that instant death would come to anyone who sought the cache."

Charles said, "A curse?"

"That was the inference. I do not believe in curses. Research shows there is always a rational explanation when some event is attributed to the amorphous concept of a curse."

Charles said, "So you're saying that there's no research that proves that curses are real. And by curses, you mean those things that can't be proven because, well, because they're curses?"

William chuckled. "Charles, that's why I teach travel and tourism. Mysticism, mythology, and theology are outside my area of expertise."

"So, the curse could be real?" Charles said.

At times such as this, it was difficult to tell if Charles was serious, obstinate, or trying to provoke a reaction.

Before William answered, Theo leaned forward, wiped his mouth with a napkin, and said, "I bet Anthony Fitzsimmons believes in curses."

I didn't know whether to laugh or agree. Instead of either, I stated the obvious, "We'll never know."

Chapter Seventeen

Theo hadn't mentioned his daughter-in-law while at the Crab Shack, so I was curious if he'd asked her to stay at his house. I conceded that after knowing Charles for nearly a decade, I was becoming more like him. I rationalized that it wasn't a bad thing, although it had gotten me in trouble more than once. With that said, I didn't see any harm in calling Theo.

Sal answered so I asked if Theo was home.

"Hey, Chris, if Theo tells you that I kicked him in the butt, it's true."

I was used to my friends' penchant for answering the phone in, shall I say, a nonconventional manner. Sal's response was a new one.

"Why?"

"I didn't mean to, Theo turned around." Sal broke into laughter.

I wanted to ask if he'd started a dial-a-joke business but was afraid it'd encourage him. I repeated, "Is he there?"

Instead of answering, I heard rustling in the background, before Theo said, "Hang on while I move to the kitchen."

The sound of Sal's laughter lessened.

Theo said, "Sorry about that. I'm making progress, breaking my brother of his exasperating habit of seeing every person as a victim of his humor. He'd never admit it, although it's clear to me that he uses humor, what he thinks as humor, as a shield against others seeing his insecurities."

"Good luck."

"I'll need it. The good thing around the house is that I can turn off my hearing aids. Oh, well, he's my brother, I love him." He paused, before saying, "I don't suppose you called to hear a joke, or me gripe about Sal."

"True. I was wondering if you talked to Grace."

"Last night. I told her there was plenty of room, that she was welcome to move in until she got on her feet." Theo sighed. "She thanked me then turned me down."

"Why?"

"She repeated what she'd told us at the hotel about coming to South Carolina to be near Teddy's dad so we could see each other. She said she didn't come to be a burden on anyone. I told her she wouldn't be a burden, that there was plenty of room, that she wouldn't be in the way. Know what she told me?"

"What?"

"She said she drove by the house yesterday, saw how big it was. I asked why she didn't stop. She said she didn't see a car in the drive, so figured I wasn't here. She said the real reason was to get a layout of the island to see a good place to set up her food truck."

"Is she still living in the truck?"

"Yes."

"What're you going to do?"

"What can I do? She made it clear she didn't want to stay here. She was polite, didn't sound angry, yet was clear about her intentions."

"Did she find somewhere she could set up?"

"She didn't say."

"Think she knows what she needs to do to operate a food truck on Folly? I assume there're health department permits, inspections, specific local regulations about opening a business. When I opened my gallery I had my friend, Sean Aker, help me through the bureaucratic maze."

"Chris, I have no idea. She had the truck in California, so I assume she knows the hoops to jump through. She seems self-sufficient so I'm sure she'll be able to take care of it. I plan to call in a couple of days to see what she's learned. I'll offer help, financial or otherwise, if she needs a lawyer to get her business set up. If she does, I'll recommend Sean."

I wished him luck a second time.

He thanked me, then added, "I was thinking after lunch about what you told us Laurie and her husband said about finding treasure. It had me confused."

"Why?"

"If Anthony thought there was even a ghost of a chance, pun intended, in finding something of value, he must've known more than vague rumors about treasure being buried, or relics from the Civil War."

Theo had an excellent point. Laurie sounded confident they were going to discover something countless people had failed to find since the Civil War ended more than a century and a half ago. Laurie and Anthony were new to the area, so they hadn't been here long enough to explore each nook and cranny. So, what did they know? How did they learn it? Even more important, if it existed, where was the treasure? I told

Theo I agreed and asked if he had any idea how they might've known.

"No. What I can tell you is Sal would have a joke about it."

No doubt, I thought.

I moved to the chair in the living room and reflected on the day that began with a funeral, continued with an awkward, tense lunch with Laurie, Dean, Gail, and Charles, then ended with a sophomoric joke and Theo making a generous offer to Grace only to have it rejected.

I was starting to drift to sleep in the chair when Charles called.

"Guess where we're going tomorrow morning?"

I didn't have the energy to ask how I could possibly know. "Where?"

"Laurie's house."

If I wasn't fully awake when he started the conversation, I was now. "Why?"

"She called and invited us to coffee."

"Us?"

"Not exactly."

"What exactly?"

"Something like, 'Charles, could you stop by the house in the morning around nine?' "

"She invited you."

"There's no reason to get so picky about it. Would you go with me? She sounded like there was something strange going on. I'd feel more comfortable with you there."

"Strange, how?"

"Can't put my finger on it. Strange."

"That helps. What's she going to say if you show up at her door with me in tow?"

"I'll let you know in the morning."

I rolled my eyes at the phone. "What do you think she wants?"

"I'll let you know in the morning."

I surrendered. He said he had to deliver a surfboard for the surf shop and would meet me at Laurie's house. She wanted him to be there at nine, so I knew he'd be there at 8:30, Charles Standard Time.

I'm certain he said, "Thank you." Of course, I couldn't hear it since he'd hung up.

Chapter Eighteen

I pulled in Laurie's gravel drive and parked behind Charles's Toyota Venza and Laurie's MINI. Charles stepped out of his vehicle. He had on navy shorts, and a long-sleeved, gray T-shirt with IPFW in blue letters on the front. I had stopped asking about the shirts years ago, although it'd never stopped him from sharing, in my opinion, worthless information about his logo ware. I was clueless about what the letters stood for and comfortable remaining that way.

Fortunately, he didn't feel the need to enlighten me. He said, "On time, good."

We walked up Laurie's steps thirty minutes early, and one person more than she'd invited. I stood behind Charles, wishing myself invisible as the homeowner opened the door. She'd abandoned her black, mourning clothes. She had on a baby-blue blouse and tan slacks, a drastic contrast from our first visit when she was in a quilted robe. Her face looked refreshed, with no remnants of tears.

"Oh," she said. "You're early," proving that she didn't

know Charles enough to know about his time quirk. She glanced around Charles. "Hi, Chris."

Charles said, "Is it okay if my friend came with me?"

I didn't expect her to say, "No."

"I suppose, come on in."

Not quite an open-arms welcome, although, under the circumstances it wasn't bad.

We followed her to the kitchen, where she asked how we liked our coffee. We said black.

"Good. I have all this food the good people of Folly have given me, but I don't have cream." She got two mugs out of the cabinet and poured our drinks. She handed a mug to Charles and said, "What's IPFW, a union?"

"Thanks for asking," he said as he glanced at me. "It's Indiana University, Purdue University Fort Wayne."

"Oh," she said.

My sentiments exactly.

"Did you go to school there?"

Further proof that she didn't know Charles that well.

"No. I thought the shirt was interesting."

"Oh," she said, for the third time. She walked us to the living room where we sat on the sofa. Laurie took the Lazy Boy.

"Did your company get off okay?" I asked.

"Yes, thank goodness. Dean has a meeting with his banker this afternoon, so I think Gail would've stayed forever if her ride hadn't been leaving. I love her to death; she'd do anything for me. As you could tell from lunch, she'd smother me with kindness, and advice. As wonderful as she is, smothering is still smothering." She turned to Charles. "That's why I asked Charles over. I wanted to apologize for getting him in the middle of our carping."

The use of *him* wasn't lost on me, so I waited for the only person she'd invited to respond.

"Laurie," Charles said. "I hadn't given it a thought. We were glad you invited us, weren't bothered a bit. Were we, Chris?"

Yes, it bothered me, yes, I felt uncomfortable horning in on her grief. Of course, I said, "No. It was fine."

"Thank you. I feel better with that out of the way."

Charles said, "Has Gail always been that pushy?"

Laurie looked at the floor. "I don't know what's gotten into her. She wasn't always that bad. Honest, she wasn't."

I didn't think she expected a response, especially since we didn't know Gail at all. It didn't stop Charles.

"You've been friends a long time. I'm sure Anthony's death struck her hard. Maybe that's why."

Laurie looked up from the floor. "You're a wise man, Charles. That's probably it."

It was the first time I'd heard Charles called wise without being followed by another word for donkey.

The wise man said, "Are you going to be okay?"

"I think so. I hope so. I don't know what I'll do without Anthony. He did everything for me. Perhaps Gail was right about me moving back to Jacksonville. I don't know many people here. And what about that bullet that nearly killed me? Somebody killed Anthony, somebody was trying to kill me, Charles. I don't know what to think. What's to say they won't try again?"

Charles looked over at me, expecting me to respond. She was talking to Charles, so I stayed out of it. He took the hint.

"Any idea who it might've been?"

She jerked her head toward Charles. "No. Why kill Anthony? I know he could be difficult. Lordy, we had our differences, but no one knew him here. So why kill him? What have we done to make someone that angry?" She jumped out of the chair and grabbed our mugs. "Let me get you more." She headed to the kitchen without waiting for us to respond.

I looked at Charles, who shrugged.

Laurie returned with refills. Her hands were shaking as she handed us the mugs. Not knowing what to say, I took a sip as she returned to the La-Z-Boy.

"Laurie," Charles said, "could Anthony's death, umm, murder, have something to do with what you were looking for out there?"

"Why? All we were doing was looking for Civil War relics."

I took a gamble. "Laurie, when we were at lunch, you mentioned that Anthony said something about you not having to worry after you found the buried treasure. What was—"

She leaned up in her chair so fast that I thought she might fall out. "You must've misunderstood. I wouldn't have said buried treasure. Heavens, that sounds like gold, silver, or something more valuable than what we were looking for. They may have worth, but nothing like buried treasure. A simple misunderstanding." She leaned back.

I hadn't heard her incorrectly at lunch. "I misunderstood. Sorry."

"Are you a treasure hunter?" She had leaned back yet her words were as sharp as they were seconds earlier.

I smiled. "Far from it. I'd never thought about it. Why?"

"Nothing. I was curious."

Curious, and ill at ease with the topic.

"I know it's none of my business," Charles said. "Are you going to be okay financially?"

"It's okay to ask, Charles," she said as her smile returned. "I'm glad you're concerned. I think so. Anthony had insisted on that nice insurance policy. I have my teachers' retirement."

"If you ever need anything, don't feel bad about calling."

"Charles, thank you for the offer. I may take you up on it. I appreciate you, umm, both of you, stopping by. I know you must be busy, so I won't keep you."

A dismissal, albeit a polite one. We stood, thanked her for the coffee, and reiterated that she could call Charles if she needed anything.

On the drive home, I asked myself two questions. First, why did Laurie really ask Charles over? She could've told him on the phone she was sorry about how he was caught in an awkward situation at lunch. That would've been as effective and easier than Charles going to her house. The second question was why did she lie about what she'd said at lunch concerning a buried treasure? The drive home was too short for me to come up with adequate answers. What I did come up with was a need to learn the truth.

———

Despite the food Laurie's neighbors had brought, all she had offered Charles and me was coffee. I parked in the drive but, instead of going in the house, I walked next door to Bert's Market to grab something to quench my hunger. I found a Reuben sandwich that I could microwave at home, and found Abraham, excuse me, Captain Gant pulling a six-pack of Budweiser out of the wall cooler. He lowered the beer to his side and gave me a vague smile of recognition.

"Hi, Captain," I said, and in case he didn't remember, added, "I'm Chris."

"Of course. I may be old, but I'm not senile."

Old, not senile, and cranky, I thought, before I said something about it being a muggy day and that it looked like it would rain tomorrow.

"We need the rain," he said.

I turned to walk away when he said, "Glad I ran into you." He set the beer on the floor. "Have you heard if the police have suspects in the damned relic hunter's murder?"

I thought it was a strange question. He was the retired cop, not me.

"No, why do you think I'd know?"

"I hear rumors. Someone said you're good friends with the chief. I thought she might've shared something."

"We're friends although she——"

"You know what she accused me of?"

Irritating interrupting came to mind. I said that I didn't.

"She questioned me a half hour yesterday, accusing me of taking a shot at the damned relic hunter's wife. How stupid is that?"

I didn't think it was stupid since I'd suggested it to Cindy. "Why'd she think that?"

"She was playing it close to the vest. Admirable, I suppose. That's how I would've handled it back in the day when I interrogated suspects. The chief didn't say why I was a suspect. I figure it was because of how I'd badmouthed the couple for meddling in the past, things they had no damned business doing."

"What'd you tell her?"

He glared at me. "Young man, it's none of your damned business what I told her." His glare turned to a wicked smile. He put his hand near my face, palm out. "I have nothing to hide. I was at a doctor's appointment in Charleston. Told the chief there was a herd of sick people in the waiting room the entire two hours. That's right, two hours waiting. Ought to be a law about that. I had to sit there listening to people cough, wheeze, spew germs. If I wasn't sick when I got there, I damned well could've been when I left. There were witnesses galore. The damned doc couldn't vouch for most of that time because he didn't see me for two hours. Did I already say that?"

I nodded. "Good alibi."

Abraham was at the top of my suspect list. Even if he didn't take a shot at Laurie, he could've killed Anthony.

"Not saying I wouldn't have had a desire to kill the damned women for her and her husband digging for buried treasure. It's pathetic how people meddle where they shouldn't. I'm not sorry someone's trying to end her meddling life. I'm only saying it wasn't me."

That was today's second reference to buried treasure.

"Captain, my understanding is that they were searching for Civil War relics. What do you mean about buried treasure?"

He looked around the store and leaned closer to me, like he was about to whisper the nuclear missile launch code. "Remember when I told you about the grandfather of the woman I was accused of trying to shoot?"

"Harnell Levi. You said he was a nut."

"Good recall."

"You said he was always talking about pirates, about treasure."

"Meddling in the past. Horrible."

I didn't want him to get on another rant about those who dig up the past. "Do you think he told his granddaughter about buried treasure and that's what they were hunting?"

"Sure do."

"People have searched here, plus on the other barrier islands for decades. They haven't found anything other than Civil War items, or skeletons. What makes you think the Fitzsimmonses would have a chance at finding something of value?"

He rubbed the side of his face and looked around again. "I didn't take it too serious at the time. Hell, I didn't take anything the old coot said serious. Didn't give it a thought, until the damned relic hunter was killed."

"Take what seriously?"

Gant nodded. "The map."

"Map?"

"In addition to running around singing show tunes, talking about Nazi subs he claimed to see, and looking like a character actor out of a B cowboy movie, when the old codger got a few of those in his system," Gant pointed to the six-pack on the floor, "he'd spout off about a treasure map that was going to lead him to riches."

"Was he serious?"

"Serious as a delusional, screwed-up, old codger can be."

"Where'd he get this supposed treasure map?"

"As far as I know he never said."

"Anyone ever see it?"

"I never heard about him showing it to anyone."

"Except Laurie?"

"Speculation, my friend. Pure speculation."

A little sucking up may be fruitful. "You're a former law enforcement officer, a good one I've heard. You have good instincts, decades of experience. Any thoughts on who had reason to shoot Anthony Fitzsimmons?"

He smiled. "Flattery, not a bad technique." His smile disappeared as quickly as it had appeared. "Back in the day, if I was looking for a killer, I'd start with the spouse. The relic hunter's wife. Does she have motive? Money's always a big one? Did hubby have a lot of it? Was he worth more dead than alive? Then there's love. Was he having an affair, or did she love someone else, and her husband was an albatross around her neck, a problem she needed to eliminate?"

"I don't know—"

He ignored me. "Then you get reasons that are flat out

stupid. Did she get mad at him because he wanted to watch a NASCAR race when she wanted to watch a Hallmark movie, or she didn't like the way he criticized her for the way she cooked pork chops? Stupid reasons, yet I've seen spouses killed because of them."

"Who else would you consider besides the wife?"

Abraham looked at his hand and held up three fingers. "My third choice would be someone who knew about the treasure, someone who wanted to get it before the dead guy found it."

"If Anthony had the map you mentioned, why wouldn't the killer wait until he dug up whatever was out there then steal it?"

"That's what I said or meant to say. How do you know he didn't?"

"It doesn't make sense that they found something. If they found the treasure, why wouldn't she have said something to the police, or to me when Charles and I found her in the car? As far as I know, the police didn't find a shovel or where digging had taken place."

Gant grinned and shrugged. "They didn't find a murder weapon either, did they? It would've been easy to throw the gun and whatever he had been digging with in the ocean. It'd been raining hard. With the land low out there, it could've flooded, washed sand and crap into wherever he'd been digging. Tons of unanswered questions, ain't there? That's why they call it a mystery."

"True."

"I'll tell you one thing, mister. It's a mystery for the police to figure out. It's nothing for a retired state police officer or a whatever you are to waste time with."

I wasn't about to argue. I'm also far from a mathematician

and have trouble balancing my own check book, yet I realized something Gant had said didn't compute.

"You said your third choice was someone who knew about the treasure hunt. Who's your second choice?"

His smile returned. "You're looking at him."

He picked up the six pack of Bud, turned, and walked to the cash register leaving me staring at the cooler and thinking how much simpler life would be if Charles and I had decided to drive to Charleston to take photos of the mansions overlooked the bay rather than traipsing off to the old Coast Guard property that fateful morning. I also thought that Abraham had a good point that whatever had happened to Anthony Fitzsimmons was none of my business. It would better be left to the police.

Finally, I wondered why that wouldn't be the case.

Chapter Nineteen

The next morning, the heavy rain that Abraham and I wasted time talking about had done its damage, and eased. A puddle the size of Lake Erie was in the front yard as water cascaded off the roof of the screened-in porch. An hour later, the rain ended, and I decided to make a visit to Barb's Books. She was standing by the large plate glass window, gazing at the traffic passing on Center Street, a practice that consumed hours of my time when the space had been my gallery.

She smiled. "Thank goodness, someone enters."

She had on another red blouse. As a concession to the summer temperatures, and the custom of many island retail employees, she wore shorts and tennis shoes.

"Slow day?"

"Including you, I can count today's customers on one finger."

"Suppose I should buy something."

She rolled her eyes. "How many books have you bought since I've been open?"

"Counting on one hand, zero fingers."

"Don't ruin your perfect record. Can I interest you in a Diet Pepsi?"

"You twisted my arm," I followed her to the office. I looked around, again marveling how different the office looked than when it was Landrum Gallery's office, snack bar, and hang out for my friends.

She said as she handed me a drink, "Let's head up front so I don't miss any of the customers who don't come in."

I was pleased she was acclimating to the quirky character of many of the island's residents. I joined her as she returned to the staring spot at the front window then shared my conversation with Captain Gant.

Barb listened with the intensity of an attorney, took a sip of Diet Root Beer, before saying, "It's interesting how he included himself in his list of suspects. That was an effective way to deflect guilt."

"What do you mean?"

"You said he smiled when he added his name to the list. It was as if he threw it in as an absurdity, like who could possibly think he was the killer. Also, he has a solid alibi for when someone shot at Laurie."

"True. Depending upon what version Laurie gives, she was either in the bedroom or in the kitchen when the shot was fired."

"You think she faked it?"

I shrugged

"The police know Laurie's conflicting stories?"

"Yes."

"They're following up?"

I was heading into a trap. I nodded.

She mirrored my nod. "So, you're stepping aside, leaving it to the police?"

The sun had started to break through the clouds, as I muttered, "Yes," and changed the subject. "Looks like it's going to be an enjoyable day."

She gave me a skeptical expression, then agreed about the weather. Before I said I should head home we agreed to meet for supper in a couple of days.

I turned onto East Ashley Avenue, where I saw a white, Chevy step van parked at the entrance to a large gravel lot that's the prime parking area for beachgoers and customers to the central business district's restaurants and stores. The van had been converted into a food truck and had a large red and brown oval logo on the side with a rendering of a hot dog slathered with mustard. Above the hot dog were the words *Hot Diggity Dog!* Underneath the cartoon-looking hot dog, it read, *Gourmet Hot Dogs*. I didn't have to be a detective to know it belonged to Theo's daughter-in-law.

I pulled in a parking space in front of Cool Breeze Bike Rental across the street from the truck. I waved at Matty, the bike rental's owner, told him I'd be just a minute, and crossed the street to the food truck. The six-foot long service window was closed. No one answered after I knocked twice. I walked around the vehicle to see if Grace was nearby. She wasn't, so I took a closer look at the vehicle.

There was a dent on the back corner on the passenger's side. I thought there would be more than that if I had to back the truck into parking spaces. The tires weren't bald, although I suspected they'd have trouble passing a safety inspection. It appeared a miracle that Grace had safely made the twenty-three-hundred-mile trip from California.

I knocked one more time in case she'd been sleeping. No response, so I headed back to my car.

Matty was leaning against my hood. He smiled. "If you'd told me where you were going, I could've saved you a trip."

The truck was Grace's only means of motorized transportation, so I knew she couldn't have gone far. "You know where she went?"

He waved in the direction of Center Street less than a block away. "When she started walking that way, I should have asked for a written itinerary and how long she'd be gone. I didn't know you'd be asking, so I didn't."

I smiled at my friend. "You don't know where she went?"

"No. Now that you're standing in my parking area, keeping hundreds of vacationers from getting to my business which will probably put me out of work, let me ask something. Who is she? Why is that oversized hot dog stand parked there? Oh, yeah, where's the lady from who parked it?"

I wasn't certain if Matty knew Theo. Even if he did, I doubted Theo would want him to know Grace's story about why she was here.

"Someone I recently met, name's Grace. She wants to open a food truck on Folly. Why'd you ask where she's from?"

"She came over an hour ago to tell me her name. She gave me the cutest smile I'd seen in years. She has a delightful accent."

"If she told you her name, why ask who she is?"

"There's a difference between a name and who someone is."

True. I still didn't want to get in an extended conversation about Theo's daughter-in-law. "She's Jamaican, came from California."

"Yep. Knew she wasn't from around here. Mighty cute sounding. Is she thinking of opening her business there?"

"I don't know."

"Hope so. She's pleasant to listen to, and look at."

"If you see her, tell her I stopped by."

"You got it. Besides, that'll give me an excuse to share

some facetime with her cute Jamaican accent, and lovely smile."

I smiled. "Since when have you ever needed an excuse to talk to someone?"

He smiled. "Now get your car out of here so real customers can get in."

Chapter Twenty

The sun had concluded its work for the day while I was on my screened-in porch watching cars pass in front of the house, many carrying surfboards. I smiled, thinking about my ill-fated attempt at surfing with Dude, when the phone rang.

"Chris, this is Matty. Did I catch you at an inconvenient time?"

Matty was an interesting man, as Folly as anyone can be. This was the first time he'd called. I was tempted to ask him to teach telephone etiquette to my friends. As great as that temptation was, I decided it was more important to hear what he wanted.

"It's fine. What's going on?"

"You were asking about the lady with the food truck, so I figured you'd want to know something's going on over there. Two patrol cars are parked beside the truck. Now, Chief LaMond just rolled up."

"Any idea what happened?"

"Nah. The good news is there aren't firetrucks, or ambulances."

That was good, although it didn't answer my question. I started the block-long walk to the truck with the phone still to my ear. "You don't have any idea what happened?"

"I don't think they're there to buy hot dogs. If you'd mosey over, you could con your buddy, the chief, into telling you."

"I'm on my way."

"Good. I'll leave it in your capable hands."

I was a half block from the food truck and saw flashing lights from the patrol cars. One of the cars was exiting the lot when I crossed the street in front of Grace's vehicle. Its door was standing open, its owner sitting on the slide-out step. She wore a pink sundress, and her arms were waving around, like she was describing something to the chief who was standing in front of her, taking notes. Grace was backlit from the light inside the truck, so I couldn't see her expression.

Chief LaMond looked up when she saw me approach, pointed her pen at me, and said, "What took you so long. You're usually attracted to commotion, like a mosquito to my lovely, ivory-hued arms."

Theo's daughter-in-law stood then turned so I could see her face. "Hello, Mr. Landrum."

Cindy glanced at me then looked at Grace. "You know this fossil?"

"Yes, mon. Mr. Landrum is a friend of, umm, someone I know."

It didn't appear that Grace wanted to get into her relationship with Theo. "What happened, chief?"

Cindy glanced at her notebook. "Someone broke in Ms. Stoll's truck. I was taking down basic information, was about to ask her if she was related to Theodore Stoll when you stuck you nose in official police business, again."

Grace's head jerked toward Cindy. "Are you familiar with Mr. Stoll?"

She was about to get her first lesson in everyone-knows-everyone on Folly.

"Most definitely," Cindy said. "Known him ever since he moved her. Your relationship?"

"I was married to Teddy, his son."

"Oh."

That threw Cindy. Now, for my contribution to the conversation. "Theo's son and Grace lived in California. Theodore Jr., Teddy, was killed in a motorcycle accident a while back. Grace has moved here to open her business." I looked at Grace to see if she wanted me to say more.

She took it from there. "I needed to leave California, thought being closer to my father-in-law could be a good thing." She waved her hand toward the truck. "Now, this."

"Was anything taken?" I asked Grace, sensing she was uncomfortable saying more about her family.

"I don't think so. I was eating supper at that place called Planet Follywood. All the money I have was with me." She tilted her head toward the truck. "Everything in there is a mess. I can't tell what could be missing."

I asked, "How'd they get in?"

She started to respond when Cindy said, "Chris, why don't you let me play cop and ask the questions?"

"Sorry."

"Grace, how did they get in?"

I turned my head so Grace wouldn't see me smile.

"The old girl has some age on her." Grace pointed at the truck. "She'd be old enough to drink in most states. Has more than a few dings. Her air conditioning works only when it wants to. Her door ain't quite as secure as Fort Know, mon."

The space between the door and the jam had a quarter-inch gap which was wider near the handle.

Cindy nodded, wrote something in the notebook, pointed in the door, and said, "Anything broken, or just thrown around?"

Grace stepped in the truck, and Cindy followed. I was behind Cindy and while the truck was old enough to drink, the interior had been converted to a food truck much later. Even with equipment strewn around, I could tell it was nearly new. Grace picked a large pot off the floor and set it on the counter.

"It had been a bakery delivery vehicle in Los Angeles before we bought it. Teddy found a company in LA that converts step trucks into food trucks. We worked with them to have the interior custom outfitted. We did some of the work ourselves. I'll pat myself on the back and say that I'm handy with tools; in fact, helped remodel a couple of restaurants in my younger days.

"Even with doing much ourselves, it was still many thousand dollars later before this became our pride and joy. The good thing about it is it's built to travel, to go over bumpy roads, to have a hard life. In other words, it would take a lot to break anything in here. At first glance, I don't see anything beyond repair."

Cindy nodded as she looked around. "Ms. Stoll, can you think of anyone who would do this?"

Grace looked at the floor as she leaned against the aluminum prep table. "Chief, I pulled onto your quaint island two days ago. I have only spoken to dear Theo, Mr. Landrum here, that nice man across the street with the bicycles, and Melody, the server at Planet Follywood. I do not know anyone else." She shook her head. "What reason could I have accumulated for someone to want to do this to *Hot Diggity Dog!*?"

Cindy picked up tongs from the floor, looked around, then

set them on the counter. "Grace, it could be as simple as someone seeing the truck; not seeing anyone around; thinking there could be money inside; breaking in to steal it; getting frustrated when he or she couldn't find anything worth stealing; then made this mess."

Grace dropped the tongs that Cindy had put on the counter in the compact sink and sighed. "I hope that it's as simple as that."

Me, too, I thought.

Cindy patted Grace on the arm. "Grace, would you like me to help put things back together?"

"Oh, dear, Chief, you are way too kind. Thank you, but no. I will have it together in a jiff."

Cindy nodded. "That's all I can do here. I'll have some of my guys ask around to see if anyone remembers seeing someone lurking around. I doubt it'll help. Anyway, we'll try." Cindy hesitated, then glanced at the sleeping bag rolled up between the driver's seat and the passenger's seat. "Grace, where are you staying?"

She followed Cindy's stare. "In the truck."

The Chief said, "Where are you parking overnight?"

Grace lowered her eyes. "Last night over on the other corner of the lot. I was hoping to stay here tonight."

Cindy slowly shook her head. "I'm afraid that's not possible. Motor homes aren't permitted to house occupants on Folly. Technically, your truck falls under that classification. Sorry."

"Where can I—"

Cindy held her hand up. "There's Walmart five miles up Folly Road on the left. Check with their manager. They let people park their motorhomes overnight in their lot."

"Thank you, Chief."

"I know you've been here only a couple of days, probably

haven't had time, but have you applied for a retail food establishment permit from the South Carolina Department of Health and Environmental Control?"

"I was going to work on the application tonight."

"Great," Cindy said. "What about a permit to operate on Folly?"

"I'll check on that tomorrow."

Cindy said, "I've pestered you enough. It's nice meeting you. Sorry it's under these circumstances." She started toward the door, hesitated, pulled a card out of her pocket, and handed it to Grace. "Give me a call if you think of anything that might help. In case you don't already know, Chris, while he's often a pain in my posterior, is a good guy. He can be trusted."

She was out the door before I could say, "Awe, shucks."

Grace stared at the open door. "She seems like a nice person."

"She's the best. Let me help you get straightened up."

"No way, fine sir. I'll do it later. It's not like it's going anywhere. Do you mind if I sit down? This has been one long day."

I followed her to the front of the truck as she moved the sleeping bag from between the seats. She took the driver's seat while I moved to the passenger's seat.

"Are you okay?"

Grace was staring out the window at the lights from Pier 101, the restaurant at the Folly Pier across the parking lot. She didn't say anything for a minute, then in her lilting voice said, "If someone told me six months ago that I'd be a widow, sitting in a ransacked food truck, staring at the Atlantic Ocean, I'd say they'd been smoking too much wacky weed." Tears began flowing down her cheeks.

Other than an occasional sniffle, we sat in silence, staring straight ahead.

Ten minutes later, in a low voice, she said, "Dawg nyam yu suppa,"

"What?"

"Oh, sorry, it's a Jamaican phrase that literally means, "Dog will eat your supper." She looked at me as she attempted to smile. "It means I will be punished, something bad will happen to me, for some reason. Like what could be worse than your supper being given to a dog." She sighed. "What did I do to deserve this?"

"Bad things happen to the best of us, often for no reason."

"Mr. Landrum, I'm so terribly sorry. You don't know me. Here I am, a middle-aged woman, acting like a sniveling baby taking up your time."

I touched her arm. "It's okay, Grace. It's okay."

"Thank you." She turned to look toward the food prep area.

"Would you like me to call your father-in-law? He has room in his house. He'd love for you to stay there. You can park the truck in his drive until you find somewhere of you own."

"No way." She sighed. "He treated me like pig dung when we met." She returned to staring out the front window. "I don't blame him. Here I was, a stranger, trying to be family. The whole time I was driving from California; I knew he and Teddy had a horrible relationship. Besides, Mr. Stoll has a right to think I must want something. Why wouldn't he think that? No way will I stay there, or ask him for anything." She slammed her hand on the steering wheel. "No way."

"Grace, I've known Theo for a couple of years. I've been with him in rough situations. I've seen how loyal he was to his friends, even when it would have been better otherwise. Don't judge him without getting to know him."

"Perhaps another time, mon. Now, I'd better get *Hot Diggity Dog!* to Walmart before she gets towed. Thank you for coming to check on me, Mr. Landrum."

She was pulling out of the parking lot before I had time to cross the road on my way home.

Chapter Twenty-One

_____

C harles and I agreed to meet for breakfast at the Dog, so I wasn't surprised to see him at a table on the front patio when I arrived. I was glad he was there because the restaurant was packed. Plus, there was a couple accompanied by their collie waiting for an outdoor seat.

"Guess who called last night," Charles said as soon as I sat.

"Mick Jagger," I said then took a sip of water that he'd had the server leave for me.

"You suck at guessing."

Amber was at the table before I could offer a second guess. She pointed her pen at me. "Found more bodies?"

"No. Good morning, Amber," I said, practicing the lost art of politeness. "How are you this beautiful morning?"

She smiled. "You're the first person who asked me that today. I'm fine." She pointed her pen at the wall between the patio and the inside dining area. "Guess what he's saying in there about Anthony's death?"

"Who's he?"

"Who's your favorite councilmember who's here nearly

each day with another councilmember, the one who'd rather spread gossip than butter?"

Finally, a question I could answer. "Marc Salmon."

"Bingo. Are you ready to hear what he's saying?"

Two in a row I could answer. The day was looking up. "Yes."

"Said Anthony was shot because he stumbled on a drug deal. According to Marc, drug dealers were bringing dope on shore out there because it's isolated, nobody'd be there after dark. Something about Anthony being at the wrong place at the wrong time."

That made sense, but I wondered how Marc heard about it. "Who told Marc?"

Amber shrugged. "Didn't ask. Needy customers keep interrupting his story. Want to me to find out?"

Charles said, "You bet."

I added, "If you can without letting him know who's asking."

Amber saluted then asked if I was ready to order yogurt.

I said, "French toast," to which she said, "Surprise, surprise."

Charles watched her leave. "You ready for me to tell you?"

I'd forgotten what he was talking about. "Sure."

He said, "Laurie."

It was coming back to me. A call. "What'd she want?"

"Thought you'd never ask. She wants me to come see her."

"Why?"

"Didn't say."

"Why do you think?"

"Get real, Chris. Who wouldn't want this charming, handsome, wise, witty fellow to visit?"

I wanted to add *delusional*. Instead, I repeated, "Why do you think?"

"No idea."

That was more like it.

"When?"

He looked at his wrist. "As soon as you're done eating."

I knew the answer to the next question before I asked. "Did she say she wanted me to come?"

"Not in those words."

"How did she say it?"

"The last time we were there, she hadn't mentioned you coming, yet she invited both of us in. See. she wants both of us."

I was ready to point out the lack of logic in his thinking when Amber returned, refilled my cup, and whispered, "Captain Gant."

"Gant told Marc about the drug deal gone bad."

"Yep." Amber grinned like she'd solved the Rubik's Cube.

Charles said, "He say anything else?"

"Yep. He said, 'Ready for the check.' " Her grin turned to a smile as she tapped the top of Charles's head before walking away.

I asked Charles, "What do you make of that?"

"He was ready to leave, wanted to pay."

"You know what I mean."

"His story makes sense. It was late, so nobody would be there. One of the cars Laurie saw could've been the person waiting to pick up the drugs. After Anthony got separated from Laurie, he could've stumbled on the deal. Then, bang!"

I looked at the increasing crowd waiting for tables. "Or, it could be Captain Gant, dreaming up the story to lead police on a wild goose chase."

"That, too."

"Charles, thanks for coming. I see you brought your friend," Laurie said as she opened the door. She looked like she was ready to go to a party in a lavender blouse, white linen slacks, and low-heel, black dress shoes.

Her comment about Charles bringing a friend was spoken with little enthusiasm, or else I was projecting awkwardness about being there. Regardless, she didn't turn me away, then asked if we wanted something to drink. We said, "Water" and followed her to the kitchen, where she grabbed three plastic water bottles out of the refrigerator. We headed to the living room.

Laurie looked at her lap, picked a speck of lint off her linen slacks, looked up at Charles, and smiled. "I suppose you're wondering why I asked you over."

Charles returned her smile. "I was curious."

I leaned back on the sofa and remained quiet.

"The last two years Anthony and I were teaching, all we talked about was moving here when we retired. We batted scenarios around like a volleyball." She picked another piece of lint off her slacks and shook her head. "We'd be retired, still in our fifties, too young to not do something. We talked about getting part-time jobs." She giggled. "Anthony wanted to work at that shop on the pier so he could look out the window and see the ocean.

"I'm a morning person and thought it'd be interesting working at a breakfast restaurant, like the Lost Dog Café, or the Black Magic Cafe. We talked about getting a boat; nothing big, nothing oceangoing, simply something we could use to explore the marsh or nearby rivers. We talked about taking an Alaskan cruise. The boat and the cruise were only dreams because we didn't have the money. She hesitated and looked down at her slacks. Apparently, she couldn't find more lint, so she looked back at us. "Charles, do you know what we never dreamed about, never gave a second of thought to?"

"What?"

"One of us being gone. Charles, Anthony's gone. Gone forever."

Charles whispered. "I'm sorry."

Laurie put her hand on her forehead and closed her eyes. "I'm scared."

Charles said, "Is there anything we can do to help?"

Laurie moved her hand from her face. "Guys, you're the only friends I have here. Sure, I've talked to people at the stores, I even know a few of their names. I was shocked by how many came to the funeral. I don't really know them."

"It takes time," I said. "When I moved here, I didn't know anyone. Then, so many people showed me kindness and true warmth that I felt welcomed."

Laurie looked at me as if she just realized I was there. "I know I must keep my head up and move forward. Maybe—"

Charles interrupted, "Teddy Roosevelt said, 'By acting as if I was not afraid, I gradually cease to be afraid.' "

Laurie cocked her head at Charles.

He said, "I get inspiration from presidents."

"Oh," she said. "I hope you, umm, President Roosevelt was right. It doesn't help now. I'm alone and, my God, Charles, someone tried to kill me." She jumped up, started toward the kitchen, turned, and looked at us. "What can I do?"

If, as I suspected, she'd killed her husband, she was a great actress. It still wasn't clear why she asked Charles to stop by.

"Laurie," I said. "Unless you remember something that you haven't shared with the police, I doubt there's anything you can do about what happened to Anthony, or the person who shot at the house. The police are good. They'll do what they can."

She glanced at Charles and looked at me. "That night at the Lighthouse Preserve is all a blur. I think I told them everything."

I remembered the rumor that Marc Salmon was spreading. "Laurie, I know the rain was heavy, the thunder loud. Do you remember other sounds?"

"Like the gunshot? I could've but didn't tell any difference between it and thunder."

"I was thinking more like a boat motor."

"A boat?"

Charles was feeling left out of the conversation. "We heard a rumor that someone may've been delivering drugs by boat to someone near where Anthony was killed."

"You're saying Anthony saw something he shouldn't have, paid for it with his life. Is that why he was killed?"

"We don't know," I added. "That's why I was wondering if you heard a boat."

"Not really."

"You don't remember anything else about the cars that were out there when you got back to the car?"

She shook her head and looked toward the bedroom door. "If that's what happened, why did somebody shoot at me?"

It was possible that if the death was drug related, the killer could've seen Laurie then figured she saw him. Possible, although unlikely since there was a gap between when she and Anthony got separated and when he was shot.

"Laurie, I'm sure the police have heard the rumor. They'll investigate."

She returned to hunting lint on her slacks, and whispered, "I hope so."

Charles said, "They'll figure it out."

"Good," she said and shook her head. "Sorry I dumped all that on you. That's not why I asked you over. Gail and Dean are coming back tomorrow for the weekend. They want to take me to supper. I told them not to. A four-hour drive to get here for supper. Stupid. Of course, Gail wouldn't listen." She sighed. "Charles, could you come with us? I'm not ready to hear Gail spend all night telling me why I should move to Jacksonville, or griping about the condition of the house, or that I need to sell it. Whatever else her gripe of the day is."

"I don't want to take time away from you, and your friends."

"Please."

Charles smiled. "Sure."

"Thank you."

The mood was broken when Charles said, "Can Chris come? He could be my date."

"Oh. I don't want to impose. I'm sure he has better things to do than spend time with strangers."

"No, he doesn't."

Laurie faked a smile. "He's welcome to join us."

She wasn't as good an actress as I thought she was.

Chapter Twenty-Two

C harles and his "date" were to meet the others at Taco Boy on Center Street. I told Charles that I'd meet him in front of the popular restaurant and was there thirty minutes early. My friend was next door to Taco Boy, leaning against the green, brick wall of the Palms gift shop. He wore a long-sleeved, royal blue T-shirt with Gators on the front, and orange shorts that matched the color of Gators.

Instead of saying "Hi," or anything normal people might utter, he pointed his cane at the outdoor patio at Taco Boy and said, "How about eating outside? It's in the shade."

I reminded him that, when we ate with the same group after the funeral, they preferred air-conditioned comfort.

He reminded me that it was twenty degrees cooler than it was after the funeral. Besides, he liked the outdoor tables which were a couple of feet from the sidewalk, so he could check out the people walking by and talk to their pets.

I hadn't been invited, so I deferred to Charles.

One of the six-foot-long picnic-style tables on the patio was available. After Charles assured the hostess that there would be three others, she seated us. A server was quick to the table, told us he was Timothy, and asked if others would be joining us. I told him there'd be more, so we'd wait for them before ordering.

"Wrong," Charles said. "An order of nachos and a Cadillac Margarita for me. I suppose the boring guy beside me wants white wine, the cheapest you have."

Timothy looked at me as I shrugged. He said, "No problem," and headed to the bar.

Charles leaned past me to set his Tilley on the wide railing separating the patio from the sidewalk. "What can I say? I'm starved. I have a feeling I'll need the margarita, and more, before the night's over."

Bud Light was usually the most exotic drink my friend ordered.

Charles said, "Do you still think Laurie shot Anthony?"

"Not as much as I did before yesterday."

"Good. I told you she didn't."

"Charles, she still could have. She has the strongest motive. I have trouble wrapping my arms around the odds on Anthony being at such a desolate place stumbling on a drug deal."

He looked past me to at the retro Christmas lights that were strung along the railing, waved at a couple passing by, then said, "I don't think she killed him. I do have a feeling she's lying about searching for Civil War relics."

"I agree."

Before we got over the shock of agreeing on something, our nachos and drinks arrived. Laurie may've been lying about something, but Charles hadn't been when he'd said he was starved. He'd stuffed three nachos in his mouth before the waiter asked if we wanted anything else. I looked at the cheese oozing out the corner of Charles's mouth and said, "Extra napkins."

"No problem."

I inwardly snarled at the server.

With Charles stuffing his mouth, I figured it'd be an appropriate time to tell him about Grace and what happened at her food truck. Eating kept questions to a minimum. For Charles, minimum meant no more than one each thirty seconds. He managed to garble out one of his most often asked questions less than a minute into my description.

"Why didn't you call me?"

There was never an acceptable answer, so I didn't try, and continued the story. By the time Charles got around to asking what kind of hot dogs *Hot Diggity Dog!* sold, I was saved when he spotted Laurie, Dean, and Gail walking toward the entry. He yelled for them as he pointed to the table, like they wouldn't know it was where they'd be joining us.

A few seconds later, they arrived. Charles slid closer to me so that Laurie could sit on our side of the bench seat. Dean and Gail moved to the other side but, before sitting, Gail said, "Don't you think it's too hot out here?" She pointed to the door to the inside dining room. "I saw a nice table in there. Let's move."

Laurie glared at her. "This is fine. Our friends are already here."

A great way to start a pleasant meal, I thought.

Dean smiled as he slid across the bench seat. Gail mumbled something under her breath then followed her husband.

She noticed Charles's T-shirt, wrinkled up her nose, and said, "I hate the Gators. Do you have to throw it in my face?"

For one of the few times, Charles was speechless. Laurie saved him when she smiled. "I'm sure that, since you're from Florida, Charles was trying to make you feel at home. Now, Charles, what's good to eat here?"

164

As if on cue, Timothy appeared to ask if anyone needed drinks.

Charles was quick to say another margarita, I said I was fine.

Each of the others ordered beer.

Charles proceeded to tell the visitors that, since the restaurant was named Taco Boy, they couldn't go wrong with tacos.

Whether Gail bought it, or she didn't want to talk to anyone who threw the University of Florida *in her face*, she didn't ask him about the multiple taco options.

Laurie asked Dean if business was good at the tire store. I suspected it was to steer the conversation away from the growing rift between Gail and Charles.

"Not bad."

"Not bad, crap," Gail said. "How about sucking wind. With Costco, Walmart, and every big box store under the sun selling tires by discounting the hell out of them, mom and pop shops can't compete."

"It's not that bad, dear."

"Tell that to our damned banker."

Timothy returned with drinks, and I was about to tell him I needed more wine, a lot more. Instead, I asked if everyone was ready to order.

Gail said, "Yeah, tacos. They better be good."

Seventeen different taco iterations were on the menu, so she wasn't going to get off that easy. Timothy did a respectable job of describing the most popular choices, did an even better job of not throwing Gail's beer in her face. The rest of us ordered, and Timothy left the table, probably contemplating a career change.

Dean smiled at Laurie and turned to Charles, "Laurie tells us you've been good friends and have stopped by the house to see if she was okay. She said you've also kept her up on what the police are doing to catch the horrible person who shot Anthony. She's here by herself and needs—"

"Needs to move back to Jacksonville," interrupted Gail.

I hoped we weren't going to rehash that discussion. Laurie had made it clear that this was her home. Couldn't Gail let it go?

Laurie reached across the table and put her hand on Gail's hand. "Now, dear, I know you're concerned about me. I appreciate that, I really do. I'll be fine."

Laurie was trying a new tact. I hoped it'd be more effective than getting angry, like she did the last time Gail shared her feelings about Laurie returning to Florida.

Gail pulled her hand away then balled her fist. "Don't come crying to me the next time someone shoots at you."

Charles leaned toward the Clarks. "How long will you be staying?"

He was trying to diffuse the tense situation. I hoped their answer would be that they were leaving after supper, if not sooner.

Charles succeeded, although I didn't get the answer I wanted, when Gail took a deep breath, faked a smile, then said, "We'll head back Sunday evening. Dean has to go to some dingy hotel in Miami all next week for the annual meeting on something about tires."

Dean added, "Independent Tire Dealers of the South."

Charles smiled. "Sounds interesting."

Really, Charles?

"Not terribly interesting," Dean said. "These meetings are critical if we're going to compete with the big guys, if we're going to stay in business."

Our food arrived, saving me from having to listen to more about tires dealers, independent, or otherwise. The taco put Gail in a better mood. She asked several non-hostile questions about how Charles and I had come to Folly, what were some of the best places to visit in Charleston, and what Laurie's plans were to remodel her house. She used neutral terms, like it needed *tender loving care*, or *a few upgrades*, rather than calling it dump like she had the last time she went on a rant about its condition.

We ordered more drinks, Timothy managed to deliver them to us with no problem. Customers at the tables around us came and went. Despite the way it had begun, the evening, the conversation, and the warmth expressed by the Clarks and Laurie continued on the uptick.

I was finally relaxing while enjoying the company when Gail said, "Laurie tells us that you think poor Anthony came across drug dealers out there in the middle of nowhere. That's what got him killed."

I said, "That's a rumor going around. There's never a shortage of rumors when something bad happens. I don't know if it's true."

Gail said, "Is that what the police think?"

"I don't know."

"I thought you were friends with the chief," Gail added, not letting it go.

"We're friends. That doesn't mean she talks about investigations. The lead on the case is a detective from the Charleston County Sheriff's Office."

Gail pointed her beer bottle at me. "I don't know what I'd do if anything happened to Laurie." She set the bottle on the table and stared at it. "I can't help but think that, if Dean and I'd been here that night instead of in Florida, Anthony may still be with us."

Dean added, "Or we'd all be dead."

"Enough!" Laurie said. "Don't ruin a wonderful evening with friends. What's past is past. I'll be fine."

Her comment reminded me of Abraham Gant's views on the past. I need to call Cindy in the morning to see if she had any information about the captain. It made more sense that he could've been the killer than the unlikely event Anthony stumbled on a drug deal.

The evening ended on a more pleasant note than it had begun. Gail thanked Charles and me for keeping an eye on Laurie. Laurie thanked us for putting up with her and her friends squabbling. I lied when I told her it was okay, also when I told Gail and Dean I enjoyed spending time with them. Charles grinned as he covered *Gators* with his hand on our way to the exit.

We got to the sidewalk where Laurie, Gail, and Dean headed one way, Charles started the other direction, stopped, and smiled. "That was fun. Let's do it again."

I smacked his arm.

Chapter Twenty-Three

A low cloud cover hung over the city, keeping the temperature mild for July so, instead of driving, I walked three blocks to City Hall. Chief LaMond's door was open a couple of inches, so I could see her sipping coffee as she flipped through manila folders. She looked up when I tapped on the door.

"Unless you've come to confess to a murder, or give me a new car, turn around and let me see your chunky butt waddle away."

I took that as she'd love to talk to me. I pushed the door open, stepped in the cluttered office, and smiled. "Morning, Chief. Having a good day?"

She pointed to a pile of papers on the side of the desk. "You know how many calls for service your itty-bitty, under-staffed, underpaid police department got the last twelve months?"

"A lot?"

"Nearly eighteen thousand."

"Wow."

"Number of citations and warnings, you know, the bad kind, not for good citizenship?"

"A lot?"

"Thirty-eight hundred."

"That is a lot."

"Ya think! That doesn't count more than seven thousand parking tickets."

"Your point?" I asked, although she would tell me whether I asked, or not.

She waved a computer printout in my face. "The point of all these numbers I have to talk to the city council about next week is that I don't have frickin' time to waste talking to you about whatever you made the trip here for."

"Sorry, Cindy. I didn't mean to—"

She threw the printout in the air. "Hell, you talked me into it. Let's walk down the street to get some good coffee, not the crap your tax dollars pay for."

Cindy jogged down the steps to the sidewalk, like someone would catch her and tie her to her desk if she dallied.

I didn't need to ask where we were going as she led me two blocks to the Black Magic Cafe, a coffee shop and break-fast/lunch restaurant. It was close to Cindy's office so she could often be found sipping a drink in the popular business whenever she wanted to escape the bureaucratic burdens of her job. She grabbed one of the outdoor tables while I went for our drinks.

Five minutes later, I returned with two colorful Black Magic mugs.

"Chris, I don't suppose you were wandering around City Hall when you happened to stumble in my office. Why did I let you buy me coffee?"

I blew across the hot liquid. "True." I smiled. "Wandering

around City Hall isn't something I often do. You should be honored you're the reason I was there."

"How lucky can a girl be? Did you forget my question?"

"I was wondering if you learned anything more about the break-in at the food truck."

"Nary a thing. I also have no idea who broke in the baby-crap-green Volkswagen minivan the night before last and stole, if you can believe this, an 8-track tape player, or who swiped two baseball bats out of the yard of a vacation rental on East Hudson last Tuesday, or—"

"Got it. You have more problems than cops to solve them. The answer is, "No clues, no cameras, no witnesses, no idea who broke in.' "

"Couldn't have said it better myself." She took a sip of her drink. "Nothing appeared to be taken, so vandalism slips a far piece down the priority list. Sorry."

"I knew it'd be a longshot."

"A longshot means there's a shot. I wouldn't give it that good a chance."

"Any news on Anthony Fitzsimmons's murder?"

"Keep with the questions, and you'll be buying me lunch, and a diamond bracelet."

"News?"

"You'll be pleased that I listen to you, sometimes. I casual-like talked with Captain Gant."

"Casual-like?"

"I didn't want him to think he was a suspect, didn't want to get his Captain Crunch knickers in a twist. I asked if he knew about the shooting. He acted insulted I asked, said that of course, he knew about it. If he said he didn't, I would've arrested him for not being a true Folly resident. Anyway, he did what he's known for. He went on a tirade about the blan-kety-blank screwballs who're digging up the past."

"Don't suppose he confessed during the outburst?"

Cindy chuckled. "Not even after he finished the rant when I teased him with, 'You sound mighty angry at Mr. Fitzsimmons. You didn't kill him, did you?'"

"What'd he say?"

"The old boy didn't see much amusement. He snarled then growled out words that sounded like, 'If you think I did, prove it.' I displayed my enchanting smile and told him I didn't think he did but, to satisfy the detective from the Sheriff's Office, I needed to ask where he was when Fitzsimmons was killed." She took another sip.

"What'd he say?"

"He said, 'Asleep, asleep by myself.' He repeated that, if I thought he shot the blankety-blank grave robber, prove it. His quote was, 'That's for me to know, you to find out.'"

"That's all he said?"

"No, he ended our fun-filled conversation telling me to get my rear in gear, go pester someone else."

"Anything else?"

"Not about Captain. Detective Callahan and I talked to Laurie again. I didn't think it'd do any good. There are only so many ways she can say she didn't see anything, or anyone, that night. She didn't vary from her previous story, yet... never mind."

"Yet what?"

"Something keeps tugging at my instincts. She's not telling everything."

"Like what?"

"Chris, instinct-tugging ain't specific. I don't know." She hesitated and looked around the patio. "Lord, strike me down with lightning. I can't believe I'm about to ask this." She sighed. "Why don't you and, yes, I'm saying it, Charles, make another run at her? For some logic-defying reason, she seems to trust you two."

I told her about last night's dinner with Laurie and her friends from Jacksonville.

"See, she's taken a likin' to Charles. She'll tell him things. He has a way of nosin' into secrets. Don't tell him I said that."

I said that we'd try.

She told me she had to get back to the mountain of paperwork.

I promised not to tell Charles what Cindy had said about him *nosin' into secrets*.

———

Black Magic was three blocks from Theo's house. I was making efforts to get more exercise, so I took a chance he'd be home and welcoming guests. The clock hadn't reached noon, so I also hoped that, if Theo was there, Sal was asleep. No such luck. Instead of Theo answering the door, I was greeted by black, wide-rimmed glasses magnifying the sleepy eyes of Theo's brother. I was amazed that anyone could be sleepy wearing a red, orange, and luminous green shirt, the same shirt he had on the last time I'd seen him.

Sal blinked twice, ran a hand through his long, gray hair that hadn't touched a comb this morning, and smiled. "What do you call a sleeping bull?"

I'd transitioned from someone at the door to an audience. "What?"

"A bulldozer." He slapped his knee and laughed.

I asked if Theo was home.

"Ah, Theo. Did you know he had to retake his driver's test?"

Why, again, did I decide to visit Theo?

"No."

"Yep, he got eight out of ten. The other two guys jumped out of the way."

I faked another smile then repeated my question about Theo being home.

Sal sighed and pushed his glasses up on his nose. "You're a tough audience. You remind me of a group of Masons I entertained back in Toledo, or was it Oshkosh? I was getting to my best material when—"

"Is Theo here?"

He stepped aside and waved me in. "Kitchen."

I waited for another joke. Instead, Sal huffed and headed toward the great room, while I went to the kitchen. Theo was standing at the granite-covered island, slathering butter on a bagel. He wore a lightweight navy-blue robe. Red and white striped pajama pants stuck out the bottom.

He turned, saw me, and jumped back. "Didn't hear you come in."

"Didn't mean to startle you."

"What? Hang on, let me get my hearing aids." He left the room, and I heard him clomping up the stairs, leaving me staring at his breakfast and listening to Sal in the great room singing "Danke Schoen." It was horrible, but at least it wasn't a joke.

An eternity later, Theo returned. He'd changed into red jogging shorts, a T-shirt with the Nike swish on the chest, plus his signature knee-high support socks. Theo and Sal's attire reminded me of men leaving a homeless shelter on their way to panhandle.

"Sorry I took so long," Theo pointed to his ear. "Couldn't find these. I try not to put them in when we're here alone."

Wiser words couldn't have been spoken. I told him I was nearby and thought I'd stop to see if there was news about

Grace. He thanked me then asked if I wanted a bagel. I declined but told him to go ahead and eat.

"Let me heat it then we can go out on the deck. It's a beautiful day." He lowered his voice as he looked toward the great room. "I don't want Sal to hear."

He poured us coffee while his breakfast was heating and grabbed the bagel, coffee, and headed at Theo-speed through the great room to the door to the deck. Sal was crooning his version of "Ain't That a Shame" that'd have Fats Domino rolling over in his grave. He ignored us as we slipped through the door onto the sun-drenched deck overlooking Theo's private pier leading to the Folly River.

After closing the door, Theo pointed toward the great room. "See why I don't wear these around him?"

"Yes, yes, yes."

"I didn't want him to hear us discussing Grace. He doesn't know I'm trying to get her to move in."

We sat in two chairs shaded by a large umbrella on the corner of the deck.

"Have you talked to her since she turned you down?"

"No, the more I thought about it, the more I think her staying here is a good idea. I called yesterday afternoon, got her voicemail. I left a message asking her to call. I'd hoped she'd call last night. No such luck."

I told him about the break-in at her food truck. He seemed shocked. He asked who'd do such a thing. I told him what little I knew. He said that he was glad the police had gotten involved but, then, I shared what Cindy had said about it being a low priority. What I didn't share was how Grace had said that she wouldn't stay with her father-in-law or her comment about how poorly he'd treated her.

"Chris, what should I do if she doesn't return my call? I feel horrible about how I treated her. I want to apologize."

"Chief LaMond told her she couldn't stay on Folly in the truck, so you might check the Walmart lot. She may also move her truck to the space across the street from Cool Breeze Bike Rental where I found her."

"I could try."

I smiled. "Or you could stay here and listen to Sal's combination concert and stand-up comedy act."

Chapter Twenty-Four

I arrived on Folly ten years ago from my hometown in Kentucky, and my life changed. Some say that it changed for the worse, most swear for the better. My existence had been uneventful before I crossed the bridge to the island the first time. I had the good fortune to be born into what in the late-40s had been considered a normal family, with two well-adjusted parents, and no siblings to fight, or compete, with.

I graduated with average grades from an average high school; attended college where I continued to earn average grades; graduated and bounced around in a few unrewarding jobs until landing with a large insurance company, where I had an average job in its human resources department. Like many in my generation, I married my high-school sweetheart; unfortunately, like many of my peers, divorced after twenty average years. I stumbled upon Folly while attending a seminar in Charleston. One visit to the island, discovering one body near the beach, and being stalked by one murderer, the concept of average was yanked out from under me.

I accumulated more friends than I had during my half century in Kentucky. By friends, I'm not talking about people whom I know casually and proclaim to be friends. I'm talking about people who would literally give their lives for me. I knew that, because on a few occasions, some almost had. As surprising as it was, I would've done the same for them.

Charles Fowler was at the top of the list. We met my first week on the island. Once I realized that he wasn't your average wacko, nor was he a killer, we'd become friends. We were also as opposite as possible. I was average; Charles was anything but. I'd worked my entire adult life; Charles had spent the last thirty-two years treating work as if it was a terminal disease. I was an introvert; Charles has never met a man, woman, child, dog, or cat he didn't want to make friends with. There are other differences, but suffice to say, we had little in common.

One thing I'd learned over the last decade was that friendships, true friendships, know no boundaries. Opposites didn't necessarily attract, yet they didn't stop us from becoming close. I also learned that my friendships, true friendships, were cemented when I shared traumatic experiences with others. That's what changed my life. Well, that and becoming embroiled in murder investigations, getting shot at more than once, getting close to becoming incinerated in a house fire, moments from drowning at the hands of a murderer, and not to mention nearly getting killed in a sabotaged automobile, and on another occasion, run over by another vehicle.

I was dragged, often by Charles, more than once kicking and screaming more, into situations, deadly situations, that should have been left up to law enforcement professionals. I'd been told that, unless I acted, those committing horrific deeds would go unpunished. As the arguments went, since I knew the victims, however slightly, I "had" to get involved. After a while, I started believing it. I suppose that's why I couldn't shake the feeling that I shouldn't, couldn't, stand idly by while whoever killed Anthony Fitzsimmons remained on the loose. The question was, What could I do about it?

There were two suspects that I'd met, Laurie and Captain Gant, plus the mysterious drug dealer, or dealers, who, to my knowledge, no one I know had met. Laurie would've had the most obvious motive: insurance. Gant didn't like Anthony, or for that matter, anyone who had the nerve to dig for anything from the past. He had motive, means, and hadn't hesitated to express disdain for Anthony. Was that reason enough to kill? Possibly, although it didn't seem strong enough. Which brings me to the drug dealer who might've been seen by Anthony, thus inflicting upon him a death sentence. Was it possible? Sure. What could I do about it? No clue.

With all that cluttering my brain, I pulled denial, one of my most often used tools, out of my tool box, and headed to Barb's Books for what I hoped to be a pleasant conversation with the lady whom I found far more fascinating than Theo, or Laurie. She was unquestionably more attractive. I was forced to observe her appearance from across the room. There were six customers in the store with three vying for Barb's attention. Two more potential customers entered while I was waiting, so I decided to return later. I left the store and came inches from bumping into Stanley Kremitz.

He stopped when he saw me, nodded toward the bookstore, and said, "Looks like books are selling like hotcakes."

I couldn't come up with an appropriate cliché. "Sure are."

"Glad I saw you," he said as he nudged me closer to the building out of the line of foot traffic. "I've been thinking of something I wanted to share. I learned the other day that Laurie, you know, the wife of the guy who was killed out at the end of the island."

I nodded.

"I learned Harnell Levi was her grandpa. Did you know that?"

I nodded again.

"I knew old man, Levi, back in the day. He was a mean old bastard, yes he was. Getting along with him wasn't a bed of roses, although somehow I managed to stay on his good side." Stanley looked around, leaned closer, and whispered. "When he was, shall I say, under the weather, he didn't have a good side."

"Under the weather?"

Stanley mouthed, "Drunker than a skunk."

"Was he often *under the weather*?"

"Yes. I didn't know him when he was a young whipper-snapper. In his twilight years, he was often drunk. I avoided him when I could, but I too had a fondness for the hops. I spent more than a few hours in local bars bending elbows with him."

Interesting story, I suppose. Now, get to the point, Stanley. "You said you wanted to share something."

"Tell you what, Chris. Why don't you let me buy you a drink at Rita's? The sidewalk isn't the place for me to share what I know."

I could count on one hand the number of times someone offered to buy me a drink, so it didn't take much effort to convince me. Besides, I wanted to know what he had to say. We walked in silence two short blocks to the restaurant's outside bar. We each ordered wine and took the first sip before Stanley spoke.

"Now to what I wanted to share. One night, I remember it clearly, Harnell and I were sipping beer, swapping tales. Other than the bartender, we were the only two in the joint. Harnell told me he knew where gold was buried on Folly. I figured it as an overdose of alcohol pickling his brain. I didn't take him seriously. Not at first, you see. I asked him to tell me more. He started rambling about pirates hijacking a ship coming from England carrying tons of gold to the good ole' US of A, which wasn't the US of A at the time. I figure a rose by any other name is still a rose. Harnell said he got the information from an old sea captain he crossed paths with, said it was a fact."

"Stanley, there've been stories for ages about pirates' bounty, gold, and everything else of value, buried along the coast. What made Harnell think it was true?"

"Chris, that's the same thing I asked him. Know what he told me?"

"What?"

"He had a map to the treasure. He said the old-timer who told him about the gold knew he didn't have long on this earth, wasn't able to search any longer, so he traded the map to Harnell for a few drinks. If Harnell was to be believed, the old-timer died three days later."

It sounded like another tall tale. "Stanley, did you see the map?"

"I asked him about it. Boy, did he get defensive. Said I wanted to get my grimy hands on it so I could steal the treasure right out from under him. He was coming close to screaming. I wrote it off as him being pickled, not really accusing me of wanting to steal it."

"If the old-timer had a map, why didn't he find the treasure?"

"Chris, that's another question I posed. I'm beginning to think you and I are as alike as two peas in a pod."

Not on your life, I thought. "What'd he say?"

"He reminded me that the map was drawn a couple of hundred years earlier, that it'd been bent, folded, wrinkled bunches of times. The next person who got it must've redrawn it. That could've happened more than once. The point being the *X marks the spot* could've gotten off during each redrawing. Also, hurricanes and storms that've hit in all that time, redefined where the beach is, changing the shape of the island. Erosion, vegetation, growing, then dying, walking paths made and covered over, all those things made the original map hard to follow. All Harnell was sure of was that the treasure was buried on what became the Coast Guard property."

"I can see that. If it'd been buried by pirates, what's to say the treasure wasn't dug up by people who had the map?"

"Two peas in a pod, yes we are. That was my question to Harnell. He figured since the map was still around it was an indication no one had found the treasure. If they had, why need the map?"

"Stanley, if pirates buried treasure it would've been a hundred years before the Civil War. That property was used by the military during that period. Later, the Coast Guard built several buildings and roads on the same grounds. Even if the person who had the map didn't find the treasure, there would've been a good chance it was uncovered by someone."

"That could be true. Hmm, it'd be unlikely that it's still out there. Yet let's say it's still buried. Remember, Harnell was the Fitzsimmons's woman's grandpa. If he didn't find the treasure, he could've given her the map."

"She and her husband could've been searching for the treasure rather than Civil War relics like she said."

Stanley slapped me on my back. "Two peas, Chris. Two peas."

My phone rang before Stanley could share more clichés.

"Mr. Landrum, umm, Chris, this is Grace. Is this a good time to talk?"

It wasn't, but I was curious. "Yes."

"I've been thinking about Theo's offer. I don't know him as

well as you do, and you've been nice to me. Would it be too much to ask if you could go with me to see him?"

I told her I'd be glad to, so we decided on a time in the morning.

Stanley had paid for our drinks while I was talking to Grace. He stood, patted me on the back, and said. "Yep, we're two peas. Birds of a feather flock together."

He turned and left. I turned and ordered another glass of wine. I'd earned it.

Chapter Twenty-Five

I called Theo the next morning for three reasons: To warn him that Grace and I would be knocking on his door at ten o'clock so he'd have a chance to get dressed before we got there; and, most importantly, to decide if he wanted to tell Sal about her prior to our arrival. Grace didn't need an impromptu stand-up comedy routine interfering with whatever she wanted to share with her father-in-law. Theo was surprised that Grace wanted to see him. He thanked me for the warning, said he'd put on his finest, and assured me Sal would be dead to the world that early in the day.

I parked behind Theo's Mercedes. Before I unbuckled my seat belt, *Hot Diggity Dog!* pulled in behind me. Grace bounded out the door, wearing a blue and white sundress, sandals, and a shell necklace. She stretched her arms over her head as she smiled in my direction.

"Good morning, Mr. Landrum."

I was only seventeen years older than Theo's daughter-in-law, yet felt ancient compared to her trim, athletic figure and cheerful demeanor. "Please call me Chris."

"Okay, mon." Her smile faded as she nodded toward the house. "Do you think it's acceptable to visit?"

"Yes. I called to make sure he'd be home. He was pleased you were coming."

Her smile returned as she followed me up the steps. Theo opened the door before we reached the top step. He'd heeded my advice. I'd never seen him so well put together. He had on a Hawaiian shirt which I'd never seen, and from the packaging creases, I suspected it was its debut. To complement his attire, he wore white shorts and tan, canvas Crocs. Black, knee-high, support stockings that I'd never seen him without, were nowhere to be seen. His legs were as white as his shorts.

"You look lovely today," he said as he grabbed Grace's hand. "Please, come in."

He wasn't as appreciative of my faded-blue golf shirt. I followed them to the great room where the host invited us to sit then asked if we wanted something to drink. Grace said tea if he had any, if not, coffee would be fine. There was no tea, so she and I settled for coffee as Theo headed to the kitchen.

Grace looked around the room with her mouth open. "Oh, my God, this is magnificent."

"It's one of the nicest homes on the island."

She looked out the large windows. "The view, incredible."

Theo returned with a bamboo tray holding three cups of coffee. "I didn't know if you needed cream or sugar, so I brought both."

We said black was fine.

"Where might your brother be?" Grace asked and looked around, as if she expected Sal to step out from behind a piece of furniture.

Theo pointed to the ceiling. "This is his middle of the night. He spent decades performing at clubs, often didn't go on stage until ten or eleven. His performances ended months ago, yet his day still doesn't begin until the rest of us are thinking about lunch."

Grace nodded. "Teddy and I had similar hours when we had the restaurant. I never adjusted well to it." She jerked her head toward Theo. "I apologize; I didn't mean to speak of your son. It must be painful to you."

Theo smiled. "That's okay, dear."

This was a much kinder, gentler Theo than Grace had been exposed to during their first meeting.

She said, "Thank you."

"Chris tells me someone broke into your food truck."

"A mess they made. I haven't detected anything stolen."

Theo nodded. "Do you know why?"

"No. It can't be because someone has something against me. I haven't been here long enough. The police believe the person was looking for valuables. When finding nothing but cooking supplies, he, or she, became angry. Out of frustration created a mess. My father would say, 'Puss inna bag,' a Jamaican phrase that means 'a cat in a bag.'"

I was pleased when Theo said, "What?" It kept me from asking, and sounding, stupid.

Grace chuckled. "Not knowing what you're getting before seeing it. You can't tell what a cat is like if it's in a bag. The person who broke in didn't know what he was going to find. It was with great fortune that all my money, as meager as it is, was in my purse instead of in the truck."

"That's frightening. Dear, do you think it's safe staying in your truck?"

"I believe so. The manager at Walmart indicated I could continue to park overnight in their lot a few more evenings. It's well-lighted."

"What'll you do, then?" Theo asked. "Have you got all the permits needed to start selling hot dogs?"

"I have the paperwork, but haven't submitted it yet. I'm afraid it may take longer than I'd anticipated." She sipped her drink and looked at the floor. "Mr. Stoll, that's what I wanted to talk to you about. You graciously offered to allow me to stay in your wonderful house until I could get my feet on the ground. I'm afraid I reacted discourteously toward the offer, I must confess, toward you. I do not want to be a burden on anyone. You don't know me. Considering the strained relationship you had with Teddy, you would have no reason to be so kind in my direction." She turned to me. "Mr. Landrum has convinced me I should reconsider being so stubborn. Perhaps he's right." Her gaze returned to Theo. "Might I enquire if your generous offer is still available?"

"Grace, your negative reaction to me was justified. I admit, when we met at the hotel, I was shocked, riddled with emotions regarding my son. I had pent-up anger from years gone by. That had nothing to do with you. I'm also old-fashioned and, while I'm embarrassed to admit it, I was shocked to see that you were, umm, Jamaican."

"Black," interrupted Grace.

Theo lowered his head.

Grace smiled. "Mr. Stoll, I grew up in Topeka, Kansas, where more than nine out of ten residents are white. My father was a black man from Jamaica. My mom's skin was as white as your legs. There is nothing you can say I haven't heard since the day I first learned the difference between red and green, blue and yellow, black and white. Dad would say, 'Yu tink she mi born big?' which literally means 'You think I was born big, or old?'" In other words, don't take me for a fool. I wasn't born yesterday."

I smiled. Theo nodded.

"Besides," she said, "I know you white folk can't dance,

can't sing worth a lick, cooking, get real, and when it comes to sports, forget it. But, hey, mon, we'll tolerate you."

Theo made the greatest response possible. He laughed, stood, leaned down, to give Grace a hug.

He stepped back. "Mrs. Stoll, I'd be honored if you would move in here. You can stay as long as you like. My home is your home."

Chapter Twenty-Six

Theo and Grace said that they had a lot to talk about. She moved the truck so I could get my car out of the drive to let them spend time alone. Theo wanted me to stay and see Sal's reaction to having a new housemate. I needed a plethora of Sal's jokes like I needed malaria. I declined and left that "fun" experience to Grace and Theo.

It was still before noon, also known as wake-up time in Sal's time zone, so I gave Charles a call to see if he wanted to make a grocery run to Harris Teeter. He laughed, saying that me making a grocery run was like our obese, iconoclastic friend Bob Howard making a run to, well, a run anywhere. He added that I could pick him up and take him somewhere he needed to go. I asked where. The answer would have to wait, he'd already hung up.

Charles was waiting for me in the parking area in front of his apartment. He slid in the passenger's seat and said, "You're late."

I said, "Where to?"

"Laurie's house."

I slammed on the brakes. "Why?"

"She called, said she wanted to talk to me about something important."

"What?"

He shrugged.

"She asked for you, not for you and me?"

"So?"

Another shrug.

Instead of getting in a discussion about the difference between asking for Charles, as opposed to asking for Charles and Chris, I said, "Don't you find it strange that she keeps calling?"

He glanced at me as he tapped his cane on the floorboard. "Sure. You've known me long enough to know strange is my thing. The real question is strange why, not that it's strange."

I understood, proving I knew him better than he thought. What I didn't understand was how Laurie would react to seeing me tagging along with the person she asked to come visit. I didn't have to wait long. She opened the door wearing a tan, button-down blouse, and navy slacks, and greeted Charles with a hug and a stare at me that would bring fear to a lion tamer.

"Oh, I see Mr. Landrum is with you."

Oh, I thought, and wished myself invisible.

Charles pretended not to see her glare. "Yes, he'd stopped by my place after you called and offered to drive. It's okay, isn't it?"

Historical revisionism was one of Charles's many talents.

"Yes. Come in gentlemen."

A plate of brownies was on the table beside the sofa with orchestra music playing in the background. She asked if we wanted coffee, and Charles said we'd love some before I had a chance to say no. She headed to the kitchen as Charles noted that the room had been straightened up since our last visit. Laurie returned, handed each of us a mug, pointed out the fresh-baked brownies, and sat in the chair opposite the sofa.

Charles grabbed a paper napkin, a brownie, and asked if I wanted one.

I declined.

Laurie said, "Baked them this morning. Thought you'd like them."

"You didn't have to do that," Charles said while wiping a crumb off his lower lip.

Laurie chuckled. "Idle hands are the devil's workshop, or something like that."

"Proverbs," Charles said.

Laurie looked impressed, so did I. I thought, unless a president said it, Charles didn't know it.

"I believe you're right," she said. "Anyway, I wanted to share something with you to get your take on it."

"Share away." Charles said then took another bite.

Laurie took a deep breath and looked at her hands folded in her lap. "That lady chief stopped by last evening. She was polite. The chief told me again how sorry she was about Anthony's death."

Chief LaMond didn't make house calls without a reason. Expressing sympathy would've been a good enough reason. "Did she want anything else?"

Laurie frowned like she hadn't been talking to me. That was reinforced when she said, "Charles, she wondered if Anthony had a gun. I told her he bought one years ago. I thought it was a stupid idea, stupid and dangerous. She asked if she could see it."

Charles said, "What'd you tell her?"

She shook her head. "I told her no because he sold it. He eventually agreed with me, finally saying he didn't need it. The chief asked who he sold it to. I told her Anthony never told me."

I said, "Why'd she ask about the gun?"

"At first she didn't say. She kept asking if I was certain I didn't know who bought it from Anthony. After a while, she said the bullet that killed Anthony and the one shot at me were from the same gun."

Charles was reaching for another brownie then hesitated. "Did she think it was from Anthony's gun?"

"She didn't know since she'd need the gun to run the ballistics test. She was thinking Anthony may have carried it with him on our relic hunt, the killer took it from him, shot Anthony with his own gun. I told her that couldn't be right since he no longer owned it."

Most likely, before she made the house call Cindy would've checked records in Florida and learned about Anthony buying a handgun. My guess was that Cindy was becoming as suspicious about Laurie's involvement in her husband's death as I was. I also found it convenient for Laurie to say that Anthony sold the weapon.

Laurie started to say something. Instead, she stood, said she would get us more coffee, and headed to the kitchen. I was left in the room wondering why she'd really asked Charles over.

The sound of shattering glass and an eardrum-shattering scream coming from the kitchen broke the silence. Charles leapt to his feet. His drink sloshed on his University of Arkansas T-shirt. He cursed and clanked the mug down on the table.

I didn't have to deal with spilled coffee and beat Charles to the kitchen. Laurie was huddled down in front of the sink. Shards from the shattered window over the sink were on the counter, in the sink, on the floor, and in Laurie's hair. Window glass mixed with broken pieces of curved glass from the carafe from the coffee maker. Hot liquid spread over the counter and dripped down the front of the cabinet.

I bent so I was lower than the windowsill and inched over to Laurie. "Are you hit?"

She was shaking all over but managed to mutter, "Don't think so."

"Can you move?"

She nodded.

I said, "Stay low, move to the living room."

Charles saw that Laurie wasn't injured. He dashed to the back door, slowly opened it, then peeked around the corner in the direction the shot had come from.

Laurie crawled to the living room, remained on the floor, and leaned against the sofa.

"Think they're gone," Charles said as he returned then squatted down beside Laurie who was still shaking. He put his arm around her shoulder.

I punched 9-1-1 on my phone, gave a quick report to the emergency operator, then went into the kitchen to see what I could see out the window. Whoever took the shot was gone, the large lot was deceivingly peaceful, as it was bathed in a beautiful, sunny day at the beach.

Laurie, with coffee splattered on the front of her blouse, moved to the sofa and was comforted by Charles.

I went to the front door to greet the emergency responders. A patrol car, siren blaring, slid to the sandy curb in front of the house.

Allen Spencer, a cop I'd known since he was a rookie on the force years ago, scampered out.

I met him at the door to assure him that no one was injured. He radioed we wouldn't need the EMTs that had been dispatched. I led him to the living room. I heard the siren from another patrol car in the distance. Allen looked at Laurie and Charles on the sofa. Laurie had her head down and didn't look at the newest arrival. Charles nodded and told the officer Laurie was shaken but okay. Spencer moved to the kitchen, cautiously walked around the glass on the floor, then looked out the damaged window.

A second patrol car skidded to a stop behind Spencer's and Trula Bishop was quick to the door. "Here we are again, Mr. Chris. What now?"

I led her to the kitchen, where Spencer was surveying the scene. Bishop, like Spencer, was careful not to step in the glass, or the coffee. Fortunately, there was no blood to avoid. I shared what'd happened, while Spencer headed outside to see if he could see where the shooter had been.

Bishop went to the living room and motioned for Charles to move to the other side of the room. Bishop replaced Charles on the sofa. In a calming voice, told Laurie who she was, then asked her what she'd seen.

Laurie tensed, as if she didn't realize that Charles was no longer beside her.

Bishop touched Laurie's arm. "It's okay, you're safe. If you could tell me what you saw, it might help us catch whoever did this."

Laurie looked down and touched her damp blouse. "Charles and Chris were here on the sofa. I went to get more coffee." She, again, rubbed her hand on the blouse. "Picked up the pot, turned to bring it in here when the window shattered. Scared the hell out of me. I screamed, dropped the carafe. Glass flew everywhere, so did coffee. I ducked, umm, Chris came in. Then… then, nothing. I was in here and you came."

"Miss Laurie," Bishop said, "did you look out the window either before it was shattered or after?"

She rubbed her forehead, shook her head. "If I did, it was

a glance. I didn't notice anything other than it was a gorgeous day. Sorry."

"That's okay. Do you know why someone would want to shoot you?"

Laurie moved her hand away from her face then turned facing Officer Bishop. "Officer, I haven't the faintest idea why someone killed my husband. I don't have a clue why someone shot at me the other day. Now—" She twisted around to face the kitchen. "No…"

Spencer stood in the doorway. "Officer Bishop, there wasn't anything out there. It's a big field. With so many trees, someone could hide and not be seen from the road, or the other houses."

Bishop nodded and turned to Laurie. "Miss Laurie, do you have family, or friends, you could visit until we get this figured out?"

Charles added, "What about Dean and Gail?"

Laurie glanced at him then turned to Bishop. "Officer, this is my house. Folly Beach is my home." She pointed toward the north. "My husband is buried over there. I'm making good friends here, like Charles and Chris. I'm not going anywhere."

Bishop smiled. "It was simply a suggestion, Miss Laurie. I don't think there's anything else we can do here. I'll call Detective Callahan to see if he wants to send a forensics team. They could look around outside, dig the bullet out of the wall. Most likely, all they'll find will be the bullet. To be honest, I doubt they could find anything outside, other than a few beer cans, nothing useful. I'll talk to Chief LaMond, and we'll increase patrols in the area. Do you want me to help clean up the kitchen?"

Laurie's shaking was now limited to her hands. She made a brave effort to smile. "Thank you. My friends and I can get it cleaned up. I'll call the chief's husband at the hardware store."

"If you think of anything, regardless how inconsequential, please give us a call."

Laurie started to stand.

"Don't get up," Bishop said. "I'll find my way out."

I followed the officer to her car. Before she got in, she said, "Chris, how do you do it?"

I knew what she meant; I didn't respond beyond a shrug.

Bishop said, "I know, I know. It's a gift, a gift like a piñata full of pelican poop. You have any theories?"

"I did until a half hour ago."

Bishop said, "You thought she killed her husband then took the shot into the house the other day to throw us off?"

"Yes."

Bishop nodded toward Laurie's house. "I suppose this shoots the hell out of that theory. Pun intended."

"Yes."

By the time I returned to the house, Charles and Laurie were in the kitchen. Charles was sweeping up glass, while Laurie was wiping coffee off cabinet doors. I grabbed a roll of paper towels to help Charles with the glass.

"Laurie," Charles said, "I know you don't want to leave so how about calling Gail to see if she could come up to stay with you a few more days?"

"I don't know. She's been so irritating lately."

Charles said, "It'd be good for someone to be with you."

"Suppose I could put up with her a few more days." She stepped around the pile of glass Charles had swept to the center of the room. She grabbed the phone from her purse. Charles swept the pile of glass into a dustpan as Laurie sat at the table calling her friend.

Gail didn't answer, so Laurie left a message for her to return the call as soon as possible. She made another call, this time to Dean. From hearing one side of the conversation, I gathered that Gail was out of town for a couple of days and probably had left her phone in the hotel room. Dean said he would keep calling his wife to make sure she got Laurie's message.

Laurie may not have been the person shooting up her house, probably not the person who killed her husband, but she knew something that she wasn't telling the police. It was time to find out what.

Chapter Twenty-Seven

The kitchen was clean. Larry from Pewter Hardware agreed to stop by to fix the window. Laurie changed out of her coffee-stained blouse, and we'd returned to the living room. She sipped orange juice between bites of brownie, which, according to Charles, were both good for her health, and her nerves.

Laurie's hands had stopped shaking, so I thought it was an appropriate time to broach the subject. "Laurie, what aren't you telling the police?"

Her grip tightened on the juice glass. "What do you mean?"

"It's none of my business. You can tell me to butt out, if you want. You told us, and the police, that you and Anthony were at the Lighthouse Inlet Heritage Preserve searching for Civil War relics."

She mumbled, "Yes."

"I've heard from friends, who know way more about it than I do, that Civil War relics seldom hold great monetary worth other than sentimental value or value to a collector or museum."

Her eyes narrowed. "So?"

"Erik Swartz, a friend of mine, told me about a conversation he had with Anthony who told him all he planned to do in retirement was to fix up the house."

She continued to stare. "So?"

"Erik said he joked to Anthony that it sounded like a lot needed to be done. My friend referred to it as a money pit. Anthony told Erik he was right, but wasn't worried, because he'd dig up the money to do the work. I asked Erik if he thought Anthony meant it as a joke. He wasn't sure. Laurie, was it a joke?"

Charles had leaned back on the sofa as I prepared for an explosion.

Laurie reached for another brownie, changed her mind, and pulled her hand back. "When I visited Folly as a young girl, my granddad told me stories about buried Civil War relics."

She was speaking low, so Charles and I leaned closer to hear.

I said, "I remember you telling us that."

"I did, didn't I? What I didn't say was that Granddad also talked about how pirates stole tons of valuables from ships. That was long before the Civil War."

"A hundred years before," interrupted Charles.

Laurie nodded. "I learned some of it was buried out where we were." A tear formed in the corner of her eye. "We were looking for it when... when it happened."

"Wow," Charles said. "How'd you know it was there?"

Laurie wiped the tear from her face then looked at the floor. "It's cursed. Granddad told me stories. He told me about ghosts of pirates watching over buried treasure. He told me anyone who tried to find it will be struck dead. I thought he was telling stories to scare a little kid. I should've believed him. The curse killed Anthony."

I remembered William talking about pirates burying treasure along the coast, possibly in the Carolinas. He also talked about a curse on anyone who digs up the treasure. Laurie hadn't answered Charles's question, so it wouldn't be long before he repeated it.

"I've heard those stories," Charles said. "How'd you say you learned about the treasure being at the old Coast Guard station?"

"Charles, Anthony is dead. Someone's trying to kill me. It doesn't matter how I learned it." She pounded her glass on the table, effectively shutting down Charles's questions.

"Laurie, I understand," I said, even though I didn't. "Who else may've known where you and Anthony would be that day?"

She leaned back and took a deep breath. "I didn't tell anyone, honest to God I didn't. I can't speak for Anthony. From what you said, he told your friend, it's evident that Anthony told some of it to a stranger. He could've told others."

Charles said, "Anyone in particular?"

She hesitated, then said, "One day, we were in Bert's Market. Met some old guy. We were buying flashlight batteries when he made some crack about them being for our apple. I think it was a joke, you know, like an Apple iPhone. Out of the blue, Anthony started telling him about us relic hunting."

I'd already heard the story from the *old guy*, Stanley Kremitz. "Did you tell him when you were going to be out there?"

"Not then. I remember Anthony telling him more than I

thought he should about what we were doing, especially since relic hunting was prohibited in the Preserve."

Charles said, "So you didn't tell him anything about specific times?"

"No. That doesn't mean Anthony didn't. Chris, I didn't know about his conversation with your friend."

"Have you met Abraham Gant, goes by Captain Gant?" I asked.

"Captain Gant. Didn't know his name was Abraham."

Charles said, "You know him?"

"No, Anthony told me about him. They about got in a fight."

I knew what the captain had said about meeting Anthony, how he thought Anthony was okay until he said something about relic hunting. "What happened?"

"Gant knew my granddad, said he liked him. Anthony and the captain were having a pleasant conversation, until the topic of relic hunting came up. The captain got mad. From what my husband said, Gant looked like he'd hit him."

Charles said, "Did Anthony tell the captain that you'd be out there that night?"

"He could've. He tended to open his mouth without thinking. That was cause for more than one argument. He didn't tell me he told Gant about it."

"You're certain you didn't tell anyone about where you were going to be that day?"

"Yes."

Laurie's phone rang. She said, "Hello," then moved to the bedroom.

Charles watched the bedroom door and said, "Aren't you glad I invited you to the party?"

"That's what friends are for. What do you think of her story?"

"Which story?"

"She didn't tell anyone they'd be out there that night."

"Even if she's telling the truth, hubby was a blabbermouth, he could've told anyone. And, what's with her not saying how they knew where to look for the buried treasure? The Preserve is a big plot of land to be roaming around hoping to dig up a fortune."

"She knows more than she's saying."

"Wow, Sherlock, you figure that out by yourself?"

I was working on an incredibly humorous, insightful retort when Laurie returned.

"That was Gail. She'll get back to Jacksonville tomorrow, will head over here the day after tomorrow."

Charles said, "That's great."

"Yes, you all can meet us for supper once she arrives."

What was it that I was saying about malaria?

Chapter Twenty-Eight

C harles was scheduled to make a delivery for Dude's surf shop, so I dropped him at his apartment then realized that I was hungry. After what I'd been through at Laurie's, I didn't want to eat at a restaurant, so I stopped at Woody's Pizza to get supper to go. Instead of ordering one of their pizzas, which I knew I'd eat too much of and later regret, I settled on a sub sandwich.

I'd opened my door when my phone rang. I considered not answering, and enjoying a peaceful meal at home, without any outside distractions. Seeing the name Cindy LaMond on the screen convinced me to answer. It's never wise to ignore a call from the chief.

"Hey, Chris, know where Theo is?"

"What makes you think I'd know that?"

"Figured you knew everything."

"That would be Charles."

"True. Charles hadn't spent time with Theo. Officer Bishop said she saw your car at Theo's this morning."

Nothing like small-town life. "I have no idea where he is."

"How about his daughter-in-law. Know where she is?"

"No, why?"

"I'm standing in Theo's drive, staring at a big ole' food truck. Its door was open, so being the good cop that I am, I peeked inside to make sure no one was dying, or dead. The good news is there were no bodies. Bad news is I'm no food-truck doctor yet, from my lay perspective, *Hot Diggity Dog!* has serious internal injuries. It may not be able to fix-up any more hot dogs."

"No one's at Theo's house?"

"Not even the one-man comedy show."

"When I was there this morning, neither Theo, nor Grace talked about going anywhere. Any idea what happened?"

I heard Cindy talking to someone then returned to talk to me. "I asked Officer Bishop to call Charleston to see if they could free up a crime scene tech. If there's nothing serious going on over there, they might send someone. It's unlikely they'll find anything. Whoever did this probably wore gloves. If not, there should be a thousand of their fingerprints. You wouldn't believe the mess."

"I'll be over," I said, hesitated while waiting for her to give me a lecture about it being a police matter, for me to stay away.

"What took you so long to decide?"

———

I parked on the street in front of Theo's house. Bishop was pulling away in her patrol car. Cindy's Ford F-150 was in the drive behind the food truck.

"Any word on Theo, or Grace?" I asked Cindy as she leaned against the truck.

"No. I called the number Grace gave me. It rolled over to voicemail. Do you know Theo's number, or if Sal has a phone?"

"I'll call Theo."

The homeowner answered and asked what was going on.

I asked if he knew where Grace was. He said that she was with him at the City Market in downtown Charleston. He was giving her a tour, and asked why I wanted to know. I told him where we were and why. He ended with saying they'd be back as soon as he could maneuver his way back to the car. Before I let him go, I asked if he knew where Sal was. Theo said that his brother had taken to walking around town sharing his unlimited supply of jokes with shop owners. He was probably irritating one of them.

I told the chief what he'd said, then asked what made the police stop at the truck.

"Officer Bishop was on patrol, saw the door open. She wanted to stop to check on Grace. Bishop knew Theo's daughter-in-law was shook after the first break in and wanted to see if she was okay. I was nearby and stopped to see what was going on."

"Good. Could I look inside?"

"Have at it." She chuckled. "Don't mess anything up."

A glance in the door told me why her comment was so funny. The inside of the truck looked as damaged as would a carton of eggs if someone took a sledgehammer to it. Not only was the equipment smashed, it was demolished. Everything breakable was broken; everything bendable bent. If the stainless-steel equipment, shelving, and cabinets had any value left, it was as scrap.

Cindy stood behind me. "Theo's cute little daughter-in-law has seriously pissed someone off."

I said, "That's an understatement."

It was hot in the truck, so I asked Cindy if she wanted to wait for Theo and Grace in my car.

She said that the air conditioning sounded good.

While we were waiting for the owner to arrive, I shared what Charles and I had learned from Laurie about what her grandfather had told her about gold being along the coast, that was what she and Anthony were looking for. I also shared what she'd said about stories that there was a curse on anyone who tried to find the treasure.

"I reckon Anthony Fitzsimmons is now a strong believer in the curse. You know those stories about buried treasure, pirates, ghosts that come in all shapes and sizes, and curses have been around for decades. So, the Fitzsimmons were out there looking for treasure instead of Civil War relics?"

I nodded.

"Which leads to a couple more questions. How in the ghost of Blackbeard did they think they could find something that hundreds, hell, probably thousands, of people who've turned over every rock, dug hole after hole, and gossiped about in local bars couldn't find?"

"I don't know why—"

Cindy waved her hand in my face. "Hold your blunder-buss, Pirate Chris, I'm not done. The more important question is if someone killed Anthony because of the gold instead of it being a random drug deal gone bad, how did the killer know the Fitzsimmonses would be there?"

"Hold my what?"

"Google it, or ask Charles. He knows everything."

I realized that I didn't care enough to do either. "Laurie hadn't told anyone here, or so she said. Anthony is another story." I shared what Erik Swartz had told me, what Laurie said about Anthony's annoying habit of talking too much, and about his confrontation with Captain Gant.

"I get it. It's no telling how many others Anthony told about hunting for relics, or buried treasure. That could increase the suspect pool to each living resident on our quaint island, not to mention ghosts residing here. It still doesn't answer how the couple thought they had the inside track on finding the treasure."

I agreed yet continued thinking that Laurie knew something she wasn't telling us; something I was determined to learn more about. My mind was wandering to how to find out, so must've missed part of what Cindy said.

"Cindy to Chris, stop daydreaming. It's possible, unlikely, I know, but possible, I said something important."

"Sorry, what?"

"I talked with Detective Callahan last night to see if he'd learned anything. He was more interested in telling me about the new murder investigation he'd caught yesterday morning. It's high profile, so the political bigwigs are pestering the sheriff for a quick close, which means that, like all, umm, excrement, it flows downhill. Callahan is supposed to put everything else aside to make the sheriff look good, good to those who vote for him. His sheriff can be persuasive like that."

"So Anthony's investigation is on the back burner?"

"Back burner, crap. I suspect it's no longer on the stove."

Theo's Mercedes pulled in behind Cindy's truck. Grace was looking in *Hot Diggity Dog!* before Theo made it out of the car.

Grace pounded on the side of the truck, screamed a profanity, jerked her head toward the rest of us, then yelled, "Why?"

No answer was forthcoming.

She climbed in the ransacked vehicle.

Theo asked Cindy what she knew.

She told him the same thing she'd told me, which was near nothing.

Grace came out of the truck, sat on the step, then cradled her head with her hands. Her shoulders sagged, tears streamed down her face. She looked like someone had run over her pet dog. I suppose that someone had.

Cindy reached out and put her hand on Grace's shoulder. "Grace, I'm so sorry. Do you have any idea who might've done this?"

She repeated what she'd said after the first break in. Other than those standing around her now, she didn't know anyone on Folly.

Theo said it had to have happened after they left for Charleston and wondered if anyone had seen anything.

Cindy said that no one answered at the house next door. The people who lived across the street said they didn't hear or see anything. Theo said he saw Grace lock the truck before they'd left. He wondered how the person got in. Cindy told him it looked like the lock was loose from the first incident.

By now, Grace had regained her composure. She came over to Theo's car, where the rest of us were standing. "Chief LaMond, what's going to happen now?"

"One of my officers is contacting the crime scene techs in Charleston. If possible, they'll get prints. I doubt it'll do any good." She looked at the side of Theo's house and at the house next door. "Theo, you have cameras out here?"

"No."

She pointed at the neighbor's house. "Doesn't look like they do, either. That'd be too easy. Grace, unless you have anything to add, I'll be going."

Grace said that she didn't.

Cindy asked if she would be here all afternoon in case a tech arrives.

Grace said, "Maybe," and Theo said that he'd be here.

Cindy, once again, told Grace that she was sorry, adding that it was a pathetic introduction to her new home.

Chapter Twenty-Nine

As Cindy left, Grace paced the driveway, alternating between mumbling profanities and asking why. Theo and I had no answers. She looked at the truck, shook her head, and said, "I need to walk off some energy. Anyone want to go?"

Theo confessed that walking around the City Market had zapped him. Besides, he needed to stay home in case a crime scene tech showed up. I said that I'd go. We walked a block in silence before she turned back toward her father-in-law's house. "I'm glad the dear man didn't want to come. I've seen potted plants move faster." She covered her mouth with her hand. "Please don't tell him that."

I shared that I was an off-and-on member of a walking group Theo was in, and that he could always be counted on to be the last to arrive at our destination.

"He may be slow," she said, "but I don't know that I've met a nicer man." She laughed for the first time since she'd returned to his house. "Anyway, not a nicer man who's got a prejudice streak, who was on the outs with my husband, who lives with his brother, who's as funny as an ear of corn."

"I'm glad you're getting along. Like I told you, Theo is a wonderful person. From what I've seen, he would do anything for anyone."

"He told me I could stay as long as I wanted to." She shook her head. "After what's happened to my truck, it looks like that'll be a long time. I can't believe someone did that."

We were in front of Barb's Books, and I nodded toward the building, "Let's go in a minute. I'd like you to meet someone."

Barb met us at the door with, "I bet you're Grace, Theo's daughter-in-law."

"How'd you know?"

Barb chuckled. "When I moved here, it took me all of fifteen minutes to learn everybody knows everybody's business. Of course, newcomers are a challenge, so that was why it took fifteen minutes in my case. It's what makes Folly so great; it's what makes Folly so exasperating. Not only do I know who you are, I know your food truck was vandalized the other day."

Grace gave Barb an inquisitive look.

Barb smiled. "Heard it from Matty at the bike rental shop, and Paul at Mr. John's Beach Store."

Grace looked at her watch. "Let's see, it's been more than fifteen minutes. Heard anything about me today?"

Barb shook her head. "No, why?"

Grace grinned like she knew a secret that Barb didn't know.

I knew where Grace was going with her question. I wasn't ready to go there, so I formally introduced the ladies and told Grace that Barb and I had been dating. Three potential customers entered the bookstore cutting our conversation short. I told Barb that I'd call later. She put her arm around

Grace's shoulder and said that she was glad to see another businesswoman on Folly.

We were crossing the street in front of the Folly Pier when Laurie came down the steps, heading our way. She gave a knowing nod when she saw me, and I introduced Grace to her. Laurie said it was nice meeting Grace before asking where Charles was. I told her that I didn't know.

Grace stepped closer to Laurie. "Oh, are you the lady who recently lost her husband?"

I thought lost was a poor choice of words, although I was impressed that Grace was catching on.

"Yes, he was murdered."

Grace touched Laurie's arm. "I'm terribly sorry,"

"Thank you. Have you lived here long?"

"Oh, yes. Nearly three days."

That brought a smile to Laurie's face, a welcomed sight.

"I'm a newcomer, too. Perhaps we can grab a meal sometime."

"I'd like that," Grace said.

They exchanged numbers, then Laurie said she needed to get home.

Grace and I continued our walk to the far end of the pier.

"Long pier," she said as we reached the two-level observation deck.

"If you stood it on end, it'd only be seventeen feet shorter than the Eiffel Tower."

Yes, Charles's penchant for trivia was rubbing off.

She looked down at the Atlantic. "That'd be a long way to fall."

I appreciated her sense of humor. "I don't think it's going anywhere."

Her smile faded as she looked back toward the beach. "Chris, I don't know what to think. Don't know what to do."

"About what happened to your truck?"

She nodded. "Why would someone do that? I don't think anything was taken. Why break in to destroy my stuff?"

"Two reasons I can think of. To steal something of value, or to try to stop you from opening."

Grace continued to look toward shore and said, "Nothing worth stealing was in there the first time, so why try again?"

"It's unlikely that that was the reason. If it was, there would've been no reason to do so much damage the second time. Grace, think back, have you met anyone since you've been here who acted strange toward you?"

She smiled. "Theo tells me there is no shortage of people who seem strange, so how would I tell the difference? Besides, I haven't been here long enough to talk to many people."

"How about anyone who's taken more than a cursory interest in the truck?"

She hesitated. "Not really. Matty, the bicycle man's been nice. A couple of the gals who waited on me at the restaurants said they'd seen the truck and were curious. There'd even been two people who stopped to ask if I was hiring." She smiled. "I didn't tell them that, if I didn't work free, I wouldn't be able to hire me."

After talking back and forth a few more minutes, it became clear that neither Grace nor I could shed light on why her truck had become a break-in magnet.

I said, "Let me change the subject. You were born in Kansas, grew up in the states, right?"

She nodded.

"I thought if the parent, or parents, were from another country, the children born here didn't share their parents' accent."

Grace gave a knowing grin. "You wonder why I have a Jamaican accent?"

"Yes."

"Chris, you're perceptive. The only accent I had growing up was Midwestern. When I started waiting on customers in the food industry, I started throwing in Jamaican phrases and lilting some of my speech. It made customers happy. Happy customers bought more food, tipped better. The older I get, the more I sound like my dearly-departed father."

"Grace, you're a good actress, and pleasant to listen to."

"Thanks, mon."

I laughed.

She said that she should probably get back to see if the crime techs had arrived.

I offered to walk her back.

She thanked me, but said she'd be fine, before adding, if she could find Folly Beach from California, she could find Theo's mansion.

I remained on the pier, enjoying the warm ocean breeze and the melodic sound of the waves as they rolled to shore. The shrill ring of my phone shook me out of what some would call a nap, I refer to it as relaxing. Regardless, it was abruptly interrupted by Charles who said, "It's on. Tomorrow night, six, Snapper Jack's. See you there."

"What's on?"

"Supper. Gail, Laurie, you, me. See ya."

I'd hoped it was a dream, although I knew better.

Chapter Thirty

Snapper Jack's is a colorful, multi-level restaurant on the corner of Center Street and Ashley Avenue, the site of Folly's only traffic light. The restaurant's central location, reputed for good seafood and live music, often attracted diners in excess of its seating capacity. Tonight would be no exception. The temperature was in the low-eighties, so I was glad to see that Charles had adhered to his thirty-minute-early routine. He was waiting for me on the sidewalk in front of the restaurant. He wore tan shorts, a tan Tilley, and a light blue, long-sleeve T-shirt with UGF in large letters and Argos in smaller letters under it.

We'd beaten the supper rush and decided to head up the long flight of stairs to the rooftop bar where we could enjoy the panoramic view of downtown Folly, the nine-story Tides Hotel, plus a glimpse of the Atlantic Ocean thrown in to heighten the experience. Two tables were vacant along the railing overlooking the hotel. Charles gave one of his lovable smiles to the hostess as he pointed to the tables. He told her that there was going to be four of us, so she gave us our choice of tables.

A server, who told us that her name was Monique, but to call her Mo, arrived as soon as were seated.

Charles was quick to order a Budweiser, and told her that he'd probably need a lot more before the night was over.

I said water was fine, that I'd order something stronger once the others joined us.

Mo headed toward the covered outside bar, and Charles said that I'd sounded asleep when he called yesterday. He wondered if old age was catching up with me. I told him that I'd been enjoying the view from the pier which led into a discussion about why I'd been there. That led to telling him about Grace's unwelcomed visitor, which, of course, led to him asking me how *we* were going to find out who'd destroyed the interior of the food truck. Our drinks arrived while I was telling him that it was in good hands, that *we* didn't need to get involved. He took a gulp of beer then conceded I was probably right.

I was making progress until he added, "That'll give us more time to figure out who murdered Anthony, figure out who tried to kill Laurie."

"Charles, that's what the police—"

He waved his hand in my face. "Her life depends on it."

"Charles, that's why it's better left to the police."

He stopped me again. "Before you start blabbing on about why it's up to the police and none of our business, do you want to go down to wait for the ladies? They don't know we're up here."

"You go. Remember, I'm the one who wasn't invited."

Whether he saw the wisdom of my comment, or didn't want to argue, he headed for the steps. I stared at the ocean and admitted that he was right, followed by wondering how we could help the police, help before it was too late for Laurie.

It was quarter after six, so I was beginning to think that our guests had stood us up, when I saw Charles and the two ladies heading my way.

Gail was looking at Charles's shirt, "What are Argos?"

Charles responded with words I'd seldom heard coming from his mouth. "I don't know."

I stood to greet the newcomers. Laurie didn't appear to care about Argos, and met me with a hug. She didn't seem upset that Charles had invited me. Gail was more fascinated with Charles's shirt than Laurie or I were.

"Hi, Chris," Gail said. "Charles was telling us that his shirt is from the University of Great Falls, that's in Montana."

"Interesting," I said, not meaning a syllable.

The server appeared and told the newcomers they could call her Mo.

With that out of the way, Laurie started to speak, but was interrupted by Gail. "She and I'll have white wine."

I was beginning to agree with Charles about the quantity of drinks we would need. I told Mo the same for me.

"Guys," Laurie said, "thanks for joining us. It's nice getting to know people here." She looked down. "Now that... now that Anthony's gone, it's lonely being in a strange place."

Gail leaned closer to Laurie. "Now, dear, I'm here with you. You know it would be best for you to come back to Jacksonville. You have many friends there."

Laurie said, "I appreciate you coming. This is my home."

I wondered how many times she'd have to tell that to Gail.

Charles said, "When did you get here?"

Gail glared at him like he'd interrupted her Jacksonville sales pitch.

"Gail arrived this morning."

It was refreshing seeing Laurie answer for Gail.

"I would've made it yesterday, but I'd been in a seminar in Saint Augustine, didn't get back until late yesterday."

"What kind of seminar?" asked Charles as Mo returned with our drinks.

Gail glanced at him. "Oh, I'm sure you'd not be interested."

"Sure, I am," he said.

Gail sighed. "It was about ways of searching for jobs, also assistance the state provides to employees whose companies are moving offshore. The company I worked for is moving operations to Mexico. I thought it'd help if I wanted to return to the workforce."

Charles nodded. "Learn anything?"

"Not really. It was boring, boring, boring."

"That's too bad," I said to get into the discussion.

"Not really. Dean's spending day and night at the store, I wouldn't have seen him much, anyway."

Laurie said, "Gail, I thought you wouldn't have to go back to work."

"Wishful thinking," Gail said. "Selling tires is getting fiercer and fiercer. Dean's store is having to compete with stores and national tire chains that buy tires by the ton."

Our drinks arrived, then Laurie tapped her friend's arm. "Let's talk about something more fun. It's so nice out tonight. Look at that view. This is my first time up here."

"It is a beautiful view," Gail said, as she turned to Charles. "Have the police learned anything about who killed Anthony, or who shot at Laurie?"

That's a fun topic, I thought.

Charles said, "I haven't heard."

Gail said, "Do they think the killer was after the treasure?"

"Gail," Laurie said, "they don't know why Anthony was

killed. I doubt the person would've shot him over some Civil War relics. Chris and Charles think Anthony may've run across guys being where they shouldn't be, something about a boat delivering drugs. Isn't that right, Charles?"

"That's a theory."

Laurie pulled her chair up to the table, sat up straight, and said, "See, Gail, it doesn't have anything to do with the map, or anything we were doing out there." She abruptly turned to me. "Chris, it was nice meeting your friend Grace. I'll call her for lunch after Gail leaves." She turned away from Gail.

I didn't bother telling her that I'd known Grace for three days. I also didn't bother trying to steer the conversation back to the topic of Anthony's death, for she'd left no doubt the subject was now off limits.

The rest of the evening, we talked about everything but Anthony, the gunshots at Laurie's house, or anything else negative. Tension seemed to fall off Laurie's shoulders. Gail stopped interrupting everything Laurie tried to say. Charles attempted to be Charles a couple of times by asking questions that stepped over the none-of-your-business line, only to be deflected by Laurie. I couldn't tell if she was trying to hide something, or was determined to keep the topics light. Either way, it turned out to be a pleasant night spent with pleasant friends, new friends.

The feeling of a pleasant evening was hijacked while I was walking home. All I thought about was Laurie's brief mention of treasure, and the word that I hadn't heard her say before: map.

Chapter Thirty-One

I woke the next morning, remembering that, somewhere in the amorphous state between sleep and awake, I thought about something that Laurie had said during supper that was significant. The problem was that, now that I was awake, I couldn't put my finger on what it was. I convinced myself that a walk next door to Bert's to grab breakfast would jar the memory to the surface. Truth be told, I doubted that it would. I was searching for an excuse to buy a cinnamon roll.

The gooey delight was less appealing when I saw Stanley Kremitz in front of the case holding the high-calorie goodies. It became even less appealing when Stanley spotted me.

He looked my way, smiled, flapped his arms like they were wings, and said, "The early bird gets the worm."

"Hi, Stanley. Worms aren't my thing. The cinnamon rolls behind you are my weakness."

"It's an expression, Chris. An expression. I was about to grab one of those, myself. Told you we were as alike as two peas in a pod."

I wouldn't believe it, even if he told me until hell freezes over, I thought in Stanley speak.

He smiled, like he'd convinced me we were alike, then said, "Any word on who killed the relic hunter?"

"No. Have you heard anything?"

"Veronica and I were flapping our lips about it last night. She told me that she heard something at the beauty shop about Abraham Gant, you know, Captain Gant."

"Heard what?"

"Gant told someone that he knew where treasure was buried, that the money didn't mean anything to him."

"Why not?"

"Suppose because he's hung up on the past staying past."

"Did the person who told your wife say that was the reason?"

"Don't think so. I'm picturing the story about what Gant said being shared a few times from one person to another, to another. The story Veronica heard, most likely, ain't the version that started going around. A chain is only as strong as its weakest link."

The story may be convoluted although, if most of it's accurate, it's further evidence that Gant knew about the treasure map he told Charles and me about.

"Did Veronica specifically say that she'd heard the word treasure and not relics?"

"That's what she heard. It don't necessarily mean it's so."

"Who told her the story?"

"Maybelle Davis. Maybelle heard it from Francis something or other, who heard it from, umm, Francis didn't remember who she heard it from."

I lost track after Maybelle when I realized that following the chain to the initial source would be as successful as catching a seagull with a tablespoon.

"Stanley, let me know if you hear more about Gant."

"Sure will." He grabbed a roll out of the case. "Gotta head out. Promised Veronica I'd take her to Walmart." He shook his head. "She'll shop 'til she drops."

I watched him go, tried to erase several clichés from my mind, grabbed a cinnamon roll, then walked among the aisles long enough for Stanley to leave. Two things stuck with me about the conversation. First, it reinforced what Gant had told us about treasure and why Anthony and Laurie had been exploring the old Coast Guard property. Second, it appeared Stanley was determined to bring Abraham Gant into the discussion about Anthony's death. This wasn't the first time he'd pointed a finger at the captain. He'd asked again if I'd learned anything about the murder. Did the cliché king want to deflect suspicion from himself?

I microwaved the roll, paid, then headed home, only to find Chief LaMond's pickup truck in my drive. She stepped out of the vehicle when she saw me coming across the yard.

Cindy pointed to the house. "You're not in there."

I smiled. "Did you use all your chiefly skills to figure that out?"

"Nope. No answer after I pounded on the door gave it away."

"If I'd been home, what would I have done to receive a visit by the finest of Folly's finest?"

Instead of answering, Cindy sat on the step leading to my screened-in porch waving for me to join her.

"Well?" I said.

"Being that you're the second nosiest person I know, I wanted to share an update on the Anthony Fitzsimmons' murder."

Charles, of course, was the first, leading the pack by a longshot. "Share away."

Cindy watched a classic Volkswagen convertible pass and continued to stare at the road. "The update is there's no update. Or, I should have said the update is there's nothing new to update. No murder weapon, no forensic evidence, no eyewitnesses except Anthony, who unfortunately is in no condition to identify his killer."

"What happens now?"

"I talked to Detective Callahan this morning. He's up to his dimples in that high-profile case plus a couple of others. He said that he was still working it but sounded as optimistic as someone teaching a frog to pilot a helicopter."

"Does he think Laurie's telling the truth?"

She shook her head again. "Not really. Short of beating a confession out of her, his hands are tied."

"What about rumors that Anthony stumbled across a drug deal and paid for it with his life?"

"That's as good a story as any. Still, no evidence to indicate it's anything but a story."

"What about Abraham Gant?"

"Decent alibi, weak motive, no evidence."

I shared with the chief what Stanley Kremitz had said about Gant then what Laurie had said during supper about a map.

"Chris, I never bought her story about searching for Civil War relics. If she had a map from her grandfather, it would've been further proof she was lying. With that said, there's no map I've seen, no evidence, with only my gut reaction that she's involved. My gut don't mean squat when it comes to proof."

"So, you came to tell me that there's nothing."

"Frustrating as hell, isn't it?"

"Yes."

"Welcome to my world." She patted me on the knee before heading to her vehicle.

I watched her pull into the line of traffic, took a bite of cinnamon roll, and wondered what I could do to solve one more murder on my little slice of heaven. I may, or may not, succeed, although one thing was clear. The solution must start with Laurie.

I punched Charles's number in the phone. When he answered, said, "Ready to go?"

"Huh?"

I smiled at the reversal of what normally happens. "You home?"

"Yes."

"I'll pick you up in ten minutes." I hit *end call.*

I was beginning to see why he had so much fun doing the same thing to me. It was time to do what the police appeared to have a tough time doing.

Chapter Thirty-Two

I met Charles standing in front of his apartment, ignored his asking, several ways, where we were going, drove to Laurie's house, and pulled in behind her MINI.

"Did you forget something?" Laurie said as she opened the door. She jumped back when she saw us. "Oh, sorry. I thought you were Gail. She just left for the grocery." She looked at Charles. "Did I know you were coming?"

Charles pivoted to me.

I said, "We were nearby, so we thought we'd see if you were doing okay. I hope we're not interrupting anything."

"I think I'm okay. Umm, come in. Would you like coffee?"

Laurie wore tattered navy-blue shorts, a loose-fitting PINK T-shirt, and was barefoot. I felt a tinge of guilt for interrupting her morning. My guilt was short-lived. I said we'd love some.

We followed her to the kitchen, where she poured our drinks then pointed to the table. She surprised me when she chuckled. "Actually, I'm glad you stopped by. I sent Gail to the grocery to get her out of the house."

Charles said, "Why?"

"That woman's driving me crazy."

Charles looked toward the front door like he expected Gail to appear. "How?"

Laurie followed Charles's gaze. "After Anthony left us, this is the first time Gail and I've been together this long. Don't get me wrong, I love her."

She looked at Charles like she expected him to respond. He didn't disappoint.

"You're great friends."

She smiled at Charles. "We are." The smile disappeared. "Have you ever known someone who wouldn't stop talking, unless they're asleep or food's stuffed in their mouth?"

Charles wasn't that bad, although he came to mind. I responded, "Yes."

"I swear, guys, I can't complete a two-word sentence without her finishing it or she's veering off in another direction before I finish." She blinked twice then shook her head.

I said, "I'm sorry."

Laurie bit her lower lip, stared in her mug, and mumbled, "Sorry, hearing me bitch isn't why you're here."

Charles leaned forward. "That's okay. We don't mind."

She was right, that wasn't the reason we were here. I said, "Laurie, the other night at Snapper Jack's, you were talking about being with Anthony at the old Coast Guard station."

She nodded as she looked up from her drink.

"You said something about a map. I was wondering—"

She interrupted, "Map?"

"You and Gail were talking when you mentioned a map."

"Don't think so."

Okay, Charles, it's time that you stepped in to add you heard it.

No such luck, so I continued, "Gail said something about you all finding the treasure. You said map."

The look on Laurie's face screamed either confusion or that she was hiding something.

"Oh," Laurie said. "I must've been talking about that map beside the entrance to the Preserve. You know, the one where you donate a dollar to help protect the area."

I knew the map she was referring to. I also knew it wasn't the one she'd alluded to at supper.

Charles finally chipped in. "I hadn't thought of that one. That could've been it." He rubbed his hand through his three-day-old whiskers. "But, honest to Pete, I had the impression you were talking about a map you and Anthony had."

She hopped out of her chair, grabbed the coffee pot, and refilled our mugs. She then looked out the repaired window.

She paced the room as I reminded myself that I could be talking to Anthony's murderer. If she was guilty, I'll be walking in dangerous territory; if innocent, I wanted her to know that we cared. Either way, I wanted her to understand that I knew there was something about a map, not the one posted at the entrance to the Preserve. Besides, Stanley Kremitz had already told me about his experience with Harnell Levi, who'd talked about a map.

"Laurie, Charles, and I want to help. If there's something you aren't sharing, then it makes it hard for us to figure out what's going on. If you're afraid of going to the police, we could go with you."

She returned to her chair, took a sip, and in a faint voice said, "I've told you some about Granddad Levi, how I spent time here with him. He was a funny old bird. He could be cranky as a screech owl. Other times, he could spin tall tales with the best storytellers. Sadly, he could guzzle more alcohol than anyone I've ever known."

That was consistent with what Kremitz had said.

"I know people like that here," Charles added, hopefully not stopping Laurie's story.

She nodded at Charles. "During one of the calmer, sober moments, he took me in his den. He folded back a god-awful colored area rug and pried up a floorboard. I never would've seen it if he didn't show me. Under the floor was a tin container the size of a cigar box. Granddad got this big grin on his face, opened the box, took out a stack of cash. I'd never seen so much money in my life. Under the cash was a folded piece of paper." She smiled as she relived the memory. "He held the paper by the edges then unfolded it like it was the original Declaration of Independence. Know what he told me?"

Charles smiled. "Said it was a treasure map?"

Laurie shrugged. "Granddad put his arm around me. 'Laurie,' he said, 'this here's the most important piece of paper you'll ever see.' I remember it like it was yesterday because I thought the cash was as important as anything gets. He said the crinkly old map was to a treasure buried on Folly more than two hundred years ago, buried by pirates. He said he wanted me to have it. I was in my teens, no expert to say the least. To me, the map looked old, although not old enough to have been drawn by a pirate two hundred years earlier."

Charles asked, "What'd it look like?"

"I couldn't make hide nor hair of it. It had all these lines, squiggles, round things that I suppose were trees." Laurie hesitated.

Hesitated too long for Charles. "What'd he say?"

"I was right. He said it wasn't the original. Whoever got it first must've made a copy so that they could carry it around with them without ruining the original. Granddad said it didn't matter. He knew it was accurate."

I asked, "How'd he know?"

"He didn't say."

"Where'd he get it?" Charles asked.

"Funny thing. Granddad wouldn't tell me. All he said was he knew it was exactly like the original."

Charles said, "Had he looked for the treasure?"

Laurie nodded. "For years. The problem was according to the map, the treasure was buried on the Coast Guard property. For most of his years looking, it was under control of the military so he couldn't snoop around. Another problem was that over the years weather changed the face of the beach, maybe even most of the island.

"Landmarks from when the pirates buried the treasure had washed away by the tides, been blown away by hurricanes, trees grew, trees died, most everything changed. When the Coast Guard built the station, much of the landscape changed, buildings built, roads added. In other words, the map led him to the general area, but no closer."

"Why'd he give it to you?" I asked.

"It was one of the few times I saw him sober. He was in poor health. I think he knew he was too ill to keep looking." She shook her head. "He passed away two months after giving me the map."

Charles said, "What'd you do with it?"

"To tell the truth, I thought it was another of his tall tales. He was always talking about strange things happening on Folly. He told me, I think he believed it, that a spaceship landed behind what's now the Oceanfront Villas. He was also convinced, during World War II, a German submarine parked off the island sending three spies ashore in a small boat. I put his so-called treasure map in my keepsake box and went on with life, going to school, going to college, teaching, marrying Anthony."

"What changed?" I asked.

"We were moving to a new house about four years ago. I found my old keepsake box in the bottom of a carton of clothes. I remember laughing when I showed Anthony Granddad's map. I told him it was the key to our fortune. I was joking. Anthony wasn't. He didn't know Granddad, so he didn't know how quirky he was. Anthony said we needed to look for the treasure. That's what we did.

"Whenever we came here before retiring, we walked through the Preserve, looking for anything looking like what was marked on the map. A couple of times, we thought something could be like it was on the map, although we never felt we were close enough to dig. All we knew for certain was that the squiggles on the map represented the ocean. It was impossible to tell distances between the circles that looked like trees. Plus, the shoreline wasn't where it was when the map was drawn."

When we found her at the Preserve, she'd told us it was their first time exploring the property. "Laurie, didn't you tell us you'd never been at the Coast Guard property before the night Anthony was killed?"

She looked at the floor. "That was sort of a fib. You were strangers so I didn't want to tell you too much."

I let it go. "What about the night of Anthony's death?"

"The day before we'd been snooping around and found what we thought was one of the landmarks from the map. It wasn't exactly like the map, but close enough to try. There were a lot of people in the area. It was illegal to dig, so we decided to wait until the next day. Hoped for fewer people. That's when…"

She put her head down on the table. Tears streamed down her face. Charles and I sat in silence. What seemed like an eternity later, she wiped the tears away. "That's about it."

"Where's the map?" I asked.

She shook her head. "Don't know. Anthony had it. He had more pockets and didn't want to be walking around with it in his hands in case someone saw us. When the police said that I could pick up his personal effects, all they had was his wallet, watch, and clothes."

"The map was gone," said Charles, stating the obvious.

Laurie nodded.

We sipped our drinks in silence. Laurie started looking at the door every few seconds. I figured she was worried that Gail would return and for some reason didn't want us to be here. I took the hint. I thanked her for sharing the story of the map then said we'd better be going. She didn't protest.

Chapter Thirty-Three

I was backing out of Laurie's drive when Charles said, "What do you think about her story?"

"I have trouble with a story about a treasure map. It sounds more like the myths that've been around for eons. Someone finds a map with an X on it, supposedly the location of buried treasure. Then, a bunch of people go on a wild goose chase. It makes an interesting television show. Great fiction."

"Your skeptic gene is showing."

"What do you think?"

"If she made it up, she inherited her granddad's story-telling skill."

"Okay, assume there was a map, that is, a copy of another map, let's say treasure was buried on the Preserve; what are the odds it'd be there after all these years? Most of the land had been occupied by the Coast Guard. They build numerous structures and had hundreds of coasties, guardians, or whatever you call Coast Guard members who were stationed there traipsing over every square foot of land. I find it hard to believe if there was treasure it wouldn't have been found."

"That may be true, although don't you think that if someone found a treasure chest filled with doubloons, it would've been big news?"

"If they told anyone."

"That's not the kind of secret people keep without bragging."

"I'll admit if she's lying, she's excellent at it. I still think she's the number one suspect. Treasure map or not, she has motive."

"Insurance?"

"Yes."

Charles looked out the windshield and tapped his hand on the armrest. "If she's guilty, how do you explain someone taking potshots at her?"

"She could've taken the first one herself. Remember, she told us a different version of where she was than she told the police. There were no witnesses."

"She couldn't have taken the second shot. We were there."

"That, I can't explain."

"See, it ain't her," Charles said, once again tapped his hand on the armrest. "What about other suspects? How about the story going around that Anthony stumbled on a drug transfer from a boat? That'd be an isolated spot for a transfer, especially since no one was supposed to be there after dark. It's easy to see how Anthony might've seen them and been awarded with a bullet."

"It's possible. It seems unlikely that the killer would wait days to take shots at Laurie. The odds she saw him at the Preserve would've been slim."

"Abraham Gant?"

"He'd talked to Anthony a few days before the murder.

From what's been said, Anthony talked about a buried treasure more than was wise, so he could've told Gant. Everyone knows Gant goes bananas when there's talks about digging up things from the past, be it treasure, or Civil War uniform buttons."

"With him being a retired cop, he'd have a gun, and know how to use it," Charles said.

"Add to that, he knew about the murder before it was widespread knowledge. He didn't have qualms about saying he was glad Anthony was dead. Cindy questioned him. He didn't have a solid alibi for the time of the murder."

Charles turned to me as I pulled in his parking lot. "How are we going to prove he killed Anthony?"

"Charles, the police are aware of everything we know about Gant. I'm sure they're looking at him."

"Didn't Cindy tell you Detective Callahan is up to his coiffured hair with other cases? When's he going to have time to investigate Gant?"

"What do you propose?"

"Hey, you're the brains of our crime fighting duo. I'm the one who goes along then stumbles into catching bad guys."

I've worked hard over the years ignoring Charles's remarks about us being a *crime fighting duo*, or that he's a *private detective*. I was clueless about what to do to uncover Gant as the killer, so I ignored his comment.

Charles stared at me and must've figured a solution wasn't forthcoming. "Here's another thought. What about Gail?"

"What about her?"

"Think about it. She could've known about the treasure map since she was such good friends with Laurie. When someone first shot at Laurie, Gail was here. Allegedly, she'd gone to the grocery. It doesn't take a genius to figure she could've been the shooter."

That reminded me of the first time I talked with Gail

when she'd said that she and Dean were supposed to be visiting Anthony and Laurie to search for relics. They knew about the search. Did they know about the treasure map?

"Charles, she was four hours away in Jacksonville when Anthony was shot."

"How do you know?"

"I don't. Do you think she and her never-speaking husband are in it together?"

"Probably not. Didn't you tell me Dean was somewhere other than Jacksonville? That was the reason they hadn't gone to visit Anthony and Laurie?"

"A tire retailers' meeting in Tallahassee."

Charles held out his arms and smiled, "Aha. Dean didn't know where Gail was. Her alibi about being in Jacksonville has more holes than a block of Swiss cheese."

Charles had a point, although I wasn't ready to move Gail to the top of the list. Time to throw out another possibility.

"What about Stanley Kremitz?"

Charles lowered his arms. "Stanley? You think he killed Anthony with a cliché?"

I grinned. "No. That would've been a slower, much more painful death. Think about it. Stanley knew Harnell Levi. According to Stanley, Levi told him about a map. Each time I've seen him since the murder, he's asked if I've heard anything about the killer then he pushes the theory it's Gant."

"I haven't given Stanley a speck of thought. I can't picture him shooting anyone."

"That doesn't mean he didn't."

"Does Cindy know your harebrained theory about the cliché king?"

"No."

"This is where if I told you what you told me you'd pat me

on the back, then say it was none of our business, that I should take my ideas, regardless how stupid, to the police."

I hated it when Charles was right. "That's exactly what I'm going to do once I leave your parking lot."

I called Cindy on my way home. She was with Larry at a plumbing supply house in Charleston. I said that I could call her when she got back to Folly. She said my call was a gift from heaven. It would give her an excuse to not "ooh and ah" when Larry showed her the latest, greatest, high-tech toilets. I shared my ideas about possible suspects. When I finished, she said looking at toilets may not have been the worse idea after all.

Despite her faux lack of enthusiasm about my ideas, she'd take me seriously.

Chapter Thirty-Four

Theo called the next afternoon to share news about Grace's food truck. He'd talked to several local restaurant owners to explain what happened. Even though they competed for dining dollars, the owners were a tightknit group that helped each other in times of need. This was no exception. They pitched in to loan Grace the equipment needed to open *Hot Diggity Dog!*

Additionally, she had received her permit so, by the next day, she would be serving the best hot dogs found anywhere east of the Mississippi. Theo had done a taste test and couldn't swear hers were the best east of the Mississippi, but said it was the best he'd eaten. He ended by inviting me to a celebratory dinner with him and Grace the next evening at Magnolias, one of Charleston's finest restaurants. He was driving and buying. I asked what time.

Theo didn't have Charles's obsession about being early. He pulled in my drive at 6:00, the time he'd said he'd be there. I slid onto the soft leather backseat in his Mercedes. Grace rewarded me with a charming smile, while Theo thanked me for joining them. I told him I was honored to have been invited. Theo had on a navy sport coat and gray slacks, dressed more formally than I'd ever seen him. Grace wore a pale-yellow silk blouse and black linen slacks. I felt underdressed in a long-sleeve, blue striped shirt and tan chinos.

"Where's Sal?" I asked as we pulled off the island.

"I invited him. He declined, thank goodness. The night will be better without a joke machine with us. Said he'd met a couple of Folly old-timers who meet at the Crab Shack nearly every night to swap tall tales, share opinions on everything from the mayor to the president, while putting away a beverage or two. Sal said they love, he put air quotes around love, his jokes and stories from the comedy circuit.

They'd get over it, I thought, then lied saying I was sorry he couldn't make it.

I'd never been in Theo's car and was mesmerized by its smooth ride as we weaved through Charleston's streets lined with stately mansions and years of history on our way to the East Bay Street restaurant. I could get used to being chauffeured. A valet met us at the door, whisked the car off while another employee held the door of the restaurant known for its contemporary Lowcountry cuisine. I wasn't certain what that meant but, from everything I'd heard about the white-tablecloth restaurant, the food was outstanding. Besides, for once, someone else was paying.

We were seated by a window, overlooking the street, and greeted by a server who, with great flourish, handed Theo the wine list. I got a glimmer of Theo's life as a successful businessman before he retired in bohemian comfort on Folly when he ordered a bottle of expensive Champaign pronouncing its French name correctly, or so I assumed. Theo told the server we were celebrating the opening of another fine restaurant in the Lowcountry. Like the professional he was, the waiter said congratulations. He didn't enquire about what he could have perceived to be a new competitor.

"Grace," I said, "how was your first day of business?" I'd asked the same question on the ride over, but Theo said for us to wait until we were at the restaurant.

She gave me a high-wattage smile. "Exhilarating, and exhausting. I underestimated the quest for gourmet hot dogs on Folly."

Gourmet was not a word often bandied around on Folly, but I knew what she'd meant. "I'm thrilled for you."

The server returned with our bubbly, adroitly uncorked it, then poured a taste in Theo's flute. Theo waved it off saying he was certain it was acceptable. The server poured each glass to a third full then continued pouring until each flute was near full.

Theo raised his glass. "Here's to Folly's newest eating establishment and its lovely proprietress."

Grace looked around like she didn't know who Theo was referring to, then she said, "If, dear sir, you are referring to me, I'm honored."

I was pleased to see Theo and Grace on better terms than when they'd met.

Theo asked if we wanted an appetizer.

I said I'd get anything that the two of them wanted.

Grace took a sip of Champaign and tilted her flute to Theo. "Anything but hot dogs."

Theo laughed and said that he didn't think Magnolias was that fine a dining establishment. He waved the server over and ordered house-made potato chips and pimento cheese with Charleston flatbread.

"Did anything surprise you?" I asked the proprietress.

"California is known for its laid-back citizens. I wasn't

certain what to expect on this side of the country. Mon, was I surprised. As dad would say, 'Gi laugh fi peas soup.' "

"Which means?" I said.

"The literal translation is, 'Give laughs for peas soup.' "

Theo tilted his head. "Which means?"

Grace laughed. "To joke around, to have a good time. Everyone, okay, nearly everyone, who stepped up to the service window seemed happy. They joked. They laughed, smiled, were cheerful. It was, how shall I say it, umm energizing to feel so welcomed. Two men came back to buy more hot dogs. They said they would tell everyone how great they were."

Appetizers arrived and, while Grace and Theo grabbed a potato chip each, I said, "Are you going to hire someone to help?"

Grace put her hand in front of her mouth as she finished the chip. "That would be preferable although, with my expenses, plus the need to replace the damaged equipment, I'm afraid it will be a long time. That's what I told two young gentlemen who stopped by to see if I was hiring. It was the second time one of them stopped to ask. I told him to check back in a few weeks."

Theo nodded, "If business continues like today, that day might come sooner rather than later."

Grace raised her flute. "I'll drink to that."

Theo and I did as well.

A half hour later, Grace was eating blue crab stuffed rainbow trout, while Theo and I were savoring grilled fillets of beef. The festive conversation bounced around from the fantastic weather of the last week; Grace wondering how many hours the carriage horses worked in a day; Theo sharing stories from his world of work; and, I told how Charles and I managed to catch not one, but two murderers because of the walking group that Theo, Charles, and I were in. Grace's laughter was interspersed with yawns. I was amazed she'd managed to stay awake. I attributed it to my charm and winning personality. I suspected it was due to her being able to relax around her father-in-law.

Grace's phone interrupted a humorous story about one of her customers who wanted to pay with a fifty-euro banknote. She apologized for the interruption then answered.

Her face turned from a frown to a look of shock as she listened to whoever was on the other end. She put her hand over the phone and asked Theo, "How long will it take us to get to Folly?"

Theo said a half hour. Grace repeated that in the phone, then hit *end call*. She put her hand over her face and shook her head.

Theo put his arm around her shoulder. "What's wrong, dear?"

She threw her napkin on the table. "That was Chief LaMond. My truck's ablaze."

Chapter Thirty-Five

Theo may be one of the slowest walkers above ground. He may need police to stop traffic on Folly when he crosses streets with the walking group. Throw all that out the window when he's faced with a crisis. In fewer than five minutes, he'd paid the tab and summoned the valet to pull the Mercedes to the side of the building. Twenty minutes later, after running two yellow lights and, don't tell anyone, one red, we were crossing the bridge to Folly. Off to the left, I saw the flashing red lights from one of Folly's fire vehicles and blue lights from a police cruiser beside Theo's house.

Grace gasped.

Theo put his free hand on her arm as he turned on his street before skidding to a stop in his neighbors' gravel drive. Spotlights from the fire engine focused on the cab of the food truck backed into Theo's drive.

Two firefighters were rolling up hoses, one from a hydrant across the street, the other from the side of the fire apparatus. A wisp of smoke rose from the truck's blackened, cracked windshield.

Grace was already out of the car and being restrained by one of the firefighters after she tried to enter the truck. The logo wrap on the side had warped from the heat. A front tire was flat, melted rubber oozed from the door.

Theo and I approached the vehicle as the words *total loss* came to mind. I was heartbroken for Grace.

Chief LaMond came around the back of the vehicle and saw us standing with the distraught owner. She approached Grace. "I'm sorry."

Grace stared at the truck, her fists were balled, her shoulders sagged. I couldn't tell if she'd heard Cindy.

Theo moved to Grace's side then Cindy came over to where I was.

"We were fortunate," she said as she looked at the totaled vehicle.

Fortunate wouldn't have been a word I would've chosen to describe what I saw. The smell of burning rubber, mixed with a whiff of burnt meat, filled the air. "Fortunate?"

"The fire didn't reach the propane tank on the back of the truck avoiding an eruption, or explosion, which could've been catastrophic."

I shook my head.

"And," she continued, "when we got here the flames were pouring out the side of the truck, coming within a hair of Theo's house. If our guys hadn't gotten water on the house when they did, we'd be looking at a crispy McMansion."

Theo was still comforting Grace.

I said, "Cindy, any idea what caused it?"

"I'll let the arson investigator figure that out, but I'd guess it was set. It got too hot too quick. We were fortunate to contain the damage."

"*Hot Diggity Dog!* has been on Folly mere days and already

broken in twice, now this," I said, more to myself than to Cindy.

She looked at the vehicle. "Don't guess we'll worry about more break ins."

"You may not want to comfort Grace with that insight."

Cindy rolled her eyes, then asked where Theo, Grace, and I had been when she called.

I explained where we were and why. Cindy muttered a profanity, then said, "Did Grace say anything about being afraid of anyone, or anything, strange happening to her?"

"Like someone telling her he was going to torch her truck?"

"That'd be a clue."

"The opposite," I said. "Her first day was a tremendous success. She was thrilled by the reception she'd received."

"I heard the same thing. I was planning on stopping by tomorrow for lunch. Suppose I'll have to change plans."

"Anyone see anybody around the truck?"

"None I know about. My guys canvassed the neighbors, who said that they hadn't seen anyone. Somebody driving by might have but, unless they do their civic duty and come forward, we'll never know."

The chief looked at her men loading the remaining fire-equipment on the truck. "I'll talk to Grace tomorrow after I have more information from the arson investigator, and she has time to get over the initial shock." She turned to head to her vehicle then stopped. "One more thing, Chris. I talked to Detective Callahan this afternoon. He said one of the other guys in his office was telling him there's been an uptick in drugs being offloaded from boats along the coast. One was caught last weekend near Edisto. He thinks there's a better than even chance the Fitzsimmonses were in the wrong place at the wrong time with Anthony stumbling on a drug deal."

"So Callahan's back on the case?"

"He's swamped. His drug guys are looking at it."

Anthony may've stumbled on a drug deal, but that didn't explain two attempts on Laurie's life. I asked Cindy to let me know if she learned anything. She said that she lived for the sole purpose of sharing everything law-enforcement related with me. I grinned as I thanked her. She mumbled another profanity then left to talk to Grace.

I looked in the truck where the smell of burnt rubber, incinerated hot dogs, and melted plastic was so strong that I had to step away from the vehicle. I couldn't fathom how *Hot Diggity Dog!* would serve another meal.

"Holy hot dog!" screamed Sal.

I turned to see him shuffle down the drive toward Theo and Grace.

He put his hand on his forehead psychic-style and said, "I see a fire sale in the future."

Theo waved his hand in Sal's face. "Sal, can it."

Sal stopped in front of Grace, leaned from side to side, possibly a result of hours sharing whatever he'd been sharing with his new buddies at the Crab Shack. He lowered his head. "Sorry, Grace. Sometimes, I'd like to smack myself for being so insensitive."

He'd have to get in line, I thought as I walked to the trio.

Grace, earning her name, put her hand on Sal's wobbly shoulder. "That's okay, Salvadore, you can't help yourself."

She was a quick learner. Theo wasn't as forgiving. He gave his brother a look that would stop a charging rhinoceros.

Sal ignored his brother's glare. "What happened?"

I joined the group to listen as Grace and Theo tag-teamed their explanation of what had occurred. Sal asked the same questions Cindy had asked and received the same answers until he asked a new question. "Was it insured?"

Grace lowered her head. "It was when we bought it. We had to have insurance in California. I didn't have enough money to keep it up. I didn't owe anything on the vehicle, so I dropped the comprehensive policy when I got here. I still have collision insurance."

Please, Sal, don't make a joke about the truck colliding with a match, or some other feeble attempt at humor.

He showed a glimmer of sensitivity when he said, "Grace, I'm so sorry."

She thanked him.

"Sal," said Theo after Sal's moment of concern. "Did you see anyone skulking around after we left for Charleston?"

"No. I headed to the Crab Shack before you got off the island. Been there ever since. I heard the fire trucks. Didn't know where they were going, or I would've followed."

Theo looked at the burned-out truck then turned to Grace. "Let's get in the house. I could use a spot of brandy."

Grace didn't say anything as she followed Theo.

Once again, Sal refrained from joking.

I walked by his side up the wide steps to Theo's house, the house spared by the quick-acting firefighters.

Theo went to get drinks, miracles continued when Sal offered to help.

Grace plopped down on the leather sofa in the great room. She twisted her hands together, looked at me, and said, "Why?"

I wish I had an answer.

Air conditioning, brandy, wine, and beer didn't reveal the answer to why someone set the fire, but calmed everyone's nerves.

Grace relaxed enough to joke that she knew today's sales were good, yet didn't realize they would be a record high.

Sal thought it was funny but didn't want to be topped so he

added, "Did you hear about the new restaurant on the moon?"

Grace tilted her head. "Don't believe I did."

Theo sighed.

Sal said, "It has great food but no atmosphere."

I excused myself on that note.

Chapter Thirty-Six

I'd agreed to meet Charles for breakfast at the Dog. I arrived forty-five minutes before the designated time, in the hope of beating my buddy. I failed. He was sipping coffee at my favorite booth along the back wall. He saw me at the door then glanced at his bare wrist as I made my way to the table.

"You're early," he said. "I'm impressed."

Forty-five minutes early, I thought.

Charles wore a blue long-sleeved T-shirt with *Salve Regina University* in green on the front. I'd never heard of the school, yet still didn't mention it. I asked if he'd been here long.

"Not long. You walk?"

"Drove."

He shook his head and sighed at the same time, his way of saying poor, pitiful Chris.

He made a walking motion on the table with two fingers. "Thomas Jefferson said, 'Walking is the best possible exercise. Habituate yourself to walk very far.'"

"Chris Landrum said, 'Good morning, Charles.'"

Amber arrived at the table in time to hear my effort at bringing civility and less presidential history to the table. She pointed at Charles's T-shirt. "It's in Newport, Rhode Island."

Amber knew how much I tried to ignore Charles's T-shirts collection.

Charles beamed.

I wanted to go back to the car and instead of walking, drive, far away. I said, "Coffee, a lot of it."

Amber chuckled, bent down, and kissed the top of my balding head. I'd never admit it to them, but this kind of disjoined conversation was one of the reasons I loved living here. Amber went to fetch my drink.

Charles watched her go then turned serious. "Chris, I like Laurie. She's nice, but seems lost. I can't imagine how it would be to lose a spouse. She's got to be lonely. Look how many times she's asked us to be with her."

I wanted to point out that she asked him, not us, but I let it go.

He continued. "I'm worried about her."

"Why?"

"Is your old age killing off so many brain cells you've already forgotten two attempts on her life? If she'd been with Anthony when he was killed, she'd already be dead. Can't you see how much danger she's in?"

"I know that. I wondered if there was something else you were referring to. Have you talked to her since we were at her place?"

Amber returned with my drink and asked if I was ready to order. I told her French toast. She pretended to be shocked at the same thing I ordered ninety percent of the time.

After Amber headed to the kitchen, Charles said, "She called me around midnight. I was asleep. It must've taken me a long time to answer because she said she was afraid I wasn't going to."

"Was something wrong?"

"That was my thought. Calling me at midnight is like calling you geezers at ten. Snoresville."

I was only two years older than Charles, both of us senior citizens by any definition.

"Again, was anything wrong?"

"If there was, she didn't tell me. Said she was sitting in her dark house, needed someone to talk to. I asked if Gail was there. She said she'd gone back to Florida. Even if she was still on Folly, Laurie said she needed someone to talk to, not to listen to." He shook his head. I took a sip as I waited for him to continue. "Chris, she didn't give another reason for the call. She sounded scared."

"Did you learn anything?"

"Don't think so, but I may've dozed while she was talking. She rambled on about the night Anthony was killed. She'd said most of it to us before. She did talk more about the map, also wondered why it wasn't with the body. Seems to me the killer took it. For some reason, she doesn't want to believe that's what happened."

Amber returned with my breakfast, plus a drink refill for Charles, before moving to a group seated across from us.

Charles looked in his mug as he rubbed his chin. "Chris, I've been thinking."

"About?"

"We know there was a map."

"Not for sure."

"Whatever. Let's say there was. Anthony had it the night he was killed, but it wasn't on him when the cops came. The killer has it. So, what's the logical thing the killer will do?"

Before I could respond, Charles said, "Try to find the treasure."

"Which, number one, may've been discovered years ago; two, the killer could've already found it; three, the map could've been a cruel joke drawn decades ago, leading to nothing."

"Yeah, yeah, yeah. Anyway, you said the police have pushed Anthony's death to the backburner, so it's up to us to solve it. We owe it to Laurie."

I was surprised, no, shocked, that I agreed. The most valuable lesson I'd learned, over my many years, was that friendships are more valuable than anything, and friends, devoted friends, would do anything for each other. Of course, it would be a stretch to count Laurie as a friend, a stretch for me. Charles didn't appear to have that reservation, but he was my friend.

"How do you propose we do that?"

"Stake out the Preserve. That's where the treasure is. That's where the killer will be looking."

"Charles, that's a huge piece of land. It's been days since the murder. The killer may have already found the treasure, that is, if it ever existed. What're we going to do if we discover someone looking? It's a long shot."

"A long shot's better than no shot. What's the downside?"

Wasting part of the life we have left. Getting countless mosquito bites. Being stuck in the woods with each other for hours. Oh, yeah, not to mention losing our lives to someone who's already killed once and tried twice other times.

After all that, I heard myself saying, "When do we start?"

Charles smiled; the smile he uses when he's won a major victory. We remained at the table another hour, getting ugly stares from customers waiting at the door for a table in the crowded restaurant. We hatched what could be considered a futile, harebrained plan to catch a killer. It was still peak vacation season, so most of the day the Lighthouse Inlet Heritage Preserve would be packed with vacationers, local fishermen, adventurous bicyclists. Like Anthony and Laurie, we'd limit our time at the Preserve to the late hours when attendance would be minimal.

At the end of our lengthy discussion, I was convinced that our chances of succeeding were miniscule. To paraphrase Charles and in terms our surfer friend, Dude, would be proud of, "Miniscule be better than no scule."

Chapter Thirty-Seven

It was four hours before Charles was to pick me up for our trip to the old Coast Guard property. The weather was perfect. Puffy high clouds meandered through the deep blue sky; the temperature was in the lower eighties; plus, a kind breeze provided nature's air conditioning. I hadn't seen Barb for a couple of days so decided a walk would do me good.

I was turning the corner in front of Snapper Jack's and nearly ran into Sal, standing in the middle of the sidewalk, looking at the traffic light. He saw me, smiled, and pointed at the light that'd turned yellow. "Why does someone believe you when you say there are four billion stars, yet has to check when you say paint is wet?"

"Ask Dude. He's the astronomer."

Sal sighed. "It was a joke, Chris."

"I know."

"You're supposed to laugh, not recommend an astronomer."

"I know."

He mumbled, "Tough audience."

"Yep. Where're you headed?"

"Nowhere, but making good time. Actually, I'm walking off my hearty lunch."

"At the Crab Shack?"

"How'd you know? Oh, wait, I forgot, everyone here knows everyone else's business."

"A lucky guess. Theo said you'd made friends with some regulars."

"One of the things I hated about spending years on the road, travelling from venue to venue, telling the same stale jokes night after night, was not making good friends."

"What about the comedians you travelled with?"

"We all knew each other, but we spent more time stabbing each other in the back than making friends. Getting to know some of the guys, and gals, at the Crab Shack is a welcomed treat. Most of them, anyway. One old gal must've fallen off her rocker before it landed on her head. One guy seems mad at everything, including everyone. Somebody told me he had a couple of businesses that went belly up. It may be true, but why take it out on me? I wasn't here when it happened." He shook his head. "Then, God didn't implant a sense of humor in a couple of them. They look at me like I'd barfed up a squirm of worms after I tell a hilarious joke."

I bit the inside of my cheek to keep from laughing, or from telling him that those were probably the people with the best sense of humor. Instead, I said, "It takes all kinds." Time to change the subject. "How's Grace?"

"Don't know. She was gone when I rolled out of bed at the crack of noon. I'm trying to get in the swing of getting up early like Theo, or you other early birds." He looked at his watch. "I'm getting better."

I'd heard enough about his quest to experience more

daylight. Time to steer the conversation back to Grace. "Was she okay after I left last night?"

"I've seen worse. Often at my performances. She's shook. She masks it with her Jamaican charm, but she's mad as hell." He glanced back at the light then at me. "Don't blame her."

"How's your brother adjusting to both of you staying with him?"

Sal tilted his head to the left then to the right. "Hard to answer. I don't know how the old boy was before I moved in, so I couldn't say which of his many quirks are because I'm there, or if he was always that way. You might've noticed I occasionally tend to tell a joke before my mind catches up reminding me it may not be appropriate."

"I've noticed."

"I'll admit, I'm an acquired taste, like opera, or bourbon. Theo's seems to be catching on. He'll occasionally laugh at something I say. To answer part of your question, I think he's beginning to adjust to having his smarter, better-looking, wiser brother shacking up with him."

I almost laughed then realized he may not have been joking. "What about Grace?"

"She thinks I'm hilarious."

Another joke?

"No, I meant how is Theo adjusting to her being there?"

"I knew what you meant. I was being funny."

So, it was a joke. Hard to tell.

"How's he doing?"

Sal rubbed the side of his head as he looked down at the sidewalk. "Theo took the death of his son mighty hard. They had an off again, off again relationship. My poor brother now knows that it'll never get better. That hurt more than he'll admit. I think when Grace arrived, it brought all of Theo's pent-up feelings about Teddy to a head. He didn't know what to think about her."

"His hurt, anger, frustration, and every other negative emotion he had stuck down in his gut erupted on the poor gal. I felt sorry for her at first. Here she was, losing her husband, moving from California, trying to start a new life, meeting her pap-in-law for the first time. Add to that, Theo treating her like she was Freddy Krueger knocking on his door."

This was the first time I'd seen Sal's sensitive, perceptive side. "Theo's gotten over most of the hard feelings, hasn't he?"

"Grace is a cutie, a charmer. Theo's happier now than since I got here."

"That's great."

"Yeah, I've made him a happy man."

"I thought it was Grace."

"Chris, it was a joke."

I smiled. "I'll let you get to your walk. Let me know if you hear anything, if any of your new friends have any ideas about who torched her truck."

He walked away without a parting joke. Was it my lucky day, or what?

Two customers were meandering through the book shelves when I entered Barb's Books. The store's namesake was helping a young lady search for something in the young adult section. Barb wore tan shorts, a red blouse and, around her neck, a silver chain with a starfish-shaped charm dangling from it. I smiled, remembering how happy she was when I gave her the necklace for her birthday.

She saw me in the doorway. "Don't run off. I've got something to tell you."

The young customer found what she was looking for. She took two books to the checkout counter. After the customer paid, Barb glanced at the other browser leafing through a book in the far corner of the room.

Barb pecked my cheek. "Good afternoon, Christopher. What brings you in this lovely day?"

"You, of course. How's business?"

She told me it had been steady, also that I'd missed William who'd left a few minutes earlier. She added that a woman brought in a box of recent best-sellers to trade. I didn't figure that those facts were what she wanted me to stay for. I reminded her that she wanted to tell me something.

She continued to look toward the customer. "Stanley Kremitz was in first thing this morning. After picking up a copy of *The Catcher in the Rye* and telling me that it was an oldie goldie, he started talking about Abraham Gant."

"What about him?"

"He hinted that Gant, Captain Gant, had been bragging that nobody was going to be digging up the past on his island. Gant said Anthony got what he deserved. The same fate would come to anybody else who's stupid enough to defile the past."

"Did Stanley think Gant was implying that he killed Anthony?"

"He didn't put it that way, yet I had the impression that's what Stanley meant."

"He say anything else?"

"This is where it got strange. After he told me about Gant, he said he'd heard you and I were dating, and you've been asking a bunch of questions around town about the murder. He said he'd bet his bottom dollar you'd be interested in what Gant said."

"Was he hinting for you to tell me?"

"No doubt."

I told Barb about how Stanley had hinted that Abraham Gant could be the killer.

"You think he's trying to deflect attention from himself?"

"Yes."

Her eyes narrowed. In a muffled voice, she said, "And you've told this to the police so they, not you, could follow up."

Not quite a subtle hint. "I shared it with Chief LaMond."

"Good." She'd made her point, knowing it wouldn't do any good to reemphasize the part about the police following up.

The remaining customer approached the counter carrying several books, so I told Barb that I'd talk to her later.

Chapter Thirty-Eight

A dozen vehicles were parked along the street, and in the public parking area near the end of East Ashley Avenue, close to the entrance to the Lighthouse Inlet Heritage Preserve. Most likely, they belonged to a combination of residents at nearby rental houses, and vacationers who'd walked to the far end of the Preserve to view the Morris Island Lighthouse. Charles parked close to the houses so, if most of the vehicles left while we were there, his car would look like it belonged to one of the renters.

It was still more than an hour before sunset. I looked at Charles, who was wearing his black, long-sleeved NYPD T-shirt he reserves for times he's either meeting with cops, or pretending to be a detective. "Okay, Charles, this is your plan. What now?"

He tilted his Tilley back on his head. "Figured we'd sit a spell in air-conditioning while we watch for somebody walking toward the entrance, carrying a treasure map, and a shovel."

"No wonder you're the detective. In case that brilliant strategy doesn't work, what's Plan B?"

He twisted his head toward the Preserve. "We amble about, walk up and down the paths, spend time near where they found Anthony, and hope to see someone acting suspicious."

"Other than us?"

"You have a better idea?"

I shook my head, slid the seat back, and lowered the back. A family of five strolled toward the Preserve's entrance as an elderly couple walked arm-in-arm the other direction. The old Coast Guard property was one of Folly's most popular sites. During summer months, there were often traffic jams near the entrance. If nothing else, we would get a chance to people watch.

Charles was unusually quiet and had leaned back. I asked if he'd heard about the fire at *Hot Diggity Dog!*"

He sat up straight, jerking his head toward me. "Fire?"

I told him about going to supper with Theo and Grace then what'd happened while we were gone.

He growled, "Why didn't you tell me earlier?"

I explained it was late when it happened. Besides, I was telling him now.

"Are you certain it was arson?"

"Certain, no. Cindy thought so, but was waiting until she got a report from the arson investigator."

He pulled a phone from his pocket and punched in a number. A few seconds later, he said, "Please hold, chief. Chris Landrum has a question." He thrust the phone at me.

"What did I do to deserve to have my peaceful supper with Larry interrupted by a call from your secretary?"

I chuckled. "I'll tell my *secretary* you were upset."

Charles leaned back in the seat like I'd smacked him.

Cindy said, "Good."

"Have you heard from the arson investigator?"

"Yes."

The phone went dead.

I handed the phone to Charles as I relayed Cindy's one-word answer.

He tapped *redial*.

This time, Larry answered. "Chief LaMond's secretary speaking. Who may I ask is calling?"

I laughed, irritating Charles, but getting a chuckle from Larry. "You may tell her it's Nosy Charles with his young, handsome friend Chris."

Larry's chuckle turned to a laugh before he said, "The chief wanted me to tell you the fire was intentionally set. If you call one more time tonight, she'll issue warrants for both of you, the charge being first degree pissing off a police chief."

The phone went dead a second time.

I relayed the longer message to Charles, adding that, if he called a third time, not to hand me the phone.

He wisely chose not to call. Instead, he said, "Who'd want to torch a food truck? Who'd possibly have a problem with Grace? She's only been here a few days, open for business one day."

I told him those were the same questions Grace, Theo, and even Sal had asked, with no good answers forthcoming.

"Know any hot dog hating pyromaniacs?"

"I don't know any pyromaniacs who hate any of the food groups," I said. "Besides, the first two break ins happened before Grace sold a single hot dog here."

"Could someone with a grudge have followed her from California?"

"That's possible, although it's a long way to come to ruin her business. If there was anyone out there, he would've done something before she headed to South Carolina. I don't know of—"

His arm flailed. "Whoa. Hold that thought. Isn't that Stanley Cliché Kremitz?"

He pointed to a lone walker heading to the stanchion guarding the Preserve.

Stanley was heading toward the entrance to the Preserve. Instead of a treasure map, or a shovel, he carried a walking stick with binoculars strapped around his neck. "Doesn't look like he's ready to look for buried treasure."

Charles looked at me like I was a blue chipmunk. "Gee, Chris, don't you know a disguise when you see one?"

I thought the definition of a disguise was something you didn't recognize when you saw it. Instead of sharing that, I said, "If it is, it's a good one. Think he'll dig up the treasure with binoculars?"

"Don't know. Let's find out."

I had to admit it. I didn't have a better plan, so we began following Stanley. We grabbed our cameras so, if he saw us, we'd have a logical reason for being there. He was walking down the paved road that bisected the property so, if he looked back, he couldn't miss us.

Stanley stopped a third of the way shy of where the pavement ended, and a thick, sandy path continued to the beach. He looked at his phone then turned off the paved area where he moved down a narrow path toward the ocean.

We followed at a safe distance. When we reached the point where he left the road, I motioned for Charles to stop. The path that Stanley had taken was barely visible from the road as it weaved through a heavily wooded area. Windswept oaks and shrubs of all sizes were intertwined, blocking easy movement through the area unless you stayed on the sandy path. "If we follow him, there's a good chance he'll spot us."

Charles said, "What's our plan?"

I didn't point out that there was no "our" plan since it was his idea to be here.

"There's another path a hundred feet or so up the road. I think it meets this one near the beach. There's less chance of getting caught if we go that way."

"I knew you'd have a plan." Charles said, as he started walking.

We reached the second path as three men emerged. Their faces were covered with sweat, their white dress shirts soaked in perspiration, their black wingtips sand-covered.

I nodded.

One of them asked if it was always this hot.

A second man said, "Knew we should've gone to the afternoon's meeting."

The third one said, "It wasn't my idea to leave the pavement, to wander through brambles."

We wished them well, watched them reach the *pavement*, then laughed at their inappropriate dress before we continued in the direction that Stanley had taken.

The methodical sound of waves crashing against the shore told me that we were near the spot where the narrow path reached the foliage facing the beach. I thought that was where the path Stanley had taken merged with our trail. I motioned for Charles to stop so we could listen for anything that'd indicate Stanley's location.

We didn't have long to wait. Mixed with the sounds of the water slapping the shore, I heard laughter coming from more than one person; at least one male, possibly two females.

Charles leaned close and whispered, "Doesn't sound like a treasure-hunting party."

We moved a few yards closer to the sounds when I saw two men and two women. Stanley, the only one I recognized, put his forefinger to his mouth, a sign to silence the group, as he pointed toward the top of a nearby tree. The others stopped talking and raised binoculars to face the tree Stanley was motioning toward. I couldn't see what was so fascinating.

"Oh, great," Charles said. "We've caught a bevy of bird-watchers."

I smiled. "Maybe the pirates hid the gold in the top of that tree."

"Funny, Sal."

That hurt.

"Do you know any of them, other than Stanley?"

He shook his head. "No, just a group of bird-watchers."

"Birds of a feather flock together," I said with my best, albeit lousy, Stanley imitation.

Charles smacked my arm, pivoted, and started back toward the paved road. I didn't blame him.

Instead of heading to the car, we decided that, while we were here, we should walk the rest of the way to the beach overlooking the lighthouse. It was worth the walk. Sunset was approaching so that the low sun behind us illuminated the lighthouse. The tide was out. The remnants of Morris Island and sandbars closer to us were exposed, appearing golden brown in the fading sun.

We took several photos of the lighthouse, the subject of countless images over the years and, since sunset was close, I suggested that we return to the car. On the way, we passed the path that led to where the lifeless body of Anthony was discovered.

Charles said that it might be a good idea to start our next casing of the Preserve closer to that spot. He figured that, since Anthony was searching in the vicinity, the map must've shown him something to pick this spot. I agreed, since I didn't have a better suggestion. When we got to the car, there were three vehicles in the area as opposed to the dozen or so when we arrived. Lights were on in two of the eight houses closest to our car, so I assumed the vehicles belonged to the residents. If my assumption was accurate, all the visitors to the Preserve, including the bird-watchers, were gone.

"Same time, same place, tomorrow?" Charles said as he dropped me off at the house.

Same time, same place, same result, I thought.

Chapter Thirty-Nine

The phone jolted me awake. I blinked twice to focus my eyes then saw that it was after 11:00 p.m. I'd been asleep for an hour and nearly fell out of bed, reaching for the buzzing, exasperating piece of technology that woke me. It portended either a wrong number or a disaster. Everyone who knew me understood calling after ten o'clock was tantamount to a declaration of war.

I managed to hit the answer button. "Hello."

The cheery, wide-awake voice of someone I would've put last on the list of people I expected to call, said, "Chris, this is your good buddy, Sal. Didn't wake you, did I? Hey, did you know that a professor is someone who walks, umm, I mean talks in someone else's sleep?"

I held the phone away from my ear, shook my head awake. "Okay, yes, no."

"Huh?" Sal said, further proof that he not only ignores what others say, but he doesn't even listen to himself.

"Never mind. Other than waking me, what's up?"

"Cranky in your old age, aren't you?"

I heard voices and music in the background. "What is it, Sal?"

"I heard something I thought you might be interested in. Remember I told you about a guy at the Crab Shack who had a couple of businesses that flatlined?"

"What about him?"

"Ran into him tonight at, umm," he said. I heard him ask someone, "What's the name of this joint?" He returned. "The Washout, yeah, that's where I am. Umm, didn't wake you, did I?"

For the second time, I thought *Yes*, wondered how long Sal had been in the bar, and said, "The man with the businesses?"

"Oh, yeah. When I got here, two or it could've been three hours ago, he was spoused, umm, soused. The old boy was soused, plus plastered when he left, maybe fifteen minutes ago."

I had the strong suspicion that Sal was well on his way to soused plus plastered. "What about the man, Sal?"

"Marember, umm, remember, I told you he had two busted businesses?"

"Yes," I said through clenched teeth.

"Guess what he told me they were?"

I was close to hanging up, yet he called for a reason. During years of putting up with Charles's quirks, not to mention the idiosyncrasies of several other friends, I'd acquired a tolerance for thinking that was not only outside the box, but so far outside that you couldn't see the box.

"Sal, why don't you tell me?"

"You're no fun. Okay, here goes, one was a miniature golf course, can you believe that?"

That bit of trivia couldn't wait until the morning?

"Interesting," I said, with total insincerity.

"The other one was a food truck."

That got my attention. "Why was he telling you this?"

"Suppose because I'm a nice guy, someone folks can easily talk to, a good listener." Sal laughed. "Kidding. Remember the soused part of my story? He was talking to me because I was sitting beside him at the bar. He could've been talking to the column that's holding up the roof on this here patio. Now that I think about it, that's what he was talking to when I sat down."

"Sal, what did he say that made you call?"

I heard him take a gulp of something, most likely beer, most likely his seventy-third of the night. "His golf course was in nowhere Ohio. His food truck was," Sal hesitated, and chuckled, "anywhere its wheels took it. It was a truck, get it?"

"Your point, Sal?"

"Has anyone told you you're no fun?"

"Many times."

"Okay, here's the skinny. He told me the reason his golf course went bust was because the only time anyone played miniature golf was in the slumber, umm, summer. Said even if the balls were orange, playing in the snow turned golfers off."

"Who would've guessed that?"

"The food truck hit the skids, figuratively speaking, I think, when the blankety, blank permit people harassed him so much, he couldn't stay open. A closed food truck don't sell much food."

He hesitated again, the music in the background got louder, and he continued, "My point is the guy told me ever since the blankety, blankety permit people shut him down, he's hated food trucks. They remind him of failing. Right before he fell off the bar stool, had to be led, or more like, carried out by two guys I didn't know, he slurred that if he had his way, all food trucks would be nuked."

"Sal, what's the man's name?"

"I'm not good with names. It's one of those Bible names. Like Matthew, or Mark, don't think it's puke, umm, Luke. Wait, something's coming to me. Got it. I know it's not John."

"Did he say anything about Grace's truck?"

"Yes, sir, he did. Want to know what?"

Sal should be glad that I'm talking to him on the phone. If I was at The Washout, my hands would be around his neck.

"Yes, Sal."

"Thought so. He said, and this is a direct quote, '*Hot Diggity Dog!* Best damned fire I've ever seen.' Think that's a flew, umm, clue?"

"Sal, are you certain he said best fire he'd ever seen? Could it have been set instead of seen?"

I had to move the phone away from my ear when Sal shouted, "Barkeep, another brewski!" I heard a bottle hitting the bar and someone in the background talking about a baseball score before Sal returned to our conversation.

"What was the question again?"

I repeated it.

"Chris, I've had a couple of beers. My mind's not razor sharp, like it usually is. Give me a minute to ponder it."

From what I've observed, in the best of times, Sal's mind was as sharp as a tennis ball, so I wasn't optimistic about his recollections.

Apparently, the *barkeep* returned with Sal's drink. My near-soused "good buddy" mumbled, "Thanks." After what sounded like him taking a drink, he said, "Okay, think I've got the answer. You asked if he said set instead of seen, right?"

"Yes."

"Drum roll, please," he said. I heard his hand pounding on the bar. "The answer is maybe."

I closed my eyes, opened them, and stared at the phone. "Maybe?"

"Yes, sir, that's my best recollection. Maybe he did. Maybe he didn't. Think that's another clue?"

Maybe, I thought, then realized the odds of me getting anything useful out of Sal in his current condition was as likely as me measuring the circumference of the earth with a yardstick. I thanked him for calling. He said that he thought I'd called him.

The phone went dead.

I fell back on the bed, wondered, no hoped, that I'd dreamed the conversation with Sal, realized I was awake, and it really was my new, good "good buddy" on the phone. I decided that I'd sleep on what Sal had said then call Chief LaMond in the morning to share what he'd almost said.

———

By 8:00, I grasped my wish to sleep on Sal's message had been elusive. I'd watched the clock pass each hour and pushed myself out of bed to head to the shower. Twenty minutes later, I felt as refreshed as I could after counting my sleep in minutes rather than hours. I punched Cindy's number into my phone.

She answered with a loud sigh before saying, "Unless you're dead, staring at a dead body, your house is on fire, or you want to give me a yacht, this is a recording. My office hours start at nine o'clock."

Not quite the mood I'd hoped to find her in, although it was encouraging that she hadn't already hung up.

"Good morning, chief. It's going to be a wonderful day."

I hadn't looked out the window, so I had no idea if it was true. Even if I had, my tired, watery eyes wouldn't have been able to see what kind of day it was.

"Yeah, yeah, Sugarmouth. What?"

I told her about my conversation with my "good buddy,"

Sal. Cindy either listened patiently without interrupting, or she had fallen asleep. I finished and said, "You still there?"

She chuckled. "Afraid so. Theo's not-funny brother was talking about Joseph Tannery."

"How do you get that from Matthew, or Mark? Oh, I get it, Joseph is a Biblical name."

"Chris, I'm many things. A Bible scholar ain't one of them. The miniature golf course gave it away."

"Huh?"

"Remember a couple of years after you moved here, somebody opened a miniature golf course on Center Street? It wasn't there long. Our guys had to arrest Joseph Tannery three times for disturbing the peace. The old boy would get drunk, stand near the entrance of the course, where he'd yell at customers not to waste money playing."

"Why'd he do that?"

"Chris, in addition to not being a Biblical scholar, I'm not a head shrink. I don't know what screws in his head came unthreaded. He told the cops he had a miniature golf course somewhere in the North. It went bust. He'd rant on that if he couldn't make it with kids hitting colorful golf balls through windmills and other stupid crap, the course on Folly shouldn't be able to."

"Who's Joseph Tannery?"

"Squatty-bodied guy, mid-fifties, jittery-like, harmless when sober. He was a big-time pain in our collective law-enforcement butts a few years back until some wise head doc suggested Mr. Tannery spend quality time in the nut house. He was gone a few years, returned a year ago, I haven't heard any negative reports on him since then."

"Did he ever mention anything about food trucks?"

Cindy was silent for a moment. Finally, she said, "I hadn't thought about it until now. When he got back from his mental respite, he caused a minor ruckus in front of Tokyo Crepes. I'll pull the report. I seem to recall him being upset because the food truck always had a line of customers. My guys didn't arrest him. Tannery apologized and went on his way. It appeared that his time having his noggin screwed back together did him good."

"That's it?"

"Pretty sure I would've remembered it if he said he was going to torch it. Tell you what, I'll review what happened at Tokyo Crepes, and see if I can find where he's staying. I'll have one of my guys ask if he wants to have a tour of our lovely police department so I can see what he knows about the weenie roast in Theo's drive."

I told her that sounded like a great idea. She told me that it was a police matter and to wring out of my brain the notion about getting involved. I told her I understood; understood, but not that I wouldn't get involved.

Chapter Forty

The phone rang two hours later, so I figured it was Cindy calling with a report on Joseph Tannery. Wrong. It was Charles inviting me to lunch at twelve-thirty at Rita's. He was buying. I should've known there was no such thing as a free lunch when he added that Laurie, Dean, and Gail would be joining us. Other than Charles, they wouldn't have been on my *A* list of people to eat with. I hesitated then he reminded me I had to eat somewhere.

It turned out to be the kind of wonderful day I'd only speculated about during my conversation with Cindy. I walked two blocks to the restaurant where I saw the others seated on the patio, enjoying the weather, two beers, and a glass of wine.

Charles waved me thought the patio's gate. He wore a smile, gray shorts, and a red and black, long-sleeved T-shirt with *FROSTBURG STATE UNIVERSITY BOBCATS* in block letters on the front. The other three at the table were dressed in traditional beach garb, not displaying allegiances to anything. Charles had pulled a fifth chair to the table and nodded for me to join them.

Laurie pointed at Charles's T-shirt, smiled, and said, "It's in Maryland."

"Oh," I said, hoping that ended the discussion about the shirt.

"Dean and I are glad you could make it. We got in this morning. Going to spend a few days with Laurie," Gail said, taking charge of the conversation. Surprise. Surprise.

Dean nodded agreement, a motion I suspected he was accustomed to making.

Kim, the server who'd waited on Barb and me during our recent visit, moved beside me to ask what I wanted to drink. I would have preferred a soft drink, but figured I'd need wine for lunch with Gail and Dean. I ordered Chardonnay.

We spent fifteen minutes sharing the niceties people who don't know each other well talk about: weather, traffic, food, and more weather. It was turning out to be a pleasant conversation, until Laurie said how glad she was Dean had taken time from his business to be here.

Gail jerked her head toward her husband and gripped the edge of the table so tightly her knuckles turned white. "Running from the feakin' bill collectors is more like it."

"Now, Gail," Laurie said as she touched her friend's arm. "Charles and Chris don't want to hear about it."

She was wrong about Charles. He wouldn't give up until he knew what "it" was.

Charles said, "That's okay, Laurie, you're among friends."

Dean blinked, then in a lower voice said, "It's no big deal. We've had a couple of financial setbacks. Nothing to worry about."

I thought Gail was going to spring over the table. "Nothing to worry about! Losing the business, losing our house is nothing to worry about?"

Laurie looked like she wanted to crawl under the table. She slowly shook her head and stared at her empty wine glass.

I caught a glimpse of Kim behind Laurie, so I motioned her to the table. With luck, an interruption might calm Gail.

Kim asked if we were ready to order.

Without checking with anyone else, Charles said that we were.

Gail started to speak, took a deep breath, then glanced at the menu. Tension subsided slightly as we went around the table making selections.

When it got to Dean, he told Kim that he wasn't hungry. He pushed away from the table and stormed out the gate.

Kim took it in stride, saying that she'd place our orders.

After an awkward silence, Gail said, "I apologize. I'm afraid the business is lost. Dean can't fight any longer. Folks, as goes the store, so goes our house. We've been living off credit cards for months. Sorry to dump this on you."

I was thinking how terrible it must be for them yet laying it on a friend who recently lost her husband seemed insensitive. I was thinking about Laurie's situation while Charles was telling Gail something about how sorry he was, when a comment by Gail joggled me back to reality.

She had thanked Charles for his sympathy and was talking to Laurie. "I'm leaving him."

Laurie stared at her friend. "What?"

"You heard me. I'm leaving Dean."

Laurie said, "Why?"

"He's having an affair."

I reminded myself that Charles was paying for this soap opera. I sat back to watch the show.

Laurie looked at the gate where Dean had exited. "How do you know?"

"Remember when we were supposed to be here with you relic hunting?"

"Sure."

Gail bobbed her head. "Dean said he couldn't come, that I should come by myself. He said he had to be at a tire meeting in Tallahassee."

Laurie said, "I remember."

"He wasn't."

"How do you know?"

"One of his tire buddies called the day Anthony was killed. He asked to talk to Dean, said Dean didn't answer his cell phone. I told him I thought my husband was with him in Tallahassee. He said he would've been if the meeting hadn't been cancelled. That wasn't the first time he'd lied about being out of town on business."

I wasn't nearly as interested in Dean and Gail's marital status as I was to learn that despite her earlier claims that she had been with her husband in Jacksonville when Anthony was killed, she wasn't. I also recalled that when I'd asked Laurie who knew she and Anthony would've been hunting for relics the night he was killed, she'd said she hadn't told anyone, which could've meant not told anyone on Folly.

I asked, "When did Dean get home?"

Gail turned to me and seemed stunned that I'd said anything. "Don't know. He was there when I got home, so I was more interested in where he'd been. He acted surprised I'd asked then gave me a song and dance about being in Tallahassee. I shut him up before he could weave his way through a pack of lies. I told him I knew he wasn't at a meeting."

Our food arrived. Laurie started on hers like she was starved. My guess was that she'd rather eat than join in the conversation. I was with her on that. Charles, on the other hand, was in his element. "Gail, how long—"

Gail pointed her fork at Charles. "Enough. I don't want to burden Laurie with my problems. Let's enjoy the weather, the food."

"That's okay," Laurie said, "I know it must—"

"I said enough," Gail said through a snarl.

The rest of our meal was eaten in peace, okay, silence, not peace.

After more than forty-five minutes of the most awkward meal I could remember, Charles paid the check.

Gail said she and Laurie needed to go to Harris Teeter to get cleaning supplies.

Laurie gave me a hug and a peck on the cheek then gave a longer hug to Charles and a super-sized peck on the cheek, more accurately, a kiss. She said that she'd call him later.

Charles and I moved to the bar to give the table to diners who'd been patiently waiting.

He told me he was still buying and added, "Wonder what took Dean so long to decide to leave Gail? That woman would drive me batty. Hope Dean's new squeeze knows he can talk."

Kim told the bartender what we'd been drinking, so he delivered beer to Charles, white wine to me, without our asking.

"Did you get what she'd said about Dean not being at the meeting in Tallahassee?"

Charles took a sip of beer. "Would've been hard to miss. I also remembered them saying they'd planned to be relic hunting with Anthony and Laurie but didn't make the trip because of Dean's meeting."

I added, "They knew Laurie and Anthony would be at the Preserve."

"Laurie said she didn't tell anyone here."

"She wasn't sure if Anthony told anyone."

Charles rubbed his chin. "Dean would've had a whopping motive to kill Anthony for the map."

"A failing store, losing his house, losing his wife."

"All good reasons. Remember, when the shot was taken at Laurie, Gail was here without Dean. He could've been with his new chick interest, or here shooting at Laurie."

"Before we accuse Dean, think about something else. Gail was already here and could've easily taken the shot. Remember what she said over there?" I pointed to the table where we'd been.

"Which part? She said a heap of hostile stuff."

"When I asked her when Dean got back from his alleged trip to Tallahassee, she said she wasn't there when he got home."

"So?"

"So," I said, "she could've been killing Anthony, stealing the map."

Charles dipped his head and tapped on the bar. "She could also have been at the grocery, getting a facial, dominating someone's conversation, or hanging with a friend making the friend's life miserable."

"True. What we do know is she was on Folly when the first shot was taken at Laurie; she wasn't with Dean when Anthony was killed."

Charles rubbed his temple. "Let's change the subject. All I get from thinking about this is a headache, a headache that started when dear, sweet Gail started unloading on Dean."

I nodded. "Do you know Joseph Tannery?"

"Whoa. I thought I'd cornered the market on abrupt turns in a conversation."

"I've learned from the best. Tannery?"

"Met him a couple of times. Don't know him well. Why?"

I shared what Sal had said about Tannery's discussion plus what Cindy had told me about the miniature golf course.

Charles stared at me. "You're taking crime-fighting advice from Sal?"

"Advice, no. Information, yes. What do you know about Tannery?"

"I remember the incident in front of the miniature golf course. I was there. I doubt Tannery remembers it. He was so drunk that if someone had walked by with a lit cigarette, his breath would've caught fire. I didn't see him for a few years after that. In fact, the next time I saw him was last week on the sidewalk. I nodded. He nodded. We didn't speak."

"Think he could've damaged and then burned Grace's food truck?"

"In the old days, he could've. I don't know about now. Do we need to find him so I can trick a confession out of him?"

"It's in the capable hands of the police."

"If you say so."

Chapter Forty-One

Hanging with Charles at the Preserve afternoon number two began a couple hours after we'd gone our separate ways from Rita's. I thought it was a futile effort. I didn't point that out when he picked me up at the house. If I'd mentioned it, he'd ask what I had better to do. I'd admit not a thing. I hopped in the car, put my Nikon on the back seat beside his.

He said, "Ready to catch a killer?"

I said sure.

There were more cars near the entrance than there were yesterday, most likely, belonging to vacationers.

Clouds had rolled in providing a welcomed relief from direct sunlight. The temperature was still in the upper eighties, yet tolerable. We followed a similar path to the one we'd taken the day before. There were no birdwatchers, and we returned to the pavement and walked most of the way to where the roadway ended, a spot where large elevated foundations left from the Coast Guard buildings had been recently removed.

During the half hour we sat on a couple of large rocks, two dozen people walked past: two groups of four, a couple of men pulling fishing carts, three bicyclists, and several couples ranging in age from teenagers to seasoned citizens. None of them carried a shovel, or a metal detector.

Charles was unusually quiet most of the time.

I asked him twice what was wrong.

Both times, he said nothing.

I didn't believe him, but knew that he would tell me when he was ready. I suggested that we walk farther up the road to explore a path on the marsh side of the pavement.

He shrugged then moved beside me as I walked a hundred yards until I saw the narrow path leading to our left. Branches provided a low canopy over much of the way, so we walked single file through the tightest spots.

The path opened to a wide area overlooking the marsh. There were burnt logs in the clearing, evidence that someone had built a fire. What wasn't there was evidence of digging. We could hear voices coming from the beach fifty or so yards to our right, plus the sound of birds squawking about something.

Charles plopped down on a large, unburnt log, removed his Tilley and wiped his forehead with his arm. "Chris, I know you think this is a waste of time. It probably is. I'm worried about Laurie, don't know what else to do. We've seen too many of our friends hurt. I don't want her on that list."

"You like her, don't you?"

He looked at the sandy soil then kicked a piece of blackened wood. "I don't know. She's nice. For some reason, she latched onto me. She calls nearly every day. Look how many times she's wanted me to eat with her."

He rubbed a question mark in the sand with his foot. "I've seen videos of an animal, let's say a dog, rescuing another kind of critter, a baby duck, for example. The baby critter starts hanging around its rescuer, follows it wherever it goes, does stuff a duck would never do if it hadn't been rescued by the dog. I was the first person Laurie saw after that traumatic night. Could she be the baby duck, me the dog? Could that be why she's acting like that with me?"

"That'd make sense."

"I've had one serious romantic relationship in my million years on earth. That's not a lot of experience, so I don't know what to think, or do. I like her, think it's possible that, someday, it could turn to something more. If she's latched on me because of the dog/duck thing, I'd be barking up the wrong palmetto tree." He looked at me. "What do I do?"

I was stuck on the dog/duck thing and palmetto tree. I hesitated before saying, "Charles, time's the only thing that'll answer that question. You need to be yourself then see what happens."

"Gee, Chris, who but me can I be?"

"What I mean is don't try to be someone you're not. Don't try to change to be what you think she wants. You being you is wonderful."

"Thanks. That still doesn't help keep her safe. The only way that'll happen is for Anthony's killer to spend the rest of his life eating slop, while looking at concrete block walls and bars. How're we going to make that happen?"

I told him that I didn't know. I suggested that we weren't accomplishing anything out here. He grumbled, made a mild case for how it might help before kicking the ground one more time, then agreed with me.

We were getting in the car when Charles pointed to an older model, black Mercury Grand Marquis parked two cars over. "That's Captain Gant's car."

"You sure?"

"Yeah," Charles said as he opened the door and stepped out. "He told me he liked it because it reminded him of the Ford Crown Vics he drove when he was with the state cops. I also remember that AAA decal on the bumper. Let's find him." He started back toward the stanchions blocking the entrance to the Preserve before I made it out of the car. He didn't stay around long enough for me to suggest that Gant may be visiting one of the houses near his car instead of being at the Preserve.

I grabbed my camera then jogged to catch Charles. He had a renewed step in his gait while tapping his cane on the pavement like he was on a mission. I was less enthusiastic since we were charging off after a retired cop, a possible murderer. By the time I caught up with Charles, he was scanning each side of the road, reminding me of a coonhound sniffing the air in search of its prey. It was nearing sunset, so the number of walkers had thinned.

We passed the spot where we'd spent time earlier when Charles said, "This way. I think I saw someone."

He pushed the branches out of his face and bent down to miss higher hanging limbs as he made his way down a narrow path leading toward the beach. We had to walk single file, so I was a couple of feet behind him when someone barked, "Stop!"

I twisted around to see Captain Gant stepping out from behind a large tree. He wore a short-sleeved black shirt, baggy camouflage-patterned slacks, and a snarl that would terrify anyone under the age of sixteen. That wasn't what caught my eye. What grabbed my attention was the silver handgun pointed at my chest.

I turned to get a better look when he said, "Don't move. Slowly clasp your hands behind your head."

I was in no position to tell him we could do one or the

other, not both. Charles moved beside me and mimicked the movement of my hands. Gant was too far away for me to grab the gun, yet close enough to not miss if he pulled the trigger.

He waved the handgun toward a log about five feet off the path. "Slowly walk over there and sit."

If Charles and I quickly split up, the odds were one of us could get to the gun. The downside being one of us would most likely be shot.

Think quickly. What other options did we have?

Better to follow his command, for now.

We did. He looked at Charles then at me, before saying, "Where's the map?"

My voice crackled as I said, "We don't have it."

He pointed the gun at my shorts. "Empty your pockets."

I wasn't fast enough. He said, "Now! Back pockets, too."

We removed everything from our pockets, placing it on the log beside us. Gant looked at our wallets, car keys, a ballpoint pen I kept with me. "Where is it?"

I knew what he'd meant. I also knew how unhappy he'd be with my answer. "We don't have it. Why do you think we do?"

"Because you took it after killing that damned relic hunter."

That was the last answer I would've expected.

Charles took a deep breath. "We thought you killed him."

Gant looked at Charles like he'd seen the ghost of Blackbeard. "You what? That's preposterous. Crap, I'm a retired cop. You know, law and order. Why would I kill him?"

"Because you hated him, didn't want him digging up the past," Charles said.

"Holy smokes, Charles, I hate lots of people. If I went and killed all of them, this island would be near empty."

Charles said, "What are you doing out here? While you're thinking up an answer, could you lower that gun?"

"Not on your life. I'm here to catch whoever has the damned map and is trying to dig up the loot." He waved the gun at Charles. "What in the hell are you doing here?"

"We saw your car at the entrance, came looking for you. Chris thought you might be trying to find the treasure."

Thanks, Charles.

Gant continued staring at us. I suppose he didn't know what to think. He wasn't alone. Beads of sweat rolled down his face.

"Captain," I said, "why don't you have a seat? Let's talk about it."

He must not have seen us as a threat. He sat on the log out of our reach, picked a sandspur off his camo pants, before turning to Charles. "I got intel someone was going to be out here digging, digging for Civil War relics or gold. What's buried must remain buried."

I was sick of hearing his tiring mantra. "What intel? Who told you?"

He turned my direction and scowled. He wasn't accustomed to being on the receiving side of an interrogation. "Bar talk. Don't know his name. He said word was going around someone got a treasure map off the dead guy. The guy said it was that nosy guy who was here when the cops found the body. That was you. If that's not why you're here, why are you?"

"It's a nice day, so Charles and I decided to walk out to where we could see the lighthouse to grab a photo, or two." I held my camera as part of my multi-media presentation.

It was a camera, not a shovel, so Gant appeared to buy my story. He rubbed his hands over his thighs, shook his head. "I'm too old for this crap. In my prime, I could stake out a spot for hours." Out of character, he chuckled. "That was back when I didn't have to pee every half hour. Damned prostate."

I nodded like I understood. Thankfully, I didn't.

He set the gun on the log, looked at me, then at Charles. "If one of you didn't shoot the guy, and I know I didn't, who did?"

Charles said, "That's what we're trying to find out."

"Did you tell Chief LaMond you thought I was the killer?"

Charles bowed. "We might've mentioned something about it."

Gant smiled. "Figures. That's why she came to my place to ask where I was when he was killed."

"Could be," Charles said, one of his rare understatements.

The Captain shook his head then repeated, "I'm getting too old for this."

So am I, I thought.

Charles didn't admit to aging. He said, "Any idea who might've shot him, other than us?"

"Probably the lovey-dovey wife. They're always the first in the line of suspects."

Charles sat up straighter. "She didn't do it."

"You sure?"

I wondered the same thing.

Charles said, "Yes."

Gant shrugged. "Suppose it's someone else, then." He nodded toward the handgun. "Fellas, sorry I pulled this on you. When I'm wrong, I admit it. Here's some advice. Instead of following strangers out here, leave it to the police. It's their job." He looked around. "I better head to the *casa* and let you get on your way."

We agreed and watched him walk away. I suggested that we wait on the log until he left the parking area before heading out. Charles said Gant was one more suspect to remove from the list. He didn't have a shovel with him today. In my mind, that still didn't eliminate him, although he was convincing when he accused us of being the killer. Add to that, he didn't appear to know the map's whereabouts. I shared my thoughts with Charles. He said, after our eventful lunch with Laurie and her "friends," his sharing his feelings about Laurie with me, the encounter with Gant and his gun, he was too tired to think straight. I wasn't far behind.

Chapter Forty-Two

The clouds that blanketed the area during the day turned ferocious overnight. Heavy rain pelted the tin roof, the accompanying wind whistled as it leaked through cracks around my ancient windows rattling the panes. I'm a heavy sleeper, so I would've missed most of the rain, and wind, had it not been for Anthony's murder bouncing around in my head. Gant was correct when he said we should leave it to the police. So why wasn't I willing to let it go?

I knew the answer, but simply didn't want to admit it. Charles and I were there when his body was found. Laurie latched onto us, no, latched onto Charles, who was my best friend. The more I got to know her, her friends, and others who were pulled into the situation, the closer I was to being involved.

The police should solve it, yet they'd already admitted the murder wasn't on top of their growing caseload. Besides, Charles and I'd already spent more time with Laurie and the potential suspects than had the police. Did I learn anything that would point to the killer? A clap of thunder rocked the house, and rocked me awake. It was a little past three and, regardless how much I wanted it to, sleep wouldn't return. I padded my way to the kitchen, started a pot of coffee, then stared at the darkness outside the rain-drenched window.

Despite Charles, and my encounter with Captain Gant and the story he'd shared, I wasn't convinced that he was innocent. His over-the-top reaction to anyone having the audacity to dig up the past made it easy for me to keep the door open to his guilt. Yet, if he was guilty, wouldn't he have the map? Then, what about the "intel" that someone told him in a bar that we had the missing document.

That brought me to Laurie. On the surface, she was the obvious suspect. Her story about getting separated from Anthony, finding the car, and falling asleep was nearly as farfetched as Gant's story that he heard about us in a bar. She was the only person we knew who'd been at the Preserve when her husband was shot. The insurance policy would've been a motive. She'd given us conflicting stories about getting separated from her husband, and more conflicting versions of where she was when the first shot was fired through her window. She may've killed her husband, but she couldn't have taken the shot when Charles and I were with her.

Was it possible that the shootings at her house had nothing to do with her husband's murder? Unlikely. Another possibility was that she had an accomplice. The second person could've taken the shot when we were there to deflect suspicion from Laurie. I tried to remember the sequence of events surrounding the shots fired into Laurie's house. Gail was there but had gone to the grocery the first time, so Laurie could've pulled the trigger. Nothing else from the first event had stuck out as being significant other than Laurie telling two versions of where she'd been.

The second shooting into the house left a larger impact

since I was there. Laurie acted terrified. Real or faked? I took two large sips and remembered something that occurred after the shooting. Laurie called Gail to see if she could come stay with her for a few days. Gail hadn't answered, so Laurie called Dean who told her Gail was out of town and may've left her phone in the hotel room. He hadn't told Laurie where Gail was. Was it possible that she was standing outside Laurie's house?

Gail was pushy, always interrupting her friend, and someone I dreaded spending time with. I'd never considered her a murderer until the other day. She knew about the map. Her husband's business was in trouble, as was their marriage. She had said that she and Dean were supposed to be with Anthony and Laurie when Anthony was killed but didn't come because Dean was at a meeting out of town. That meant she could've been on Folly for all three incidents.

It was still raining, although the torrential downpour had eased. I must've drifted asleep in the chair. The sky had lightened, my clock indicated sunrise was minutes away. I stood. My back told me that not only had I fallen asleep, I'd fallen asleep in an awkward position. I got dressed and remembered the Captain's advice about leaving it to the police. I decided to tell the chief what'd happened with Gant in the Preserve and my suspicions about Gail. I also decided that I was hungry so the call to Cindy could wait until after breakfast. I drove to the Dog, which had just opened. The heavy rain had kept the crowds away, so I had my choice of tables and headed to my favorite. Kimberly, one of several friendly servers, was quick to the table with coffee and a cheerful greeting, both welcomed.

My need to call Chief LaMond ended when I saw her coming in the door. She took off her raincoat, wiped water off its shoulders, looked around the dining room, saw me, and came my way.

"Went by your house, and your car wasn't there." She slid in the booth opposite me. "Figured I'd find you here. What're you buying me for breakfast?"

"You went by the house to see if I wanted to take you to breakfast?"

"Nope." She nodded to the entrance. "That inspiration came when I got here, saw your car, and my stomach growled."

Kimberly was back at the table, so Cindy said, "Coffee, and the most expensive breakfast on the menu, whatever it is."

I told the server that I'd stick to French toast, even though there were more expensive options.

Kimberly headed to the kitchen, and I said, "Glad you're here. I've got something—"

Cindy put her hand in my face. "Cool your jets, me first." She didn't give me time to protest. "After you told me what Sal said about Joseph Tannery, I had my guys go to his apartment to invite him to the station for a chat. He wasn't home, so they went looking for him. They didn't have to look too hard. Dispatch got a call from a concerned citizen, who said he almost got run over while he was minding his business, whistling 'Dixie,' and walking in front of the post office."

She shrugged. "I added the 'Dixie' part. Anyway, it seems a car was weaving all over the place after it nearly squashed the concerned citizen. My guys took the citizen's statement then went looking for the weaver."

"I assume they found a car owned by Mr. Tannery."

"Yes, detective-wannabe. It was in the front yard of the house across the street from Theo's place. The driver was passed out under the influence of gallons of alcohol. My guys knew I was looking for Tannery, so they called me at home. Since I was sworn to serve and protect, I went to see Mr. Tannery in his then-current state of passed out."

"What happened?"

"Let's see. First Larry, my dear, sweet, hubby was pissed I was leaving. Now, don't worry, I made it up to him later. How is none of your business." She grinned. "Back to Tannery, he was coming to by the time I arrived. The boy smelled like a brewery. I asked him if he knew where he was. He said, 'I'm right here.' I asked him if he knew where 'here' was. I asked that since he was directly across from Theo's with the charcoal-broiled food truck in his drive. Know what he said?"

"What?"

"Interesting you ask. He looked out the window at the truck then mumbled something that sounded like, 'I had one of those.' So, I asked what he had. Here's the good part. He said, 'Tood fuc...' He giggled. 'I mean food truck.' Before I could stop him, he blurted out that the damned bank took it back then added, this is an exact quote, 'If I can't have one, neither can that wiener woman. Ha, ha. Burnt to a crisp. My finest hour.'"

Our food arrived. Cindy attacked it like she hadn't eaten in days. "What can I say? I'm a growing girl."

My safest response was no response. Instead, I said, "He confessed to torching Grace's truck?"

"Close enough, especially after he said something about trashing it twice before the fire. I read him his rights, although I doubt he understood anything I said. I suggested that, as soon as he sobers up, he should find a good lawyer and, because I was so nice I was going to provide him a bed for the night with a heart-unhealthy breakfast." She stared in her mug then slowly shook her head. "Chris, I don't think he even met Grace. Her truck represented something bad that'd been burning inside him for a long time. Sorry."

"And burned Grace's dream because of it."

"Yes. I'm glad you told me about what he was saying, or

what you said Sal said he was saying. If you hadn't, Tannery would've been charged with DUI, never questioned about the fire. As much as it galls me to say it, thanks."

"Sal deserves most of the credit. Regardless, you're welcome."

She took another bite of her expensive meal, wiped her napkin across her lips, and said, "What did you want to tell me?"

I realized that what I'd been thinking in the middle of the night seemed more significant then than now. I shared an abbreviated version of my thoughts on Laurie and Gail.

Cindy listened, although she kept shaking her head. I didn't blame her. When I started telling her about our encounter with the Captain at the Preserve, I thought she was going to hop on the table.

"You were where? You were doing what?"

I repeated that Charles and I were trying to catch someone digging for the fortune. She said she thought that's what I said, then spent what seemed like hours lambasting me for my stupid, idiotic, dangerous, plus a few other words I prefer not to repeat, actions. That was all before I got to the part where Gant pointed a gun at my stomach. That's when she fell back in her seat, bowed her head, rubbed her temples. Her hand covered her face so, when she made strange sounds, I couldn't tell if she was laughing or crying. I sipped water and waited.

Cindy finally moved her hand from her face, pulled her shoulders back, leaned closer to the table, and said, "Chris, are you and Charles okay?"

I told her that we were.

"Do you want me to arrest Gant?"

"For what?"

"I'm sure I can find some archaic law that prohibits sticking a gun in someone's bellybutton, even if the recipients are total idiots, while trying to rob said idiots of a treasure map."

"Let it go. He thought we'd killed Anthony. It wouldn't do any good having him arrested. I appreciate your concern."

"Okay, but you and your lamebrain friend are still idiots."

She got no argument from me.

Chapter Forty-Three

I called Theo to see if he and Grace were home. They were, and he said he'd be delighted for me to visit. They would be more delighted when I shared what I'd learned about the arsonist.

Instead of Theo, Grace greeted me at the door with a smile and a hug. "Wait until you hear the news," she said before she bounced up and down like a teenager telling her best friend that the coolest boy in school had invited her to the prom. "Pardon my manners, please, come in."

Grace turned to Theo, who'd moved beside her. "Can I tell him, or would you like the honor?"

Theo put his arm around her shoulder. "Grace, Chris asked to stop by. Why don't we let him tell us why?" He motioned for us to join him in the great room. "Then, you can share the news."

Grace was so excited that I wanted her to go first, until I imagined what I had to say was more important.

Theo offered coffee. I was already two cups past my limit, so I declined.

Grace sat opposite me and wrapped her arms around her legs. She was straining to hold back her glee.

"So," Theo said, "What brings you out this morning?"

"Is Sal here?"

Theo pointed to the ceiling then tilted his head and rested it on his hand. Asleep, I translated.

"Why?"

I began the story of Sal talking to me about the person he'd talked to in the bar and how that led to me talking to Cindy. By the time I got to the part about Joseph Tannery parked across the street, both Theo and Grace were sitting on the edge of their seats, staring at me. I seldom had this attentive an audience. I admit, I savored it longer than I should have before continuing the story ending with Tannery confessing, well, almost confessing, to trashing the truck then starting the fire that put Grace out of business.

Grace formed a confused look on her face. "I don't know who this Tannery person is. Did he know me? Did I somehow offend him?"

I shook my head. "Grace, it didn't have anything to do with you. It could've been any food truck. He's unstable. He took his anger out on your vehicle."

"Thank God," Theo added. "That's a good thing. Grace, you have nothing to worry about."

"I'm blessed," she said, before turning to Theo. "Can we tell him now?"

Theo smiled at her then nodded. Grace returned his smile and said, "Theo's setting me up in a restaurant. A real one. No wheels."

"Great. Where?"

Grace turned to Theo who said, "You know that little restaurant on West Huron just past what used to be the Wish Doctor?"

The restaurant had operated under several different names since I'd been on Folly; none lasted more than a year or two. I said that I knew the spot.

"I bought the building. It's a mess on the inside, but—"

Grace interrupted, "Not too big a mess for me. Teddy and I did a lot of renovating. No big deal for this tomboy."

Theo continued, "I'll be covering expenses until Grace gets on her feet. Heck, I may even wait tables."

With Theo's walking speed slightly faster than a live oak, I thought, *never in a million years.*

I mumbled, "That's an idea."

Grace clapped her hands. "Daddy would say, 'Enough fi stone dawg.' "

I said, "Which means?"

"Enough to stone a dog."

Theo said, "Which means?"

Grace chuckled. "An abundance of something. I'm blessed with an abundance of love, opportunity, family."

Theo asked before I did, "What's that have to do with stoning a dog?"

"Don't know. Think maybe it means that I have so much that I can do idle things, like stoning a dog."

It still didn't make sense. I also didn't think it was a good saying to throw around canine-friendly Folly.

"Grace, when do you think you'll be opening?"

"Theo doesn't own the building for another month, but the man who does says we can get in tomorrow to start working on it. I'm so excited."

"Grace, tell Chris what you're going to name it."

Her smile widened. "Teddy's Place."

Theo bobbed his head. "Isn't that wonderful?"

It was, and I told them so. My phone's ringtone interrupted their excitement. The screen read, *Charles.*

"Chris, this is Charles. Is this a good time to call?"

The voice was familiar, but the words didn't sound like any I'd ever heard from my friend.

"Umm, sure."

"I'm at Laurie's house. Could you come over?"

"Now?"

"Absolutely."

The conversation was getting stranger by the second. "Charles, is everything okay?"

He laughed like I'd said something funny. He said, "Nah."

"You can't talk?"

"That's right. How quick can you get here?"

"Five minutes; ten, tops."

"A half-hour, good." He hung up.

I excused myself to confused looks from my hosts and was in the car seconds later. The rain was pouring harder than it had been overnight. It was still hours before sunset, yet the sky was midnight dark. Water stood on the road, so I had to swerve to miss the deepest puddles.

I called Cindy as I turned on Laurie's street. I wanted her to know where I was going, and why. I got her voice mail, left a brief message, asking her to come to Laurie's house, that something might be wrong.

I was tempted to wait for her to call back, yet Charles's tone screamed he needed help now, not later.

Chapter Forty-Four

Laurie's MINI, Charles' vehicle, plus two cars with Florida plates were in the drive. I assumed that they belonged to Dean and Gail. I pulled off the road short of the house to wait for Cindy's call when I noticed the front door standing open. No doubt, something was wrong. I pulled in the drive, then stopped as close to the house as I could manage. There was a large puddle behind the closest car, so I had to park partially in the yard to avoid the tiny lake. Heavy rain continued, the wind howled. Whoever was inside may not have heard me.

I grabbed an umbrella from the back seat. The rain was blowing sideways and was so strong I had trouble opening the car door. A lightning bolt startled me enough that I was tempted to return to the car. The rapidly-expanding, large puddle was between me and the house, so I had to walk around it. I was afraid that the umbrella would blow inside out before I made it to the porch. My clothes were soaked by the time I got to the steps.

Through the open door, I saw it was darker inside than outside. Someone yelled, "Help!"

A pool of what looked like blood was in the doorway. I yelled, "Hello!" No one responded, or no one I heard.

The wind whipped around the side of the porch. Not only did I feel like I was in a wind tunnel, the sound of the blast of warm air made it impossible to hear anything in the house. I stepped around the pool of liquid as I moved to the living room. My eyes were getting accustomed to the darkened room. I wished they hadn't.

A woman was face down on the floor to the left of the door. I couldn't see her face, but her hair was the style of Gail's. There was a steady path of blood from the pool at the front door to the body. It looked like she'd tried to get to the door, was shot or stabbed, then made it back to where she was now before collapsing. She lay still, dead still.

I shook the sight out of my head as I looked around the room. Dean was on the floor to my right. He was in a seated position with his back against the wall. His left hand was covered with blood and was clutching his stomach. His eyes were closed. I started toward him when he opened his eyes and whispered, "I'll be okay. Check on Laurie." He nodded toward the door to the kitchen.

I turned to look in the direction that he had motioned. The light over the sink was bright enough for me to notice another body. The person was backlit, but I assumed it was Laurie. I stepped closer. The homeowner was lying face up with no visible wounds. She wasn't moving. I bent down to feel for a pulse when I heard a mumbled, agitated voice from the far corner of the kitchen.

Charles was on his side with his back to the cabinets. His hands were behind him wrapped together with the cord from a shattered lamp leaning against his side. A dishtowel was stuffed in his mouth.

Now what do I do? Was Laurie alive? Do I try to help her before untying Charles? Do I dial 9-1-1 instead of waiting for Cindy to return my call?

Charles was making louder noises and shaking his head. I stood, took a step toward my friend, when I heard the front door slam. Charles mumbled louder as I reached to untie his gag.

"I'd recommend not doing that," said someone behind me.

I jerked around to see Dean five feet away. He appeared well enough to be pointing a handgun at my face.

"What's going on?" My gaze went from the gun to his bloody shirt then to his hand dripping blood.

He looked at his hand. "Oh, the blood. It's Gail's. She didn't need it." He grinned. "Your friend there said it'd be a half hour before you showed so, when I heard you pull in the drive, I had to improvise. I wiped my hand in the blood beside my dear wife's silent, silent for once, body to look like I'd been shot. Had to buy time to figure out what to do. Worked, didn't it?" His grin turned to a smile.

I found nothing humorous in his comment. I was so shocked that I didn't hear my phone ring.

Dean did. He held out his bloodied hand and motioned for me to give him the phone.

I took it from my pocket, saw that the screen read *Cindy*, then handed it to him. Without lowering his gun, or taking his eyes off me, he dropped the phone then stomped on it. The screen shattered. My hope for a rescue shattered with it.

Dean motioned me to take a seat beside my gagged friend. I couldn't think of a better option, so I sat, my arm touching Charles's side. I knew that Dean wouldn't have known I'd been suspicious of Charles's out-of-character call enough to leave a message for Cindy to come to Laurie's. Our only hope was to stall long enough for her to get here.

"Dean, what happened?"

His smile disappeared. He glanced in the living room. "All I wanted was to save my store. I'm no killer." He shook his head. "Huh, don't suppose history will agree. Gail and I knew that Laurie had a map she got from her grandfather. I never knew him. Years ago, he convinced Laurie the map was authentic, that there was buried treasure.

"Laurie told us the story so many times I could recite it word for word. We knew they'd been looking out near the lighthouse for landmarks marked on the map. Anthony said that things had changed so much they didn't know if they'd ever find it."

Come on, Chief. Where are you? Time to stall longer.

"If they didn't know where to look, why'd you show up that night?"

"Anthony called, all excited. Said they'd found something he thought would help them find the treasure. He didn't say what. He said four sets of eyes would have a better chance of finding it than two. Said he'd wait for us before going out there. I knew that Gail wouldn't go along with stealing the map, or the treasure, from Anthony and Laurie, so I told her the story about going to a meeting in Tallahassee. I came here instead. I called Anthony to say that we wouldn't be coming. Told him to go without us."

"What happened?"

I was there before they arrived, parked in one of the drives near the entrance to the whatever you call that end of the island. The weather was like tonight, so I figured they wouldn't recognize my car. I was also afraid they wouldn't show. There was a break in the rain when they got there."

Still no sign the police were on their way. I was close

enough to Charles to where I could move my left hand behind his back without Dean noticing. The electric cord was wrapped tight. It was possible, with enough time, that I could wiggle it enough to loosen its grip. *With enough time.*

"So you followed them on the old Coast Guard property?"

"It was getting darker by the minute. I didn't know who was more stupid, them for coming out on such a horrible night, or me for following. Either way, we were there. My plan was to wait until they found something then step in to steal it. I wasn't going to kill anyone."

I wondered if he thought that Laurie and Anthony would let him steal the treasure without protest. How did he think he wasn't going to have to kill them?

"I understand," I said to stall.

"You've got to believe me," Dean said. He hesitated then shook his head. "Then it all went south. The rain started again, everything was black. I heard them debating what to do. Anthony finally said for Laurie to stay where she was. He'd find the way out, then come get her. He left. I don't know how, but he saw me while he was pushing through the underbrush. He grabbed a thick branch off the ground, pointed it at me, and asked what I was doing out there. I could barely see him, although, from what I could see, he knew I was up to no good."

Dean took a deep breath. "I started to explain how I needed money. Out of the blue, he lunged at me, raised the branch over his head, like he was going to clobber me." He looked down at his gun. "I ducked, pulled this out of my pocket. Pulled the trigger."

I took that brief opportunity to scoot closer to Charles, getting a better grip on the electric cord. From where I'd been, I managed to loosen it slightly, while Charles was twisting his hands for me to get a better grip on the jumble of wire.

Still no police.

"Why shoot at Laurie?"

"When I was there that terrible night watching the two of them arguing, Laurie stared directly at me. She didn't say anything. From what I've heard, she didn't mention it to anyone. Hell, maybe with it raining so hard she didn't see me. I couldn't take a chance that she'd remember later. I'd already killed her husband. Who'd believe I was defending myself. She had to go." He nodded toward Charles, then at me. "I didn't know you and your friend were with her the second time. I came to the wooded area beside her place from the road behind her house. I didn't see your car. Sorry if I scared you."

He's standing there after killing his wife, me not knowing what happened to Laurie, Charles being tied up and gagged, pointing a gun at my face, and he's apologizing for scaring us. I'm not looking at a rational man. Where were the police?

I said, "What happened tonight?" I was making slow, painstakingly slow progress on unknotting the cord.

Again, he tilted his head toward the living room, and snarled out, "She." He hesitated, took a deep breath, then continued, "She called to say that she knew what I'd done. I thought she was talking about killing Anthony. I drove up here to talk to her before she blabbed to everyone. Didn't know what I was going to do. Honest, I didn't." He took another deep breath. "I got here, found the three of them huddled in the living room, talking. Figured she'd told Laurie, and your buddy. Know what they were talking about? Know what she thought she knew?"

I shook my head as I continued making progress with the knot.

"Said I was having an affair. She was going to leave me. She didn't know a damned thing about me killing Anthony. Can you believe that?"

That didn't explain how the day turned violent. A huge sense of relief filled me when I heard Laurie moan, saw her hand move. Charles's hands were seconds from freedom. I had no idea what we would do then. I had to keep Dean talking.

"Then what happened?"

He shifted his gun's aim to Charles. "Gail said your friend's nosy. I got here, and Gail pounced on me with both barrels. She started screaming about my affair. Laurie tried to welcome me. Gail wouldn't let her get in a word."

No surprise. He waved the gun back and forth between Charles and me.

"She said something about going to scream it to the world, then went to the front door, screaming the entire time. I snapped." He looked at the gun. "I yanked this out of my pocket. Pulled the trigger. Pulled it twice." He gave a sinister grin. "It felt good. She stood there, opened and closed her mouth with nothing coming out. A first. A first ever. She staggered to where she is now and collapsed. Laurie screamed and ran to Gail. Your friend started toward me. I pointed it at him. He stopped, put his hands in the air. Smart man."

I thought I heard police sirens in the distance. Or was it wishful thinking? I'd pulled the last bit of electric cord from Charles's wrists. I was afraid that Dean had seen Charles's arms moving. Fortunately, he was distracted by his story.

Laurie moaned. Dean glanced at her. "She screamed again and ran toward the kitchen to go out the back door. I took three steps toward her. Smacked her with the gun. She hit the floor like a sack of potatoes."

"Why am I here?" I asked.

"You and your friend have been nosing around. From what Laurie told me, you were good buds with the cops. Sooner or later, you were going to figure out what was going on. Charles was the only smart one in the room. That's why he's still alive and Gail isn't. Laurie will have the headache of the century. I told him to call you."

The sirens weren't my imagination. They were also not close to the house. Dean must've heard them as well. His eyes darted around the room. "Time's up."

Any hope Charles and I had was running out. I gave an abbreviated tilt of my head toward the back of the house.

Charles responded in kind. I figured that, if we separated quickly, then Dean wouldn't have time to shoot both of us. Either Charles, or I, could get to him. It was the same plan I'd rejected when Captain Gant had confronted us. This time, I didn't have options.

I rolled to my right.

Charles hurled the electric cord at Dean as he jumped up. The cord missed Dean but distracted him enough that he didn't fire the weapon. Charles reached for Dean's arm.

I dove for his legs. I expected a bullet to tear through my body.

Instead, Dean knocked Charles's hand away and twisted around enough to point the gun at my friend.

I slammed into Dean's left leg with my full weight. His leg buckled, throwing him off balance enough that he didn't get a shot off before falling awkwardly to the floor. I landed on Dean. The impact with the floor knocked the wind out of him.

Charles kicked the gun out of his hand.

Dean pushed up with his elbow, kicking my side before twisting toward Charles then punching him in the stomach. I reached to grab one of Dean's legs before he stood. I missed.

Charles was doubled over, gasping for breath. Dean would get away. There was little Charles, or I, could do to stop him.

Out of the corner of my eye, I saw movement beside Dean, saw a tea pitcher shatter over his head. Glass rained down on Charles, me, and Dean who staggered before collapsing.

Laurie towered over the three of us.

I could've hugged her, would have if Charles hadn't beaten me to it. His arms were around her before I caught my breath. He helped her to a kitchen chair.

She slowly touched her head where Dean's gun had smacked her.

I lowered myself back to the floor then felt my side. I'd bet ribs were broken.

The next thing I remembered was Officer Trula Bishop, along with an officer I didn't know, storm into the kitchen, weapons drawn. I was alive, so were Charles and Laurie. That was way more important than the pain in my side.

Epilogue

"It seems like an eternity since Dean tried to bump us off," Charles said.

"Two months, three days," Laurie said, having caught on to Charles's penchant for accuracy.

It was the night before the grand opening of Teddy's Place. We were seated around two large, round tables in the newly painted and appointed dining room. Grace had put together the special event to celebrate not only her opening, but to honor her father-in-law for giving her the chance to carry her husband's legacy to the town where his father lives. She also wanted to celebrate Laurie's life being spared.

The gathering planned for six of us had expanded to nine, including Theo, the guest of honor, Charles, Laurie, Sal, Stanley Kremitz, Abraham Gant, Barb, and me and, of course, Grace who doubled as chef host.

I'd suffered two broken ribs. It had only been a week since I wasn't reminded daily about them. The doctor, who looked like he should have been in elementary school, said that, because of my "advanced age," recovery would be slower than for younger people. At least he didn't say because I was ancient.

Laurie had a concussion, suffered from headaches and occasional memory loss. Her doctor said that it would take months, possibly longer, before she fully recovered. Charles was keeping a close eye on her. He claimed it was what friends did. I knew it was more. Not only was Charles keeping an eye on her, Grace had moved in with her. Instead of paying rent, she was helping fix up the house. They'd become friends with one thing in common. They'd both suffered untimely losses. They had one significant difference. Laurie knew how she wanted to fix up her house, yet didn't have the skills. Grace was an experienced remodeler. Theo had been sad to see her leave his house but was pleased that she'd made a friend.

Wine, beer, and bourbon flowed freely. There was an ample supply of iced tea for Laurie since her doctor said she shouldn't drink alcohol until her concussion subsided. The appetizer was shrimp with cheese, and little pieces of something red stirred in the sauce. Grace tried to explain what it was but, considering my culinary skills, she would have been as successful explaining to me the Big Bang Theory in Hungarian.

I explained to Stanley, whom I hadn't seen since Anthony's arrest, how Sal had been instrumental in catching the person who torched the food truck. Sal beamed when Stanley patted him on the back. Sal thanked him without cracking a joke. I don't know why it took me this long, but I realized that Sal had used jokes to feel needed, or wanted. Perhaps there was hope for him.

After we'd finished a fantastic steak and lobster entrée, Grace said that she wanted to say a few words. In her lovely, albeit fake, Jamaican accent, she praised Theo for accepting her and for the financial backing of the restaurant.

Theo choked back a tear and said, "That's what family is for. Teddy would be proud."

Grace wiped a tear from her cheek. "Yes, he would."

I could tell that she wanted to say more, but she shook her head and rushed to the kitchen. I suspected that she didn't want us to see her crying.

Stanley leaned across the table and said, "One thing confuses me. Did anyone find the treasure? What happened to the map?"

Laurie looked to see if anyone was going to answer. No one did, so she said, "We didn't find anything. Anthony thought he'd figured it out but, when we got to the spot where he thought the map indicated it should've been buried, the ocean had eroded most of it away. He thought he'd been reading the map wrong, but also thought he knew where we should go next. That's why we were out there, regardless of the weather."

Stanley said, "What happened to the map?"

Laurie shrugged. "Anthony had it when we went out there. The police didn't find it, so I figured whoever killed him took it."

Stanley said, "What did Dean do with it?"

Laurie said, "Don't know. Don't care. If there's treasure, it's cursed. I never want to hear about it again."

Captain Gant had been silent most of the evening, so I was surprised when he said, "Remember when someone broke into Dean's car?"

I doubted most of the people in the room remembered. After the police arrested Dean, his car was left in Laurie's drive. With everything going on, and Laurie suffering a concussion, no one seemed to pay attention to the vehicle.

Two days later, Chief LaMond went to Laurie's house to ask her more questions when she noticed the car's rear passenger's window had been smashed. Laurie didn't know anything about it. The chief had it towed.

Charles and I nodded. Laurie said that she remembered.

Gant sat up straight, took a sip of beer, and looked around the room. "The past must remain in the past. There is no map."

Laurie said, "There was."

"No more," Gant said, grinned, then took a sip of his drink.

About the Author

Bill Noel is the best-selling author of seventeen novels in the popular Folly Beach Mystery series. Besides being an award-winning novelist, Noel is a fine arts photographer and lives in Louisville, Kentucky, with his wife, Susan, and his off-kilter imagination. Learn more about the series, and the author by visiting www.billnoel.com.

CPSIA information can be obtained
at www.ICGtesting.com
Printed in the USA
BVHW040142060220
571591BV00004B/8

9 781937 979836